TOM

And The

IntraEarth Invaders

BY

Victor Appleton II

THE NEW TOM SWIFT INVENTION SERIES

Tom Swift And The
IntraEarth Invaders

By Victor Appleton II

It has been a couple years since Tom Swift solved both the mystery and aftermath of a loss of helium in the undersea mines he once discovered. Since then not much of anything has happened that might be considered newsworthy in Helium City. In fact, he and his friend, Bud Barclay, haven't even traveled down there in all that time.

Things are about to change!

A deep thrumming vibration begins to make itself noticed in Helium City. As it comes and goes, Tom designs and lowers a series of probes meant to discover what is coming from deep inside or even under the giant cavern filled with liquid helium.

In order to explore the many possibilities—and impossibilities—Tom and Bud undertake a new adventure that sees them being lowered into the cavern.

What they find shocks them both, but they try to make a bad situation better. What they get is a bad situation getting more and more out of hand!

This book is dedicated to all my fellow Tom Swift fan authors. You might find it hard to believe, but—and even if you don't count Scott D's 32 excellent re-imagined books—we have created more than 40 new Tom Swift (and Sandy Swift and Thomasina Swift) novels between us. So, Scott D., Jon, Michael, Scott L., Leo, Adam, and Tom, Well done!

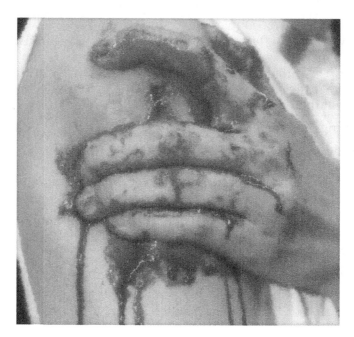

He pulled his right hand away, and Bashalli let out a shriek. Tom had been shot! **PAGE 152**

TABLE OF CONTENTS

CHAPTER   **PAGE**

AUTHOR'S NOTE:

It seems that I have been writing all my life. Actually, if you take into consideration the random scribblings from my first through fourth grades, then I have been at this for about fifty-three years. As Bud Barclay would say, Jetz!

I have been pleased to write new adventures of Tom Swift and all of the other people who help him be the successful young inventor he is. With this 13th story I honestly thought that I had hit a wall. What to do after this one. Generally I have had three story ideas sitting in wait for me to complete the current book. But as I finished number 11 I realized I had just one more "in the hopper." Then, as I neared the halfway point in book 12 I panicked a little.

I had a vague idea for this book but after that...???!!!

Luckily for me I dream a lot and remember most of what comes into my head as I slumber. So, now I have titles, front covers and even plots for the next three books waiting. I plan to get to those before the end of 2015.

After that?

Panic time!!!

Quality paperbound copies of all of this author's works may be found at the following web address:

http://www.lulu.com/spotlight/tedwardfoxatyahoodotcom

Paperbound and Kindle editions can be purchased from **Amazon.com** and NOOK versions from **BarnesAndNoble.com**

Tom Swift and the IntraEarth Invaders

FOREWORD

Ask an astrophysicist and he/she will say that space is the great unknown. Ask an oceanographer and she/he will say it is our own oceans and even some lakes that are unknown. Ask me and I'll tell you that I don't believe we have even scratched the surface of either.

Now, if you were to ask Tom Swift he might say it all depends on what year it is, what month, what day and even the precise time that determines what is least explored.

Even the places "we" have been to can change. Or, our methods of looking at things changes over time, and we get a clearer picture of things we know about or a view of something we haven't yet seen. All of it is exciting; a little of it can be terrifying.

That is the kind of predicament Tom and Bud find themselves in with this story. Lightly explored territory suddenly requires a lot more, and closer, study to solve a big mystery. What they find shocks the young inventor but he tries to make the best of it, until—as they say in Britain—everything goes pear-shaped.

Victor Appleton II

CHAPTER 1 /

IT SEEMED LIKE A GOOD IDEA

FRESH FROM his latest adventure and still with much to do around, and with, his High Space L-Evator—and the large space station currently under construction at the terminus of the elevator to do even more than his original Outpost—Tom Swift leaned back in one of the only two pieces of furniture that sat in the disused, window-wrapped, old control tower at Swift Enterprises. The room, like the inventor, sat atop the Administration building.

Unlike the inventor, it had been superseded by a tall, more modern control tower set at the absolute center of the four-mile-square industrial and scientific research facility located in upstate New York, just outside of the town of Shopton.

Nearly two years earlier Tom had unofficially claimed it as his own, a haven away from everything including phone calls where he could sit and work or just think without being disturbed. The triple panes of shatterproof glass kept out all but the loudest noises.

Today he was making a few notes and sketching out some changes to the forthcoming space station's interior design.

His L-Evator, the very first true space elevator, stretched from its anchorage point in the waters off the Galapagos Islands up to a point 30,000 miles above the planet. At that location, his gleaming, golden spacecraft, the *Sutter*, was churning out an almost never-ending stream of outer hull panels that were being assembled into an enormous tube some six hundred feet wide and sixteen hundred feet long. Eventually this would be filled with at least five levels of work, living and recreational spaces built all around the inside of the hull.

Tom was currently making a change to what he planned would be two docking stations—one on each end of the disc—where any suitably outfitted ship could connect and allow transfers in a full atmosphere.

The current Outpost in Space sat in a lower geosynchronous orbit and only featured three-man airlocks; supplies and people had to transfer over by floating in the vacuum of space. Nothing could come in that didn't fit in the current air locks.

He tapped the end of the pen on his pad a few times, smiled at what he had come up with, and laid the pad on the small table to his right.

Getting up from his chair, the young inventor stretched and

walked over to the windows looking to the South.

In the near distance, a little more than a mile from the southern wall of Enterprises, was a brand new complex nearing completion. It was the forthcoming Swift MotorCar Company and would be turning out cars in about four months. The first of these would feature one of Tom's unique Y4 engines, power plants that had a trio of 4-cylinder groups arranged in an upside-down Y formation all connected inside to a single drive shaft. The small displacement of just under one liter was compensated for by an incredible amount of torque and ready power.

Since the announcement of the coming car line, more than one million inquiries—some arriving with unsolicited deposit checks that were returned—had been received.

Tom smiled as he thought about this.

He was still smiling two minutes later when he heard the lower door open and footsteps coming up the stairs.

Bud Barclay, Tom's dark haired best friend and brother-in-law —and one of Enterprises' top test pilots—gave a polite little knock on the edge of the half wall at the top of the stairs.

"Can I come in, skipper?"

Tom sighed. It had been a wonderful and relaxing several hours, but he realized it was time for him to come back to the realities of work.

"Sure, Bud. What's up?"

Bud came up the final step and walked over to Tom. They stood there looking out the windows for a few seconds.

"Well, you may not have noticed it, and nobody blames you, but you missed the momentous occasion." When Tom turned to face him with a slight frown, the flyer continued. "Final *Racing Pigeon*? I brought her over from the Construction Company a couple hours ago and your dad gave a little speech and declared that she was a wonderful bird but her time had come. Ring and bells?"

Tom's shoulders slumped. He had completely forgotten. The *Racing Pigeon* was the successor to the Swift's first and extremely popular *Pigeon Special* line of private aircraft. After nearly a decade the original model had been discontinued only a year after the introduction of the "racing" version with its more powerful engine and slightly swept wings.

However, like all good things that model had now given way to the *Pigeon Commander*, a scaled-down airframe based on Tom's SE-11 Commuter Jet—known affectionately as the Toad for its over-wing dual engines and underslung fuselage giving it a notably amphibian look when viewed from the front. The *Commander* was still a propeller-driven aircraft, but used a pair of air-cooled Y4 engines, giving it a top speed of over 300 knots and a flight ceiling of 28,000 feet all while consuming nearly ten percent less fuel.

"Ah, gee!" Tom exclaimed. "I completely forgot. Here it is, Tuesday and—" He stopped noticing the barely disguised grin coming out on his friend's face. "Hey! It isn't Tuesday. It's Monday. What gives?"

Now, Bud laughed. "I'm sorry, Tom. Your dad told me to come get your head out of the clouds and back to Earth. I know how concentrated you can get so I decided to have a little fun with it. It seemed like a good idea at the time, as they say. Don't be mad. Your dad really wants you to be there for the ceremony tomorrow."

Tom laughed. "I'm not mad, *Budworth*," he said. Using Bud's formal first name was something that only Bud, Tom's wife Bashalli, his sister Sandy—Bud's wife—and Tom did. Bud used it when he was being self-deprecating; Sandy used it as a precursor to being angry at something he might or might not have done; Tom used it as a friendly scold, and Bashalli used it in formal situations.

"Come on," the inventor told him. "Let's get down to the big office. I want to tell dad about the few changes I've sketched out for the new space station."

"The Big Cheese?" Bud asked.

Tom groaned. "Another of your pun names, Bud?"

"Well, other than the color being grayish white, the design sort of reminds me of an extra tall wheel of cheese. Have you got a better or more official name for her?"

Tom had to admit that he did not. "Just no calling it Space Station Cheddar!"

They entered the large office Tom often shared with his father, the world-famous inventor, Damon Swift. Mr. Swift wasn't there so Tom poked his head back out of the large office door.

"Trent? Do you know where dad is?" Tom blushed a bit instantly realizing that Munford Trent, their secretary and executive assistant, would know *exactly* where Mr. Swift was. At all times!

"He left for the Construction Company about a half hour ago. He wants to personally supervise the final touches on that last-ever *Pigeon Commander*. I think he has his eyes on it as a personal aircraft."

Tom grinned. He knew that his father, who had designed the original *Pigeon* and then the *Pigeon Special* and had a hand in Tom's redesign, felt a strong affinity for the airplane line. Those planes had, after all, paid the bills during a couple of the lean years when Tom was younger and had been solid performers for years and years.

"Thanks. If he calls, can you tell him that Bud and I are on our way over?"

"Certainly, Tom."

Tom motioned for Bud to get back up from the comfortable chair he had just sunk into in the conference area of the office. "Come on, flyboy, we're off to see that last plane."

When they arrived and entered building three, home of the assembly line for the aircraft, Tom saw that his father was laughing. They walked over to him and saw that he had his cell phone to his other ear.

"Yes. Yes, we can do that, as long as you are certain that is what you want... Of course... Yes, that is also possible... Fine. We'll be looking for the purchase order later today. Thank you, again, Jon. Goodbye."

After slipping the phone in his jacket pocket, the older inventor turned to the two younger men.

"Well, that was an interesting call. The president of Centennial Aircraft out in the Pacific Northwest just called me. He'd seen the announcement of our final little birdie here—" he looked over at the airplane that was now having one of a series of decals added to the fuselage declaring it **No. 3985**, "—and wants us to keep them in production, sell at least fifty of them to his company for resale and let them license, build and sell them from that point on. He believes they can sell another three or four hundred of them in the next four years. How about that?"

"Do we want to do that?" Tom asked.

Mr. Swift told them how much the other aircraft company was willing to pay per plane and in license fees and that they would take full responsibility for all testing and transportation of the finished planes.

Bud gave an appreciative whistle. "Jetz!" he exclaimed. "Isn't that just about what we've been selling them for?"

"Only about ten thousand less and we can manage to absorb that given that we spend, on average, six thousand in advertising, promotion and flight testing per airframe."

Tom grinned at this father. "So, there is life left in the plane after all."

Mr. Swift shrugged. "Our own sales fell with the *Commander* intro, so it seemed like a good idea to get out while the getting is good. Well, it appears that I'll never get the absolute final one of these."

After having a word with the team applying the decals—telling them to omit adding the other one stating **Final Ever Pigeon Commander**—he followed the boys out of the building where they parted ways driving back in their own cars.

On the way to Enterprises Bud suggested they take a detour into Shopton.

"I would like to stop by The Glass Cat to pick up some pastries for dinner tonight," he told Tom. The Glass Cat was the little bakery and coffee shop owned by Tom's other brother-in-law, Moshan Pandit. Tom's wife, Bashalli, had been working there when the two first met, and although Moshan and his father had been initially against the beautiful Pakistani girl even dating him, they had warmed to Tom and even embraced him as brother and son once the wedding had taken place.

"Dinner?" Tom asked.

Bud looked over at his friend and went, "Tsk-tsk."

"What? Another false dig at me?"

"Another brain fail, skipper? You and Bash are coming to dinner tonight at Casa Barclay as are your parents. Sandy is preparing her piece of resistance, a baked ham to be served, so I have been reliably informed, along side of roasted potatoes, artichokes, a delightful out-of-season fruit salad and tasty pastries courtesy of Moshan."

Tom was well known for forgetting about dates and events. He often wondered how he had managed to keep Bashalli after all the times he had let a dinner date or weekend picnic slip past. In fact, if it hadn't been for Bud, who feared the wrath of Sandra Swift when stood up, constantly reminding him of his social responsibilities, well...

"Oops! Thanks for the heads up. I'm sure that Bash will have my 'going to the Barclays for dinner' clothes all set out by the time I get home, but it will be a pleasant change of pace for me to give her a call before then just to let her know I... *remembered*."

"Always here to help, skipper," Bud said with a grin.

They entered the shop and were greeted by the smiling new girl who manned the counter and the espresso machine. Moshan was a wonderful baker but he realized his forte was not in dealing with customers. When he heard Tom's voice he came out of the kitchen.

"Thomas. Bud," he greeted them warmly.

They explained the reason for their visit. Moshan smiled politely and waited for Bud to stop speaking. "Yes. I have been told about this by my little sister. Three days of calls every few hours. 'Have you remembered to prepare special desserts for Sandra's party, Moshan?' And, 'Do not forget, Moshan, that Sandra and Bud are having a dinner on Thursday!' So, yes I already know all about it. Just a moment, please."

He was laughing as he went back into the kitchen and came out with a large, pink box of the type pastries seem to usually be delivered in.

"Bashi told me to tell you to not peek." He handed the box to Tom. "I trust Tom to follow his wife's commands, but I believe *you* might try to take a look," he said pointing at Bud. "So, I have glued the box shut and both Sandra and Bashi know to check." He smiled at them and then wished them well.

Knowing that the baker was correct, Bud never said another word about it as they drove back to Enterprises.

Tom spent the last of the afternoon putting his new sketches into the Computer Aided Design software on his computer. He sent the files along with a note explaining what he was hoping to accomplish to the five department heads who would have some input into the changes as well as being the ones responsible for making them eventually happen.

He even remembered to call Bashalli at her job at the advertising agency in Shopton where she currently headed all the creative work. She was thrilled when he let her know he was looking forward to the evening.

"Oh, Tom. You cannot believe how nice it is to hear that you have remembered. And I am certain that Bud had nothing whatsoever to do with this or that Sandy pestered him to remind you. At least I choose to believe that. I love you!" and with that she had hung up.

Moments later his TeleVoc beeped in his brain. The combination brainwave analyzer and subtle jaw and muscle movement detector was both a silent communicator—the wearer only needed to think and silently move their mouth to send a message in a computer simulation of their actual voice—and the best security device Tom had come up with. Worn under the shirt collar each pin was registered to a specific individual and their unique brainwaves. Anyone not wearing one on any Swift grounds, or attempting to wear someone else's, set off an alarm.

"Tom here, Arv," he answered. Another benefit was that the name of the incoming caller was announced before a connection was made.

"Hey, skipper. Want to come over and see what Linda and I have cooked up?"

"If you and Linda Ming are associated with it, I'll bet it's a doozy. I'll come over in ten minutes. See you then."

When he arrived Tom could see that Linda—an expert in miniaturization of electronics—had been having a little fun.

On hearing the inventor coming down the hall, Arv had mounted a device that looked suspiciously like a modern version of a pogo stick. He wasn't jumping up and down at the moment, just standing on the two foot pedals, balancing with no apparent effort.

"Why, if it isn't my old friend, little Arvy Hanson with a new toy," Tom said as he walked over to get a closer look. "What is little Arvy going to show uncle Tommy today?"

"I will let the lovely Miss Ming describe it to you while I demonstrate," came the chief model maker's reply. With that said he flexed his knees and then straightened them sending the stick jumping a few inches into the air, back to the ground and then back up the same distance.

"Hello, Tom," the petite Chinese woman greeted him. "I had a few spare minutes the other day and came up with an idea to modernize this old toy."

Arv was now bounding effortlessly up a full foot. Tom noted with undisguised amazement that the end of the stick didn't seem to touch the ground. He pointed that out.

"Right. Well, after I downsized the repelatrons we use in your space elevator system I got to wondering what else I might do on an even smaller scale, so I reconfigured everything to fit up inside that inch-and-a-half tube. The best part is that Arv showed me the prototype for that self-balancing cane you built for Chow Winkler awhile back. I've incorporated that capability as well."

Now Tom realized what he was seeing. "So you combined the self-balance ability with an intermittent repelatron?"

She smiled and nodded. "Yes. All the electronics except for the actual emitter sits fairly high up in the stack while a long and thin Swift Solar Battery takes up the bottom third. That keeps the center of gravity low." Her eyes went wide and she blushed. "But, you already know that. Sorry for treating this like a Basic Science 101 lecture."

"Not to worry," he told her. "Tell me more."

"Okay. The operator selects one of two possible materials to repel: concrete or asphalt. We chose not to try for dirt as there are too many combinations and did not have the space for any detect-

and-adjust capabilities. Anyway, after that it's just a matter of giving the first little push and then using the right-side handle to select the height to jump."

Arv jumped closer and said, "It sort of defeats the purpose of the pogo stick, and that is to get kids really tired, but it also has a practical side. Up at the Mars colony everyone that wants to go exploring must either hike or check out one of the electric cars or the tri-copter. There are so many people and so few cars and even fewer certified to fly, so we think this could be a boon to them for getting out to explore without exhausting themselves."

"Can they carry anything on their backs?" Tom asked. "I know the thing has self-balancing capabilities, but how much can it do if used up there?"

Arv looked blankly at his young boss but Linda smiled and replied, "For starters, this can move up to two hundred twenty pounds on Earth and easily five or six hundred on Mars. A quarter of that can be twenty-five percent off center, but I think I can build in the ability for the rider to adjust for higher off-balance loads. I'll just make the stick adjustable to lean forward a bit."

Arv stopped jumping and handed the stick to Tom. The inventor hoisted it up and was delighted that it only weighed about ten pounds. He put on foot on a pedal and stepped up onto the thing. Linda pointed out the repelatron material selector switch and the click-to-set height adjustment. In seconds Tom was off and using the stick like a pro.

By the time he stepped off three minutes later he had tried heights of up to four feet. And, while his knees needed to do some work as shock absorbers, the effort was no greater than walking up a moderate hill.

He left them promising to come back the next day with Bud. "If anyone can shake bugs out of something like this it's Bud Barclay," Linda had stated.

Dinner at Bud and Sandy's house was mostly a success. The ham was delicious as was everything else, except for the artichokes. Having never cooked one, Sandy had simply put them into the microwave and set it for ten minutes. At the seven minute mark the first of them exploded from the build up of steam inside the "choke" area. By the time she realized what was happening, two more had become sticky fibery messes covering the inside of the oven.

Bud was sent to the store for green beans. She knew how to handle green beans.

The following morning Tom invited Bud to meet him in Arv's

workshop. By the time he arrived, Tom was hopping up and down at the three foot level. The flyer stood, mouth agape, staring in amazement. He quickly begged for a chance to ride what he called, "Linda's Mr. Bouncy Stick." Tom obliged, and after a minute of basic instruction the dark haired young man was jumping up and down, his face frozen in a silly grin.

"Watch this!" he called out as he set the stick to rise a full five feet. "I used to do this on an old spring-powered model."

With that, he crouched down low as the stick came to the ground, pushed off giving it extra lift and leaned far backward, yanking the top toward him. It was a move that he perfected as a young teen that ended in a perfect backflip and landing.

On the old style stick.

What he hadn't counted on was the stabilization feature built into this one. He managed to launch himself nearly six feet into the air, get the bottom of the stick swung up and over his head, but that was when the gyros took over and it remained upside down as he plunged, head first, toward the concrete floor!

CHAPTER 2 /

JOURNEY INTO SPACE

THE NEXT thing he knew, Tom was barreling into his side in a tackle that would have done any football player proud. Together they crashed to the left in a heap with the pogo stick shoved the other way. The lightning-fast reaction on Tom's part saved Bud from serious injury. Had his head slammed into the ground there was no telling the sort of damage he might have sustained.

Linda and Arv raced to their side, helping untangle arms and legs and making certain nothing was broken before carefully easing them both into a flat position.

"I'm calling Doc Simpson," Arv announced and glared at Tom until the inventor's attempts to argue stopped.

The young medico arrived carrying one of the portable 3D imaging devices Tom had invented. He gently slipped the receptor board under Tom's neck and shoulders, positioned the three armatures with the signal emitters above the inventor, and a floating image immediately appeared in front of him, courtesy of another of Toms inventions, the 3D Telejector.

After looking a moment and giving out the occasional, "Hmmm," and "Ahhhh," Doc wiped one hand across the floating image and the machine turned off. "You're clear. Now for Bud."

The procedure was repeated with the same proclamation of no damage. "You do have one tiny blood vessel that broke under the scalp and that's going to give you a goose egg for a few days. Just keep your fingers off of it. Okay? So tell me, what in the world happened here, anyway?"

Sheepishly, Bud related his attempt at making a flip. "I forgot that the thing likes to only be straight up and down. Guess I overcame that for the first one hundred and eighty degrees and then it took over. By the way, thanks, skipper."

When the doctor departed Tom asked Linda to check the pogo stick to "...see if Bud broke anything."

They all had a laugh when they turned to find that the stick was standing upright about five feet to the side.

"It might not be a commercially viable product, but see what you can do to make it Bud-proof and we'll have the lawyers see what they think. In the mean time I agree that this could be a boon to our colonists on Mars. Heck, even to the non-Enterprises' folks based on the Moon. I know they've made overtures about buying a couple of our old repelatron donkeys."

The boys left soon after that, each heading in a different direction. Since the most recent *Pigeon Commander* wasn't going to be the last one, Bud needed to fly it the one mile to Enterprises and then give it a series of shakedown test flights.

Tom went toward the Administration building and the shared office.

"Your dad has a delegation from Japan in there, Tom," Trent cautioned him as he was about to reach for the doorknob. "He didn't specifically tell me to keep anybody out, such as you, but I think they are in some rather tense negotiations over their space program."

"Okay. Thanks for the warning. I'll just head down the hall to my lab if anyone needs me."

Rather than going straight into his large and well-equipped laboratory, located next door to the office, Tom walked farther down the corridor, stepping over the moving ride-walk belts that ran down the center, before entering a small kitchen.

"Hey there, Chow," he greeted the older man who was standing at one of his stoves stirring something in a pot.

The man, dressed in another of his outlandishly gaudy western shirts—this one a bright yellow number with blue and red prairie dogs appearing to run up and down the sleeves—let the spoon go and turned around.

"Wahl, say thar, youngin'. What's goin' on? Yer shirt and pants is all dusty and dirty. Ya been wrasslin' steers?"

They both chuckled at the thought.

"No, Chow, Bud and I had a little run in with a loco bucking pogo stick." He told the cook, in non-technical terms, what the stick could do and how Bud had put it to a test beyond its capabilities.

"Dang! Wish I'd-a been thar," the cook said. "It'd be worth th' price o' admission ta see old Buddy Boy going bee-hind over teakettle like that! Lemme know the next time he tries that mount. Let him know old Chow'll come over ta show him how it's done!"

After a little more small talk Tom got to the point of his visit. "I'm going to head up to where the new space station is being built. I plan on taking the L-Evator and wondered if you'd like to come along? I'm sure we can bring up some special supplies and the men and women up in the *Sutter* would appreciate some of your cooking. What do you say?"

Chow looked at the floor and then into Tom's eyes. "Never

thought I'd say this, but I gotta ask the missus, Tom. Now that Wanda's got her hooks in me, she's kinda been askin' me ta stick around. O' course, I don't mind that at all, but I'm supposin' that yer not just-a asking ta take me on a three-hour tour, huh?"

Tom laughed. "No. Even at top people-carrying speed it's a good day up and another down. I suppose we could take the *Challenger...*"

"Nah! I'm ac-shully lookin' forward ta ridin that el-ee-vay-tor o' yers. Only question I got is whether I'm gonna need ta take all my pots 'n pans 'n that sort 'o stuff. Plus, does the el-ee-vay-tor have a refrigerator? If not, then I s'pose I kin pack my things in a dozen or so coolers."

"Sorry, old-timer. That's one of the things we never thought of. Since almost every load going up or coming down is just cargo, we only built two smallish cabins. Mostly for a pilot, when needed, and a few people. In fact, each cabin has seats for only six people. Everything else gets put into sealed containers."

Chow removed the ten-gallon hat that perpetually sat on his bald head and fanned his face. "Sooooo, how're ya gonna get loads o' people up to that new station when it comes time ta fill it all?"

"Well, I will build several large people containers—maybe three of them—to put on the cargo platforms. I believe each one might carry something like thirty-five people. So we can take up about one hundred and five per trip."

Chow nodded. "That'll do it!" he proclaimed.

"I'll tell you what I'll do. For this trip you and Bud and I can go up in the *Challenger*. That'll make it a day trip. But next time we go I will plan far enough ahead and get my mom and Bash and Sandy involved to keep Wanda company. The four of them can have a ladies night or two. What do you think Wanda will say to that?"

Chow beamed. "I think that's the nicest thing ya can do, Tom. Wanda'll love that. So, when d' we leave on this here whirlwind trip?"

"The morning after tomorrow if you can be ready by seven."

"Count on it!"

Tom wandered back down the hall. He was just in time to watch his father bow to and shake hands with a group of Japanese men and to have Trent escort them down the hall. As Damon turned he spotted Tom. He made a "come here" motion with his right index finger.

"Good meeting, I hope," Tom inquired.

They walked into the office and Damon said, "It all depends on how you look at it, Son. For instance, if you only refer to the outcome, then it was a moderate success. If you look at the problems dumped in my lap up front, it seems to be an amazing success."

Tom could tell his father was bothered by something. "I'm guessing it was only a qualified success, then."

"Yes." Mr. Swift detailed how the meeting began. It started with the delegation practically accusing the Swifts of sabotaging their efforts to get a giant, new weather satellite that Enterprises was building into orbit. The matter was eventually solved only to some small satisfaction once the Japanese realized that their original specifications had been incorrect, and when the engineers at Enterprises had attempted to get clarification nearly a full year earlier, their requests had gone unanswered.

It was a bureaucratic goof on the part of the Asians; their cultural protocols would not allow them to directly answer "underlings," and their internal requests for formal communications had been stonewalled by a now-deposed elderly Minister of Technology who still held resentment over what he felt was an affront to his family by another U.S. business six decades earlier!

This delegation came to Shopton under the impression that more than six hundred fifty-million Yen—about seven million dollars—had been accepted by Enterprises with nothing to show for it in return.

After a tour of the clean room in the Electronics building where Damon showed them the completed shell of the satellite, he brought them to the office to explain why they had not previously been called to inspect the progress.

"It all comes down to their refusal to adapt to Western ways when dealing with foreign companies and specifically with people who they feel are below their station."

"But they seemed to be okay when they left. Right?"

"Practically. I was able to impress on them that they must insist that all our communications be answered as fully and as quickly as possible. No running things past a compliance minister. Just real, honest answers."

They discussed the implications of the delay, and Damon stated that it wasn't as bad as it could be. The project had originally been provided with a three-month "slippage" window; they were just outside of that but only because Damon had made some executive decisions that allowed development and production to continue rather than stop and wait.

"What's new with you?" he asked his son.

"I'm heading up to the *Sutter* to watch as the first complete ring of panels of the new station get joined together. That's one forty-foot-wide ring down, just three hundred ninty-nine to go plus the two ends."

"Uh-huh. Plus all the interior build, plus, plus, plus!"

They laughed. It was a tremendous undertaking with a breakneck schedule. But having completed his High Space L-Evator was making things much easier than his first Outpost, a space wheel built from the hollowed shells of its own supply rockets.

The space elevator also made it a breeze to bring down many of the metals and minerals Tom and his people had extracted from a series of asteroids moved, temporarily, into a near-Earth orbit, mined by the *Sutter*, and the unused materials returned to the asteroid belt.

"Yeah, there's lot to do," Tom admitted, "but the good news is we are just about a week ahead on the schedule and could pick up even another week in the next month. We hit the jackpot with what we mined up there, and if you add in Hank Sterling's giant panel forming equipment being able to crank things out nonstop, I'm more than satisfied right now."

"When do you go up?"

"Day after tomorrow." He mentioned how Chow's marital status meant the trip would be a quick one.

"Oh, how the wild and free suddenly find that having a lifetime helpmeet can put the reigns on your adventures. Too bad he and Wanda didn't get together when they were younger. She might be as open to his going out for a few days as Bashalli or Sandy are."

They looked at each other and giggled a little.

"Okay. Not so much Sandy, but your wife is extremely understanding, Son."

Preparations were simple. The *Challenger* always stood ready for flight out on Fearing Island, the former four-mile-long, mile wide bump of scrub grass and seagull resting site that the Swift organization had leased from the U.S. Government for at least 100 years. It was now the site of both the Oceanic/Submariner division as well as serving as the spaceport for the small fleet of spacecraft designed and built by Tom and his father.

When the boys and Chow arrived the morning of their flight, Tom headed over to check on the ship while Bud and Chow went to assure that the chef's requested supplies were ready to be loaded aboard early in the morning.

"We've got it all set for you, Chow. Those lucky dogs up in the penthouse get all the luck!" a young supply technician told him.

Bud's head swiveled quickly around. "Penthouse?"

With a shrug the young man, perhaps a year younger than Bud and Tom, replied, "Sure. That's what everyone is calling it. You know? First floor... lobby, second floor... workout room... all the way up to top floor... penthouse. All out!"

The flyer walked over to the young tech and placed an arm around his shoulder. "Normally, it is my duty to come up with the puns around this organization," he explained, "but in this case I approve. You tell whoever came up with that it has the Barclay seal, okay?"

As he and Chow exited the Supply building they were in time to watch as Tom's giant aircraft, the *Super Queen* came in for a landing. Normally she would drop straight down on her repelatron lifters, but she came in low and fairly slow for a more traditional landing.

"She must have a belly full o' heavy stuff ta be comin' in like that!" Chow commented.

Later they found out that the two huge cargo pods carried in her belly were full of items to be taken down to the Galapagos Islands and the anchorage point for the space elevator. The *Super Queen* had been crisscrossing North America picking up food and other supplies from various states and up in Canada as well as six nuclear power pods they had loaded out in New Mexico at the Swift's nuclear research and power facility, the Citadel. These would be used to run various pieces of equipment in and around the station during construction.

When takeoff time came, the trio climbed aboard, performed their preflight checks—including Chow who did a complete check to ensure that everything in his galley was either in a closed cabinet or tied down—and agreed they were ready.

All systems were reported as good to go, so Tom radioed the tower and announced their status.

"We're good here, Leo," he called to the tower operator. He thought for a minute and then asked, "Hey, Leo? Didn't I promise to take you up on a future flight... something like two years ago?"

"Well, sort of. I mean I never thought you'd have the time and all..."

"Listen. I can hold here for about thirty minutes. Can you get a relief controller in and then hustle over here in that time? We're going to be gone about fifteen hours."

"Oh, gee! Uhhh, let me see. Adam Sparks owes me a shift or two. I'll call him right now. Get back to you in three."

"That's awfully generous of you, skipper," Bud told him. "I mean, Leo's a great guy but he's never been up in space. Are you sure he won't, you know, toss his cookies all over the place? Not good if you put him in a suit!"

"What you may not realize, Bud, is that our Leo grew up on the ocean. His grandfather and father ran deep sea fishing boats. Leo once told me that he's never felt even the tiniest hint of motion sickness. I think he'll be fine."

The radio crackled to life. "I'm on my way. Thanks, Tom. This is really amazing!"

Five minute later the fifty-five year old man climbed up the ladder to the hangar deck and entered through the lower airlock. When Tom remotely cycled the inner hatch he stepped inside and was up in the control room a minute after that.

While Bud got the man into one of the seats that could (almost) magically appear up from the deck, Tom called to the new control tower operator. "*Challenger* ready."

"Roger. You are cleared. And, give my regards to Lucky Leo, will you?"

"Will do." Tom pressed the necessary controls and the ship rose on her silent repelatrons. Moments later she broke through the cloud layer at twenty-one thousand feet and was lost to view by anyone on the ground.

The flight was routine and Tom even gave his guest a few minutes sitting at the controls. Although Leo had never driven anything more powerful or fancier than a family sedan, he was able to pick up on enough to try a simple, wide spiral maneuver.

"I give you back the controls, Tom. You've made my day. Golly, you've made my *year!*"

As they approached the top of the L-Evator, the huge asteroid keeping the anchor cable straight was the first thing they could see. That was followed by the golden gleam of the *Sutter* and finally the relatively thin ring of the new construction.

"That looks pretty fragile," Bud stated.

"Yes. In the overall scheme of things it is fairly frail, but I wouldn't suggest that you try to give it a punch. Not only is that material strong enough to deflect a three-inch meteorite, it now has enough mass that even in the *Challenger* we might have trouble if we bumped into it."

Tom parked the ship about five hundred feet away from the *Sutter* and set the controls to maintain position. They headed down to the hangar where everyone helped Chow get his supplies out of the large hangar door and on their way drifting to the other ship.

Bud had to grab Leo as he was paying no attention to where he was going; the view of the planet below was spellbinding.

They got the to large airlock at the back of *Sutter's* vertical "sail" and pushed everything inside. Chow's supplies were moved to the large common room by two of the ship's personnel while the three men met with Zimby Cox, the current commander.

"I'd ask if you're having a good time, Leo," Zimby told him, "but I don't think you can stop grinning long enough to answer!"

Everyone thought it would be best if Leo remained in the *Sutter*; there was a lot to see on board and out the view ports, and the chances of him getting into trouble would be minimal.

He agreed.

His first look "down" at his home planet had caused him to feel something he had never experienced. It was a sense of what a small spot he filled in the universe. A sense of incredible loneliness. It was the same sense practically everyone felt on their first space walk.

And now he only wanted to be able to collect his thoughts in somewhat familiar surroundings. He quite happily took the suggestion while Tom and Bud flew around outside inspecting things. Their first stop was front end of the *Sutter* where slightly curved panel after panel were being pushed out at the rate of about one every forty minutes. As quickly as they came out two of the workers using what looked like motor scooters without wheels took them in tow and moved them the two thousand yards out to where another team positioned and heat-welded them to the other panels already forming the space station.

Three panels later came a third team with one of Tom's stranger looking contraptions—an inspection tool that checked each and every millimeter of the seals to ensure they were complete and to the strictest specifications.

Tom met again with Zimby to discuss how everything was progressing and how the construction people were faring. After learning that everybody was fine they called the workers inside for Chow's special dinner. By the time the *Challenger* was readying to depart everyone was begging for Chow to stay behind. Not a woman or man didn't appreciate the cook's talents in the kitchen.

When the ship pulled away heading back down to Earth practically everybody had suited up and were outside lined up to wave them farewell.

*   *   *   *   *

Tom was jolted from his sleep by the sound of the bedside phone ringing. His hand snaked out from under the pillow and moved back and forth until he grabbed the receiver. He generally set the ringer to OFF, but the night before something had told him not to.

He hoped it was only a crank call.

After trying to get his vocal cords responding and sounding vaguely human he picked up the receiver.

"Hello?"

"Son? It's dad. At the risk of sounding like an old comedy routine—something way before your time but it just hit me—there's trouble at mill. Actually, it's trouble down at Helium City."

Tom was instantly awake. Helium City was the extraction and delivery facility located hundreds of fathoms below the surface of the Atlantic Ocean. It was the world's premiere source of ultra pure helium. Any hint of trouble down there was like waiving red flags and honking horns to the inventor.

"What sort of trouble, Dad?"

"Would you believe signals from *the center of the Earth?*"

CHAPTER 3 /
"TROUBLE AT MILL!"

TOM WAS speechless. He sought to make sense of what his father had just told him.

"Uh, signals?"

"That's the word we got from the station manager, Peter Crumwald. I just got the call from Communications. Let me read the message. 'H.C. to S.E. P. Crumwald. Mysterious thrumming coming from under us. Echo pattern shows possibly hundreds of miles below. Center of planet? Team here nervous. Please visit ASAP.' That's the sum total of the communication. What do you suppose it could be?"

"I don't know but Peter isn't given to making wild claims. I'll grab Bud and we'll head down to Fearing at first light. We ought to be at the City before noon."

There had been no need to try to compute for a different time zone. No matter where they were located—except for the Citadel— all Swift facilities including the underwater city, the colony on Mars, and the Outpost in Space used the same time zone as Shopton. It made for the best possible schedule; nobody had to stay up all night to get in touch with someone eight or eighteen zones away.

"Can you get back to him and let him know we're coming? I'll call Bud and then we'll all try to get another four hours of sleep. I think we're going to need it!"

Tom hung up and then dialed Bud and Sandy's number. His sister answered.

"I see by the caller ID that this is the number of my dear brother, but even he wouldn't dare call at this ungodly hour of the night. So, who is this?"

"Sandy. No time for pleasantries. Wake that snoring bulk next to you. We may have trouble."

Tom heard the rustle of bed covers followed by the sound of a hand smacking against flesh. With a startled grunt Bud evidently woke up and exclaimed, "Hey! Stop it! You've ruined my dream about that TV actress and a bunch of puppies..." Bud must have realized that something wasn't right. "What?"

"It's Tom," Sandy told him. "He says there's trouble. Take the phone and say good morning Tom," she directed.

The receiver was fumbled with a little before Bud's sleepy voice came closer to the mouthpiece. "Trouble, skipper? What's going on?"

Tom told him about the mysterious noises coming either from below the helium well—and the implications that might mean given the previous drilling into and theft of huge amounts of the precious gas by an evil industrialist—or possibly inside it.

"Inside? That's impossible!" Bud declared.

"Impossible or not, flyboy, you and I have to get out there this morning. I'm calling Fearing Island to get a seacopter set up. I'll pick you up in—" he took a look a the clock, "—five hours and ten minutes. Go back to sleep after setting your alarm."

He returned the handset to its cradle. Bashalli's hand came around from his back to stroke his shoulder. "I know that you will, but I must tell you anyway, that you need to be careful. I expect you home for dinner. Okay?"

Tom patted her hand before reaching for the light switch. "Okay! But, I can't promise it'll be tonight's dinner."

When he arrived at Bud's house the flyer was standing at the curb, two steaming cups of coffee in his hands and a small suitcase at his feet. He handed Tom one of the cups, tossed his bag in the back seat and climbed it. "What?" he asked seeing Tom sitting there still holding the cup. "Put it in the holder and let's get going."

Tom inclined his head down to the cup holders in the center console. There sat two cups of hot coffee already.

"Bash had the same idea," he said.

Laughing, Bud turned around and put his cup and the one he took back from Tom into holders in the back seat.

They raced into Enterprises eight minutes later and drove straight to area above the underground hangar. Tom had decided that the faster speed of the *Sky Queen* was called for as it would see them arrive a full hour earlier than if they took the next fastest aircraft.

The jet had been raised to ground level by the night crew and all the preflight checks had been made. Even so, Bud made a quick circuit of the undercarriage before climbing in, sealing the lower hatch and heading for the cockpit. He had barely slipped into the right seat than Tom moved the throttles and sent the jet skyward.

After a quick flight they landed at the closest point on the tarmac to the submarine docks. They walked the final two hundred feet and nimbly jumped from the dock onto the side of one of the small models of the seacopter. It was identical to Tom's original in size, but featured so many refinements inside that piloting it was the difference between driving an old Rambler and a new Ferrari.

They lifted off and were soon scooting across the ocean. Even though this model was capable of flying at altitudes near twelve thousand feet, Tom decided to remain within one hundred feet of the surface.

An hour later he slowed the seacopter, lowered her to the water and reversed the giant ducted blades that filled the center of her hull. The seacopter was sucked under the waves and down into the depths. A quick underwater sona-call announced their upcoming arrival. The communications woman in the deepsea hydrodome in which Helium City was locate called back, "Great, Tom. Peter has been pacing the floor since last night. He'll meet you at docking lock two."

As the two young men stepped out into the large expanse of the hydrodome a very worried-looking Peter Crumwald came up and shook their hands.

"You can't imagine how nervous we've all been. What with that theft a couple years ago by Atlas Samson..."

He didn't need to tell Tom or Bud about that. The industrialist and shipping magnate had wrested command of the underwater facility in a political move and deposed Peter, all as a ploy to cover for one of his specialty submarines drilling and then syphoning off a large amount of the stored helium below the city.

Samson was stopped but the damage had been done. It was only by sheer luck that Tom managed to pierce a rocky membrane at the bottom of the original well chamber releasing an entirely new source of the gas.

It was Samson's son, Haz—never agreeing with his father's business tactics—who currently commanded the Swift's Mars colony.

As the three men walked over to the small Administration structure Tom inquired about the noises.

"Well, they come and go and not at regular intervals. We've tried to analyze the sounds but can't match it to anything in the database. Plus, if I didn't believe differently, I might tell you that it almost sounds like some sort of signal. Like Morse Code but not." He stopped and looked at Tom. "To top it all off, it ceased about five hours ago and we haven't heard a thing since."

"Well, Peter, don't let that bother you." Tom cocked an ear. There was nothing to hear at the present time. "Can I assume your techs have recordings for me to listen to?"

Crumwald nodded. "About two hours of them. Come on."

They made a little turn to one side of the Administration building and entered the Communications building.

Bud greeted the operator. "Hey, Daizie May! We hear you've tuned into a new progressive rock station." Dora Jean Mays was a pretty and petite woman of about thirty. She had known Bud's family out in California for years before they both ended up working for the Swifts.

"Well, hey yourself, stranger," she replied getting up from her board and giving him a little hug. "I hope Fearless Leader here had filled you in on the disappearance of whatever the heck our noise is. Oh, and hi, Tom. Sorry for not greeting you first. Anyway, I've got a bunch of those sounds digitized."

She handed them both headphones and then tapped out a series of instructions on her computer.

After a few seconds Tom sat down, fascinated by what he heard. It was a vibration more than a noise and it sounded to him more like a didgeridoo along with an unidentifiable something else. The tones were constant and rose and fell without rhythm. But Peter was right. Something about it reminded Tom of an audible code.

He pulled the headphones off. "You've obviously run this through the audio analyzer. Have you also tried the Navy to see if their sonar and underwater database can match that?"

Dora looked at Peter. They both shrugged. "Never thought of that, Tom. I'm sorry," she told him.

"Don't worry about it. They might have just stonewalled you anyway. Let me contact Admiral Hopkins to see if he will okay it."

Since it was still only 8:12 in the morning, Tom decided to wait until at least 9:00 before making the call. It would be sent to the surface to an almost undetectable buoy, and from there by powerful radio beam using Tom's Private Ear Radio system—an un-tappable form of communication—to the Outpost and relayed back to Washington D.C. It meant a delay of just under two seconds in each direction, about half that of sending a message to the Moon.

When Dora put the call through the radioman at the Navy Yard in Norfolk, Virginia, told them that the Admiral was onboard an about-to-be decommissioned frigate off the coast of North Carolina. He offered to set up the connection, but Tom thanked him and said they would make a more direct call.

Dora then rerouted things and was in communication with the *USS Schofield* two minutes later. The Admiral came to the radio room immediately.

"Tom. Great to hear your voice," he said even before the inventor spoke a single word."

"Hello, Admiral Hopkins. I would like to chat but we have a potential situation at *The City*." The way he spoke the final two words sent a chill up the Admiral's back. It was the code name for Helium City, and the U.S. Navy was the primary government security agency tasked with its welfare.

"Where are you, Tom? I can rendezvous with you in... hang on —" he held the microphone away from his mouth as he asked to be connected to the Bridge, where he inquired at to their best time to get to the point above the hydrodome. A minute later he came back on the radio. "We can be over you in nineteen hours. Will that do?"

"I'm not certain you need to rush here, sir." He explained his desire to tap into the Navy's audio database and gave him the basic reason why this was necessary."

"Absolutely. I'll radio the necessary orders and clearances. I would still like to get a chance to listen to those noises myself. I believe I will come over in any case."

"Well, sir, if you are determined to come here I'll have Bud Barclay pick you up in our seacopter. I believe he can be there in about one hour. I presume that the ship you are on has a helicopter flight deck?"

The Admiral told them it did and said he would ensure it was prepared to have Bud touch down. "I'll be ready," he promised before cutting the connection.

It took most of the hour of Bud's flight to retrieve the Navy man before Dora was able to get the computer connection with the Navy's audio database. She had carefully created a dozen twenty-second snippets of the sounds. These samples were fed into the Navy's computer one at a time. Each one required two minutes to be checked against the nearly fifty thousand individual sounds available.

Sample after sample went in, and the results were identical:

No known match for audio sample

They had just thanked the operator at the other end when Bud signaled that he and the Admiral were about to touch down on the surface above them.

"See you in fifteen minutes, skipper."

Tom and Peter met Bud and his guest as they exited the airlock.

"Nice to have you come down, sir, but I'm afraid to report that both your database and ours can't match up the noises they have been experiencing down here." They headed for the communications room.

After letting him listen to a few minutes of the sounds, everyone, except for Dora Mays, headed for Peter Crumwald's office.

Sitting down with a cup of coffee, Admiral Hopkins rubbed his face. "Okay. For starters, and I'm no expert, but that doesn't sound like any unauthorized drilling." He looked around that they agreed. "Fine. Tom mentioned a sort of signal pattern and I can agree with him. It also sounds like some very muffled speaking." He looked and the others sat there with astonished looks. "Ah, you didn't pick up on that? Well, as a one-time Navy diver—five lifetimes ago it seems—I heard my share of people trying to speak underwater. Let me see if I can give you an idea."

The reached to the water dispenser and picked up three cups, nested inside each other. Into these he shoved his handkerchief. Then, placing the loaded cup to his mouth he began to softly and rhythmically speak.

The results were almost blood chilling.

"Bu-but that sounds kind of like the signals, Admiral!" Bud exclaimed.

Setting the cups down and retrieving his handkerchief, the Admiral nodded. "Not quite but similar I thought. Oh, and for the duration of my visit down here please everybody call me Horace. It's not a great name but I am so tired of admiral this and admiral that."

Peter was the first to speak. "Well, Horace, I believe this calls for us to revisit our communications room and see if we can clean that audio up a little."

They spent five hours with Dora trying to get a cleaner sound, but all attempts failed. In the end it was decided to give up for the time being. No further sounds had been heard and it was well into the afternoon.

"Admi— sorry, Horace," Bud began as they ate a very late lunch, "how far could a voice travel underwater?"

"Hmmm. Well, human voices don't have a lot of volume, nor do we communicate within frequency ranges that offer great long-distance travel. While some whales can be heard thousands of miles away, an un-amplified human voice that is totally immersed in water, under even the best water conditions, can only reach about three hundred yards. Of course, put the person's mouth in an air bubble and the range nearly triples due to the build up of pressure waves. Why?"

Tom spoke up. "I think I follow Bud's logic, Horace. It would help to know potentially how far these signals have traveled. We need to do some research!"

Tom and Peter, because they had a good idea of what to look for, divided the task of locating the potential travel distances of voices through different medium. Air, water, rock and even liquid and gaseous helium.

All but the helium came up with no greater distance that that of water.

Helium, however, especially in liquefied form, could allow certain frequencies—the lower range of which included deeper male human voices—to travel up to several miles.

"When you get back from your run to drop the Admiral off," Tom said to Bud, "can you make a wide and a narrow circuit of the area just to be certain we don't have any *guests* out there."

"Sure. What if we do?"

"Go back topside and call in the Navy, then get back here pronto!"

While Bud returned the Admiral to his ship, Tom studied the results of the research and did some calculations. Anywhere from two to five miles seemed to be the answer.

Bud's seacopter search uncovered no submarines or anything else out of the ordinary in an area extending to twelve miles from the city.

By the time he returned, Tom had come to a conclusion.

"We need to create a speaker or other broadcast device to lower into the cavern below us and broadcast back the signals we've received. At least, some of them."

"To what end?" Bud asked.

"My hope is that if—and this might not be the case—these signals come from some living source, they will hear it and try to get into contact with us."

Bud shivered. "Living? Down there! What if this is someone or something with less than friendly intentions?"

Tom pondered this. "As much as I am loathe to do it, I think that Helium City needs to be evacuated of everyone but me while I try my experiment."

Bud shook his head, and Tom noticed that Peter was doing the same.

"Listen, guys. While I appreciate your support I don't intend on just sitting here in case of a problem. It's going to take a few days and I need get things ready to try this in my workshop back at Enterprises, but we'll come back with a flotilla of seacopters and jetmarines, one of which I will be sitting in—*solo*—when I start the signaling. First sign of any problem and I detach from the lock and get out of here. Happy?"

"No, but can we talk you out of it?" Peter inquired.

"I only answer to a higher authority, my wife, Bashalli. I promised her that I would not take unnecessary chances and I intend to live up to that. Emphasis on the word, 'live.' "

"But, we do have to go home before you try this. Right?" Bud asked, concern showing on his face and evident in his voice.

Tom nodded.

"Fine. Then at least you're gonna have a couple of days where Bash can work on you and maybe beat some sense into you!"

It was agreed they would remain in Helium City until the next morning. Tom secretly was glad as he hoped the mystery signals, or whatever they were, would begin again.

Everyone was on alert so it took almost no time when, at a few minutes past three in the morning, the thrumming sounds started up. Tom hadn't undressed so he just slipped into his loafers and ran out the air lock door heading for the Communications building. The midnight to 8:00 am man was on duty.

"Hello, Tom," he said as the inventor slipped into the seat next to him, picking up the extra headphones.

"Carl. I see you are recording. How much did we lose at the front end?"

"Less than two seconds. I've been twitchy all shift and had my finger close to the record button."

Tom put the headphones on and listened carefully for nearly five minutes. Half way through, Bud and Peter entered the room but opted to stand to one side so as not to disturb the others. As suddenly as it began, the noise stopped. He pulled the phones back off and set them on the desk.

"Did you hear about Admiral Hopkins' theory?" Tom asked.

"Word gets around. Something about deep sea voices?"

Bud stepped forward. "It was more than that. He said it sounds like what he used to hear as a deep diver when somebody tried to talk under water."

Now, Tom shook his head. "I think he might be incorrect on that, folks. If Carl will replay that, listen carefully. Imagine those are supposed to be voices. I didn't hear a similarity."

They listened to the entire thing. Once it finished, Peter said, "I think I have to agree with Tom. Unless those are the sounds of about a dozen people all muttering in different languages into overstuffed pillows... well, I didn't hear voices. That's all."

Tom requested that the entire set of digitized audio files be sent to the computers in the seacopter. He intended, as he told them, to have the giant Swift bank of computers do a complete comparison of everything.

"If there is anything that gets repeated or any sort of pattern to the sounds, I'll find it. Plus I can run it through more filters than you have in your system. Perhaps I can draw out things we aren't hearing right now."

When it came time to leave Carl was off duty and met them at the airlock.

"Got everything all snug and safe in your computers, and I made this high sample rate disc for you. Might give you something to listen to in your car," he said with a smile.

Tom thanked him and Peter, and asked that Dora Mays also be told that he appreciated her assistance.

As the seacopter rose toward the surface Bud asked a question he hadn't felt comfortable bringing up inside the hydrodome.

"Does your gut tell you this is probably just some natural phenomena, like rock slides way down inside the well, or something that might be bad for us all?"

Before he answered, Tom took a deep breath and let it out slowly.

"I don't honestly know, Bud. I hadn't considered the rock slides deep in the well theory, but it is something I'll keep in mind. What my gut is telling me is that this might require I go down myself to see what is happening. Find the cause."

Bud shook his head, saying, "Not *you*, Tom. You and *me*!"

CHAPTER 4 /
RETURN OF THE STRANGE BUZZING NOISES

WHEN TWO days went by with no more reports of noises, Tom began to believe more in Bud's rockslide theory. Upon their return, he sat down with Mr. Swift and went over the audio files and related some of his thoughts.

"For the time being, Son, I would prefer to caution against any sort of plan to rebroadcast those noises back into the well. For one, we have never made a thorough survey of the caverns, just a cursory look around the upper chamber but literally nothing in the lower level. We don't even know if there are just the two chambers."

Tom had been thinking about his plan and already had come to the conclusion that the rebroadcast idea wasn't the first thing they might attempt.

"Yes, I know. About the very last thing I want to do is bounce audio waves all over down there. If anything is loose it might break away. As I told Bud on the flight back to Fearing, what if we blocked off the lower chamber by accident. We'd be in a fine fix then."

"I agree. So do you have an alternate idea?"

Shaking his head, Tom had to admit that nothing specific had come to mind. "Although, I suppose that I might create another probe to go much farther down into the lower chamber and take a look. I don't think I can use the probe design from two years ago because everything lower is mostly liquefied helium. Nothing will 'fly' through that!"

"Certainly, but how will you be able to see anything? As you know, the deeper anything might travel down there, the more pressure the liquid helium is under and the thicker it should be."

"Well—" Tom rubbed his jaw and thought a moment before he continued, "I think I may be able to repurpose some of the instruments and sensors from the probe I sent into that magma bubble over near Rhode Island. If those could see through hot magma, a little icy cold helium bath ought to be a breeze. Of course, since they burned up I'll have to build new ones, but that should give me the opportunity to make some enhancements."

Later that day he was sitting at the desk in his small office and lab next to the floor of the underground hangar where his first large-scale invention, the *Sky Queen*, was kept when not in use.

The *Queen*, also known as his Flying Lab, was a triple-deck behemoth of a jet with vertical take off and landing capabilities and featured everything from well-appointed laboratories to living quarters for up to thirty people and even a hangar at the back end that could carry many things, including a miniature helicopter and one-man jet.

Now, as he looked at the computer screen he was making a mental list of which of the sensor arrays from his volcanic probe might be suited for this job.

As well as suitability he had to take into consideration overall size. The first time he needed to look inside the helium well a special capping system—more like an airlock—had been installed down into the upper chamber and a tightly folded robotic probe lowered into the cavern where it unfolded and flew around. The issue was the lock was only about 12-inches wide. On the other hand, his magma probe had been several feet in diameter and needed to be that large to fit in most of the sensor arrays and the heat shielding.

Even without the heat shielding—and cold shielding would need to take its place—the "guts" of that probe spanned nearly 44-inches.

I definitely need to get Linda Wong working with me on this, he thought to himself. *But, I also think we're going to need a bigger hole to shove this through!*

Tom sent Peter Crumwald an email asking him to talk this over with his engineers. He ended the message with:

> See if they think that we can use that pressurization system again to hold the gas down while we swap out the current pass-through lock system for one that might be as wide as four feet in diameter.

Only time and a bit of their expertise would tell.

Next, he called the Modeling department. He was a little surprised and also pleased to hear Linda's voice answer.

"Hi, Linda. It's Tom. I may have another project right up your alley. Care to drop down to my underground office, or should I come over there?"

"You know, in all the time I've worked here I've never stepped foot down there. Unless you tell me that it is a dark, mysterious cavern of terror, I'd rather come see you there than sit in my office for the next hour or so. See you in five?"

"Five it is!"

Tom straightened up the splayed out papers on his desk and

called up three diagrams from the magma probe on his screen. Very soon he could hear the elevator coming down. He was glad she had decided not to attempt the stairs. At over eight somewhat steep stories they could exhaust anyone not accustomed to them. Even coming down. Going up was nearly an entire exercise workout.

Her heels clicked across the floor until, at what he knew would be the halfway point, they stopped. He rose and went to the door.

"She's really impressive when viewed from underneath," he commented. It broke her out of her trance, and she turned to face him.

"I don't know what to say, Tom. Of course I've see her flying away and landing many times, but that has always been from a distance." She started walking toward him as she continued, "Up close like this... well, I suppose the words 'awe inspiring' just about fit the bill. Perhaps, just plain 'Wow!' Oh, and nice little place you keep her in." She smiled at him, and he ushered her into the office.

Tom explained the basics of the situation.

"Yes. I've heard about the noises. Nobody knows what they are?"

"Not yet," he admitted. "Here. Take a little listen." He tapped a few keys and soon the sounds were coming from the stereo speakers in his monitor.

Linda listened with a mix of curiosity and confusion.

When Tom turned the noise off, she said, "That doesn't sound like anything I've ever heard. Now I *really* want to help if I can."

Tom explained what he wanted to do and spent twenty minutes giving her a visual and descriptive tour of the former magma probe. She asked questions all along the way and listened attentively.

"What do you think?" he asked as he finished the rundown.

"I think you have far too many possibilities and too many needs to get everything into a single probe, at least as long as we have to work within the fairly narrow constrictions of your airlock thing."

He nodded. "I figured that would be the case. We've been calling it a gas lock, by the way. That's not really important here but once I take you down to Helium City they will look at you wondering why we didn't let you know."

"Then I shall remember that. So, this gas lock is very narrow and is also not all that long. I'll go back to my desk with the list of sensors and things you want to accomplish and see what the most efficient use of space will be. Right off the top of my head I'd say you're looking to at least two probes but more likely three. I'll assume that you want to capture some gas samples from various depths?" She looked expectantly.

Tom groaned a little and nodded. "Right." He made a note on his papers. "Forgot that one. I guess we need to plan on one probe that does practically nothing other that take samples at, oh, every five hundred feet or so." He grinned as she stood up to leave.

"Uh, Tom?" Linda turned and asked before leaving. "I haven't run into him lately, but how is Bud doing? And, by that I mean both the pogo tackle and... well, you know. How are he and Sandy doing?"

Linda, before her previous departure from Enterprises, had a small crush on the younger man and had made her feelings known to him including a couple kisses. He still blushed any time he came close to her.

"Bud's bruises are about gone," he said. "My shoulder still hurts where it connected with his left hip, but neither of us sustained any real damage. As to the happy couple... that about describes it. Sandy is happy that she got the man of her dreams and Bud is happy to have her. I know there is a little discomfort between you two, but give him time. Unless you make some foolish play for him he will get back to being a colleague and friend soon enough!"

"Nah. I'm over him, now." She thanked him and left.

While they had been talking, Peter Crumwald sent a return email answering Tom's questions about the pressurized building.

> Sorry to report but engineers think we're nearing the limits. Do not advise widening current hole.

It was unfortunate news but Tom had expected it.

The next day Linda Ming called to say she had a few things to discuss, and Tom offered to come over. When he arrived she was just printing out a few pages.

"I think I've got a handle on the three probes we need, Tom." She sat down with him on a sofa to one side of the room. Handing him the first printout she explained, "This is the easiest of the three. It is the sampling probe. On the assumption that you will want a cubic foot of gas at each level I can fit eight containers, valve assemblies and either pressure releases or a simple computer to let you trigger things from upstairs. At your suggested five hundred foot intervals we can sample the upper four thousand feet."

As she was telling him about the specifications of the sampling equipment a question came into his mind.

"Linda, since we really don't know how deep the caverns are, is there some way to trigger them on the way up? As in, we lower the probe until it stops, take a sample, and let the computer figure out the proper spacing for the remaining containers?"

"Sure. In fact that would give the computer time to take an ongoing series of pressure measurements on the way down. If we can maintain electronic contact with it you can even change things once it hits bottom."

"Fine. Let's plan on that. Now about the other sensors."

Linda handed him the other two printouts. The first showed an array of five sensors including a revolving video camera with light system, a sonar imaging system, an infrared imaging system, temperature and viscosity collectors, along with data collection memory and transmission equipment.

The second showed just two sensors taking up about ninety-five percent of the space. These were a detailed listening and audio processing device and a unit that could flip down and shoot out smaller probes in a 360-degree arc around the main body.

He raised an eyebrow at seeing this.

"That, Tom, is yet another way to find out the size and shape of the lower cavern. It will be so dark and the helium so dense that no light and possibly very little of the sonar will penetrate."

"What will this do, then?"

"Ever heard the story of young Samuel Clemens and his riverboat days?"

"Do you mean his being the depth rope boy? Knots tied in the line every six feet and he'd toss it in, see which one was showing and call out, 'mark three, mark four, mark twain.' That?"

Linda smiled and nodded. "Yes. This unit can shoot out, using high-pressure nitrogen, probes to a distance of about five hundred feet. If we can't see anything, then we ought to be able to tell at least if the cavern is narrower than a thousand feet. The probe tips each have a little camera and light source in five bandwidths, and a temperature probe."

"So, it shoots them out, takes a look and a feel and then... do these get pulled back in?"

"They do and can be shot back out I believe two or three times. That's the limit to how much nitrogen we can carry."

"Get me some detailed drawings of these probes and we'll talk the project over with the applicable departments."

She agreed to have the diagrams ready in two days.

"Oh. Tom? I have found a way to keep Bud Barclay from bashing his own head in on that pogo stick I came up with."

"So have I," he told her. "Keep him off the thing!"

"Well, that... yes, but I also have come up with a way to safely allow people to do tricks like he tried. I can program the thing to react much faster to keep anybody from getting into trouble, but then give the handle an override button. Push it in and get perhaps five seconds to do a trick before it self-stabilizes again. What do you think?"

Tom rubbed his jaw in thought. "Tell you what. If you have time, work on that and come up with a final product. Also, I've dropped the ball on calling the Mars colony to ask if they could use something like it. Will you do that?"

She told him she would do that once the cavern probe diagrams had been completed.

While she got work on the final designs Tom visited the three departments that would ultimately build the sensors and probes to her specifications. They all agreed to be ready for the first of the projects and would devote the appropriate personnel to everything he needed.

Even with that it would be nearly three weeks before the probes would be ready to take down to Helium City.

With little to do to add to the work, or take on himself, Tom decided to investigate what might be required should he decide to mount a manned probe into the caverns. After all, both controlled and autonomous probes could only do so much. It was like that in most areas of science and exploration.

For the remainder of the day he kept to his underground lab and office. There, he cleared an area of the floor about eight feet across, picked up a roll of masking tape, and laid out a cross about six feet in diameter. He then marked the tape every six inches until he had a grid to use for setting up various-sized capsules.

While in Africa some years earlier he and Bud had been lowered in a sphere into what became known as the caves of nuclear fire. The sphere shape had been needed to keep the enormous heat and pressure inside the fiery cave from collapsing everything.

He believed that a sphere would be needed in the case of the helium as the deeper it would go, the greater the pressure. If this were to be lowered into any cavern from an open-topped area, he could make it nearly any width. But, as he picked the tape roll up again—with the intent of marking out a circle to designate the outer width of his sphere—he stopped. Just how wide *could* he make this new sphere?

It would certainly be limited in width. And, even if he gave up the notion of it being completely round most probably it could be no taller than about the current 12-feet inside length of the gas lock.

He picked up two small chairs sitting against the wall and placed them facing each other. If he wanted to give the occupants—and he knew that Bud would not allow this to be a one-man (Tom) machine—about ten inches of leg room, then the minimum capsule width needed to be nearly five feet. It would be even wider if the occupants sat side-by-side. So, two persons—facing was written on his notes.

He took the tape and created, as well as he could, a circle of five feet. Anything else he came up with would almost certainly need to fit inside of that outer dimension.

He was standing to one side when he came up with a question to which he had no ready answer. A call down to Helium City and Peter Crumwald was necessary.

"Peter, it's Tom in Shopton. I've got a question. How much weight do you believe the ceiling of the upper cavern can support?"

"Well, obviously it's already supporting everything we've got down here. And it just so happens that we sunk the three pipes into the well close to dead center of the top of the cavern, and that also happens to be about the thinnest area, just the eleven feet from our floor to the cavern ceiling. As I said in my email, that is really our limit for that spot. The structural guys here have been asking for months if we would remove the pressure building to lessen the load. Why do you ask?"

Tom explained that he didn't wish to place undue stress on the upper wall. He didn't tell Peter but he was also feeling a little nervous about the probable concentrated weight of any larger probe and the effect drilling for a larger gas lock might bring.

"Do me a favor when you get the chance. This may be for nothing but can you get a team outside the dome with ground penetrating RADAR or some sounding equipment to find a likely spot for an additional entry lock? I'd like to find somewhere with perhaps thirty or even fifty feet of solid rock to go through."

Peter promised to get it done in the following five days.

Tom looked at his watch and decided that it was too near time to go home to work out the logistics of creating a new gas lock for any possible excursion into the caverns, so he made a few notes, turned off the lights and went up to his car.

Bashalli generally managed to beat him home by half an hour or more, but when he pulled into the driveway, her car wasn't there. He shrugged and went in through the front door. As he passed the small desk and telephone he noticed the blinking red light from the answering machine. He pushed the **PLAY** button.

"You have one call. Today... five thirty-seven p. m."
Beeeeeeeeeeeep!

Hello Tom? It is Bashalli. I missed you at work and your cell phone did not answer so I am leaving you this message. I will be home at about seven. I am sorry, but we have a possible new client from over in Oswego and my team must put together a presentation for tomorrow. I love you. Bye!

He went upstairs and changed into a clean tee-shirt and shorts, then grabbed a soda from the refrigerator and sat down to watch some television.

The news was just wrapping up the international portion and turning to U.S. stories. The first three were merely continuations from things that happened the previous day, but the fourth one made him sit up and take notice.

"In Florida, a religious leader who goes by the name of Reverend Walter Speers has gone public today with an incredible claim... and a warning. Our sister station WSLG in Ft. Lauderdale files this report."

The scene changed to a woman standing outside across a busy street from a very large building. On top sat a cross and the words **Heaven Only Takes Repenters** emblazoned in six-foot letters just below it.

"This is Haley Brandenburg in Ft. Lauderdale. I'm standing in front of the church of the Reverend Walter Speers. Speers began his career as a small town evangelist in Arkansas before purchasing a bankrupt television station and turning his efforts, as he puts it, to televising God's message."

The scene now changed to some old stock footage of the inside of what might be any church with a man dressed in black standing in front of a rough wooden cross and waiving his arms about. The reporter's voice continued over the new pictures.

"Reverend Speers held a press conference today in an adjoining building to the actual church which he refers to as 'my temple.' "

The scene changed again, this time to a shot of an older, somewhat wild-eyed—Tom thought—man standing in front of several microphones.

"I've warned you, all of you, about the sins of this world and how the time is coming. Time and again people have refused to believe me. Well, now I'm here to tell you that the end is at our doorstep! There is someone among us who is associating with the very devil himself. Together, they plan to destroy all of us!"

He paused for effect and shook a finger at the assembled

reporters.

"I'm talking about *Tom Swift*!"

Tom's blood froze.

"This young man is not content to go digging under the surface of the Earth. No. Now he is about to release Satan on this world! I have credible proof that he is in communication with the underworld. A recording of one of the messages was delivered into my hands. It has an unearthly sound. It is the sound of sin!

"And so I say to you, repent and come unto me. Send me your name and send me a donation and I will see that you are saved! And, if Tom Swift is watching this, be warned. Tinker with the Devil and *you shall be punished!*"

CHAPTER 5 /

MR. TOAD'S WILD RIDE

TOM SAT there a little dumbstruck. To begin with he had never heard of the reverend, nor his church. Then there was the matter of the implied threat toward Tom. However the thing that bothered him most at that moment was the apparent leak of information and classified recordings of the noises down under the sea floor.

His phone rang while he sat trying to decide what to do.

"Tom? It's Harlan," his chief of Security said. "I don't suppose that you have your TV on by any chance?"

"Yeah. And I just saw that man in Florida and his telling the world that I might be part of something that will destroy them. What is it with these fanatics?"

"Fanatic is right. Speers is not an ordained minister of any religion other than his own, and he is the only one in his church so designated. He's one of those pay-as-you-go types. I have his website up right in front of me. For general blessings and, quote, 'protection from the Devil' it *suggests* a donation of one hundred dollars. Direct flight to heaven, two hundred. Cash preferred. Automatic annual, semi-annual and monthly payments available. If you feel that you have sinned at some point it jumps to two-fifty and goes up from there."

"And he has a following?" Tom asked incredulously.

"Evidently that *church* in the news story gets about a thousand people sitting inside to hear the man each Sunday paying an *honorarium* of ten dollars per person. And, he broadcasts on several of the larger satellite and cable systems into a potential of about fifty-million homes every night from about two to three a.m."

"What about his 'You will be punished' thing?"

Harlan sighed. "I'm afraid that we can't do anything about it other than to notify the FBI that we find it to be a threat and want them to keep an eye on the man. Not much else we can do unless Legal says sue the man. However, what we can do is track down whoever it is that gave him the recording, assuming he actually has one."

"Keep me in the loop, Harlan. And, see if you can find any way to tell if that Speers has followers here in the area. I've gotten very tired of thugs and criminals coming in from out of town to try to do me harm, but at least you can spot a stranger. I'd hate to find myself smiling at a local only to discover they are so devoted to this man they are willing to hurt me or anyone else over something like this."

As they were hanging up, Bashalli came in through the front door. She had a worried look on her face.

"Did you hear that lunatic from Florida?" she asked after giving him a quick peck on the lips.

"Yes. I just got off the phone with Harlan Ames." He told her about the conversation.

"I do not like this at all!" she declared with anger flashing in her eyes. "How dare that, that *person* tell people that you are doing something like that? Or to say that you will be punished. My family escaped an entire nation of horrible people like that and their stupid followers, and I don't wish to go back to those conditions. What can you do?"

"Possibly nothing, Bash." He took her in his arms. "As much as I hate to be threatened like this, it isn't the first time and probably will not be the last. It is something that people in the public view have to put up with. Besides, he's obviously a crackpot who is trying to make money out of this."

"Well," she told him, not the slightest mollified, "he had better never show his face around here. Moshan would probably kill him."

Bashalli's older brother was exceptionally protective of his sister. He now thought of himself as Tom's older brother as well.

"Let's hope and assume it will never get to that point. So, tell me about your meeting," he suggested hoping to change the subject.

She sat down and composed herself before telling him about the new furniture super store just being constructed in the city located on the banks of Lake Ontario.

"It is part of a larger chain and they like to have a local flavor for the first year or two. Then their big agency in Los Angeles takes over, but if we do well we could receive a longer term contract to work with them. It will be very good money for the agency."

They talked about this happier news until she stood up and went to the kitchen to cook dinner.

By the following morning Tom was over his feelings of anger at the Florida evangelist and was more bothered about any possible betrayal of trust among the people both at Helium City and on the surface who might have provided a recording to the man. With nothing he could do along that line, he plunged into his potential manned probe project.

Before the end of the day Tom was nowhere closer to deciding on what a capsule might look like than the day before. He was about to call it a day when the phone rang.

"Tom. It's Trent. You have a rather nervous caller on line two. The caller I.D, says he's in Washington D.C. Can you take it?"

"Sure. Thanks." Tom pressed the button. "Tom Swift here. Who am I speaking with?"

He heard the shaking intake of breath before an equally shaky voice began.

"M-m-mister Sw-Swift? M-my name is Ju-Jerrod Lewis. Uhh, I work in the ma-ma-master tape v-vault in W-wa-Washington."

"Well, Mr. Lewis, take a deep breath and then try to collect yourself. What is it you wanted to tell me?"

The caller took a deep breath and then a second one before continuing. "Thank you. I am very nervous as you probably guessed. You must hate me right now. I'm afraid that I might be responsible for that money grubber down in Florida having part of the recording you sent us for identification."

The hairs on Tom's neck raised. He fought the urge to yell at the caller.

"At the risk of making you more nervous, Mr. Lewis... Jerrod... I need to conference call in my head of Security so he can hear your story. Please do not hang up. If this was an honest mistake then you have nothing to fear. Hold on—" Tom quickly got Harlan on the line. "—I assume you are still there, Jerrod, so please go on."

"I won't get arrested?"

"It depends on what you can tell us," Harlan told the man.

"Okay. Right. You see my girlfriend is sort of a nut when it comes to what she calls 'getting into heaven.' So, she really took to this Florida guy. Sends him twenty bucks a week. Anyway, she and I have been drifting apart for a few months and I thought I'd impress her with a little listen to sounds from inside the planet."

"So you copied a top secret recording, played it for her, and then what?" Ames was sounding very perturbed now.

"Her eyes got all sparkly and she told me that I was a really great man. Then, after I fell asleep I guess she sort of sent herself the file and left. Next thing I know I'm called on the carpet down here about it. I know I'm going to lose my job, but I don't want to be put in prison. I mean, it isn't like treason or murder anything, right?"

"No. Not treason, but your actions have caused both a huge security problem as well as a personal threat against me," Tom told him.

"You did an incredibly stupid thing, Mr. Lewis," Harlan said. "You will and should lose your security clearance, and that means your current position, but more idiotic things have been done in the name of love so I suppose I can have a talk with your bosses to see if there is some other spot for you there."

"It took guts to call, Jerrod, so thanks," Tom said. The caller gave them as much information about his now ex-girlfriend as he could before he hung up.

"You still on the line, Tom?"

"Yeah. I figured you might want to talk."

"Okay. I'll call the FBI to let them know we found the leak, give them the girl's info so they can go put a little fear and reality check into her, and then get onto this Lewis' boss to see if his career can be salvaged."

"Thanks, Harlan. I appreciate it."

They both hung up.

Four days went by. On Saturday Tom received a postcard from his car dealer regarding an important software update and asked if he could please bring the sedan by Monday morning. He called their service department and made an appointment.

The man had sounded so eager to know Tom was coming in that the inventor decided this must be a very important update.

On Monday he phoned his father before the older inventor was to leave for work and asked if he might come down and pick Tom up.

"Certainly, Son. I'll be down there in twenty minutes. Bye!"

Tom had never seen the man who greeted him at the service counter but the paperwork was completed and he was told it would take that day and a bit of the following morning to perform the work.

"We can offer you a loaner, sir," the man told him. Tom spotted his father waiting outside so he declined.

"Wish it didn't take so long. I'll be back tomorrow," he promised.

As they drove out of town heading for Enterprises Tom began to wonder about the lengthy time for something seemingly as easy as a software update. He brought the subject up.

"Perhaps they have a few cars to get through today and yours is at the bottom of the list. Or, the whole thing might need configuring after the car has been test driven a bit. Whatever it is, I'm certain it is nothing to worry about or you would have heard or read about a major problem with that model."

"I suppose."

They drove the rest of the way to work in silence. Once inside the Executive gate, Tom thanked his father and said he would walk over to the underground hangar.

About the only thing of interest that day was the report from Helium City regarding a new possible drilling location. Tom called down to see what was up.

"Hey, skipper," Peter greeted him. "So I sent a few people out on a scouting party. They had your requirements plus two of my own. First, any place they looked at had to be within sight of the dome. Nothing behind small hills or too far down the slope of the hill we're on. Second, no sites with notable sea life that would need to be moved."

"Did they find anything?"

"Sure. Nine spots. Five of them are too deep to drill though. More than eighty feet. I still have them charted if you want us to take a closer look, but we were concentrating on the ones in the thirty to fifty foot range. So, of those four, most are no farther from the edge of the dome than ninety-five feet. Just one is at one hundred twenty-seven feet. They all look like good candidates. The rock under the silt is solid and should take drilling without issues."

Tom was about to thank him when Peter added, "Of course we didn't go out to the site where Atlas Samson drilled sideways into the upper cavern and stole all the helium. It is out of our line of sight but has the security system you installed out there so we can keep an eye on things."

Tom wondered silently for a moment before inquiring, "Why did you think of that location, Peter?"

"Well, it is already known to be solid yet drill-able, and the two-foot bore they sank could fairly easily be widened, but the main reason is that your dad had us erect a pressure building about twice as large as the one inside the dome and seal it down as tightly as we could. The shaft has a small crack in it, a natural one by the way, that leaks about twenty cubic feet of gas a day. He wanted to make certain that there are no bubbles that might be detected, so we go over there once a week and fill up a couple of pressure tanks and bring the gas back here."

"Well, I'll be," Tom said. "Okay. Does that building have power?"

"It does."

"Could it hold back the pressure when we get the hole to the cavern?"

Peter paused. "Probably not with everything wide open, but assuming you come up with an ingenious way connect a drill to a tether so it can be retrieved back into the hole after breakthrough, and seal the upper end during the drilling, we can managed the pressure."

"Thanks, Peter. This may not come to pass, but I want to have as many options open as possible. Also, please thank your team for their work. I'll keep you advised. Bye."

Tom walked to the Administration building and the shared office.

Mr. Swift was speaking on the phone to the team in Japan for whom Enterprises was finishing up the new satellite. It had been planned that the NSA, Nippon Space Agency, would launch that atop a brand new class of rocket, but reports from a day earlier said the test rocket exploded just a mile into its test flight.

"So, if you can please tell them," Damon sat patiently explaining, "that we are still on track to deliver right at the end of the extended time line. Also let them know that we can assist after the disaster of the test launch. We can place the satellite on our recently completed space elevator, take it up to the precise orbit point and then move it into position so that the orbit insertion rockets can get it moving at the right velocity. It can be placed within about a thirty-foot measure of accuracy as oppose to the Earth launch placement of within about two hundred meters. I'll expect your return call. Thank you, Yoshi-san."

He turned and smiled at Tom. "I hope my mixing feet and meters won't confuse them. The program managers are in a real tizzy over their non-working launch vehicle."

"What you told them ought to soften the blow. Besides, if we do it for free then they save millions on a rush job of the second rocket."

"Right, and there's no guarantee it will be any better. So, what's on your grinning-like-the-Cheshire-Cat mind?"

Tom told him about the potential for a manned probe in case the robotic ones didn't get them the information they needed. By the end of the hour that they discussed things, Damon Swift was almost completely on board with Tom's ideas.

He went home that afternoon feeling happy.

Tom laughed when he saw Bud's convertible pull up behind his own car as they arrived at the main gate of Enterprises Tuesday morning. The pilot leaned out his opened window and called out to Tom.

"Skipper. I need to ask you something. Don't drive off."

"Okay," Tom turned and shouted back.

Inside the gate he pulled over to the right about fifty feet and stopped his car. Bud pulled along side.

"What's on your mind this beautiful morning?" Tom asked.

"I've got an assignment from the little woman. You might recall her. Blond? Kind of pushy when she wants something?"

"So I've been led to believe," Tom said back feigning seriousness. "What sort of mission are you on?"

"I've been told to tell you that she hopes you and your lovely wife might join us for dinner at the House of Barclay this evening, with a retry on the artichokes—steamed this time—followed by a spot of dancing at the Shopton Yacht Club. Evidently a brother of a friend is singing there this very night. Oh, and she's already cleared it with Bash, so you really have no choice."

"Okay. Have you got time to have coffee right now?"

"Sorry, skipper. I've got a couple of demo flights today. One this morning, ten minutes from now, and one a bit later on. Maybe we can grab something in between. Say, eleven?"

"I'll see, Bud. Have a good one."

"Ta!"

Bud put his car into gear and drove off. As he did, Tom could swear he heard laughter.

They met a little before noon with Bud telling him all about how dinner that evening was going to be a barbecue and that Tom should bring a bathing suit as the Barclay's had just installed an above ground pool. "And, remember your dancing shoes!"

"How was the morning demo?" Tom asked, curious that Bud hadn't mentioned it at all by the time they had been sitting for ten minutes. Generally, when a contingent of thirty airline executives, especially when they came to Shopton from as far away as Sri Lanka and got the Barclay demo treatment, the flyer had all sorts of tales to tell.

"Not a lot to tell. But it was demos, plural. I had to take them up in four groups because their three interpreters had to go along each time. One for the really big wigs, another for the smaller wigs and one for me. All in all they were impressed enough to want to talk to the Purchasing folks about getting maybe five of them. The thing that cemented the deal was when they were all standing around the front of the plane. The interpreter said they really like how it looks, just like that amphibian we all see." Now, he grinned. "Want to know what they call you now that they've had a ride in the SE-11?"

"Go ahead," Tom replied cautiously, unsure if this was going to be another Bud joke.

"They all were calling the great Tom Swift, Mister Toad! Guess they've never read the book or seen any of the old Disney stuff."

After giving a little groan over the name, Tom said, "They probably haven't paid attention to those sort of things. Well, I'm glad they enjoyed the air tour and think enough of the jet to consider buying a few."

After a couple minutes Tom asked, "Want to come into town with me?"

"Test run of one of the new Swift Auto models? Errand of mercy? Going in to visit Bash?"

Shaking his head, Tom answered, "None of the above. I had to drop my car off at the dealership yesterday for some sort of software recall. A computer glitch that could cause something horrible like butterflies to spontaneously come pouring out of the vents." He smiled at Bud. "Actually it is a software update but they couldn't get mine finished yesterday. It's ready now and I sort of need a ride in. Got the time?"

Bud looked at his watch and nodded. "Just barely. I've got a demo flight in a Toad for the folks at CanaDair. They might be ordering thirty of them so I want to be on time."

"Great! Let's go."

The two left the cafeteria and headed for the small parking area next to the underground hangar. Bud's little two-seater was parked in the closest spot, so they climbed in and were driving out of the main gate a half minute later.

Fortunately for Bud's appointment, the dealership was on the Enterprises side of Shopton, so he dropped Tom off in front and roared away giving his friend a wave over his right shoulder. The rather bored woman at the payment window took Tom's credit card, processed the payment for the oil change he'd asked for as if it were a labor and by the time he turned around, his car was waiting in the covered staging area just outside.

He climbed in, noting that an addendum to the Owner's Manual was sitting on the passenger seat, and started the car. It might have been his imagination but it sounded a little smoother than before. With a shrug, he put the car into Drive and pulled out and onto the street.

"I think I'll head through town and take a little test run past the airport," he muttered to himself. After stopping at a downtown grocery store for a can of cola, Tom got back into the sedan and headed north. Less than a mile farther on as he got up to thirty-five, the car lurched forward and started to accelerate.

Worried, Tom pressed on the brakes. Nothing happened except that the car continued to move faster. He was passing fifty in seconds. He shoved at the shift lever trying to get the car out of Drive but it wouldn't budge.

Although the road was fairly straight he noted that his speed now was exceeding sixty and continuing to climb. The car had a push-button ignition and he stabbed his finger into it with no results.

He had to concentrate on the road as the first of several curves approached, now at nearly seventy. He made the first curve just as Bud and the Toad flew overhead. He really hoped that Bud would notice that something was seriously wrong and call for help. The second and third turns were less smooth and the rear end began to slide out on the third one. Tom fought the steering wheel and managed to regain control, but he was now going eighty.

The next curve, an S one, was a half mile ahead. At his increasing speed he calculated he would get there in eighteen seconds. Again and again he stabbed at the ignition and then pushed with all his strength at the shift lever.

Nothing. As he neared the S curve and ninety miles per hour, Tom knew he was in very serious trouble!

CHAPTER 6 /
"COLOR ME SURPRISED"

AS THE out of control car entered the first part of the curve, Tom was thrown to the left side, and the partially full soda can jumped from the cup holder and was flung into the window, cracking it. His upper body hit the door and his legs slammed up and under the dash and into the center console. His right knee hit something hard.

It hurt but he fought to ignore the pain; he had more important things to do!

He got back upright in time to throw the car into the other half of the curve and almost managed to keep control. He was tossed around again, and once more his right knee bashed upward and into something. He realized it had never hit anything under the dash before and took a second to reach under to locate the offending item. His hand felt a hard, plastic square.

With some sense of panic setting in, he grabbed the box and yanked it down with all his might. It popped out of the car's data port and now sat in his hand. He didn't have time to study it. If it was the source of his troubles, removing it had solved nothing. Even now that it had been removed, the car still raced onward passing ninety and less than a mile from some very dangerous curves rated at just forty miles per hour.

Tom patted his shirt and without looking down—he didn't have the luxury of being able to take his eyes off the road now—and pulled his ballpoint pen out. Using his right hand and his teeth he managed to get it apart and took the metal-encased cartridge in his hand. Quickly he jammed the tip up and into the data port, giving it a fierce wiggle around.

He was rewarded by a small shower of sparks cascading down and burning his hand, but it had done the trick. The engine shut off. The car began to slow but now he had to contend with a total lack of steering. This model was a steer-by-wire one and no power meant no ability to turn. He tested the brakes and was relieved to find that he had some, if considerably sluggish, braking power.

Tom practically stood on the pedal and got the car down to under twenty by the time he reached the first of the sharp curves. Luckily for him, this one curved to go around a small hill on the side he was driving and not down into the twenty-foot ditch on the other side of the road.

The car went a few yards up the hill, dug the front bumper into the soft ground, stopped for a second and rolled backwards just as the Toad roared overhead again. Bud wiggled the wings and performed a sharp sliding turn so that he could come back over Tom's car in just a few seconds.

By then the Inventor had opened his door, climbed painfully out, and stood waiving at Bud to let him know he was all right. The flyer made one more wide, sweeping turn and used the plane's landing lights to Morse Code Tom with: called help r u ok

Tom gave Bud a salute as the Toad passed over him for the final time.

About six minutes later Tom heard a siren and soon saw one of Shopton's police cars speeding toward him. It pulled behind his disabled car and the officer jumped out.

"You okay, Mr. Swift?" the young man asked.

Tom nodded finding that he was panting after holding his breath from trying to walk on his hurting knee. The pain was subsiding, and he nodded. "Yeah. A little shaken, but no real harm." He stepped forward and his right knee reminded him again that it had recently been violently involved in the discovery of the mysterious box. Tom hopped back a few feet and reached into the car to retrieved the box from the passenger seat. He dropped it into his front pants pocket.

He limped as he walked over to the police car. "Can I please get a lift out to Enterprises?" he asked.

"Sure. Golly, are you sure you're okay? I mean you're limping something awful!"

Tom favored the young officer with a rueful grin. "Yeah. Just a little bang on the knee that my doctor will take care of. Thanks!" On the way through town Tom phoned Munford Trent and described where his car could be located.

"Can you get a flatbed truck there with one of Harlan Ames' people to check the car out and bring it back to Enterprises, please? Tell Harlan I have a little electronic dongle that was plugged into my data port. He ought to find that interesting. Thanks, Trent."

"Is that something the police should know about?" the officer asked.

"Not yet. If my Security people turn up anything out of the ordinary you guys will be the second ones to know!"

Within an hour of getting back to Enterprises Tom had a heavy, elastic wrap around his knee, an injection into the joint to ease the swelling and pain—that had hurt more than the actual injury when Doc Simpson stabbed him with the long needle—and was taking a call from Harlan.

"That little box was a disabler computer that infected the car's four computers with a nasty 'shut everything down' virus, and then took over the engine management. It appears it was meant to keep accelerating you until you crashed, and then a small accelerometer inside would set off a little squib of plastic explosive, destroying the box. Luckily you didn't hit that hill too hard. It also disabled the airbags. We estimate the explosion would have taken out anything within two feet, including your legs!"

Tom knew that there would be no answer to his next question, but he asked anyway. "Any idea where it came from? I mean, it obviously wasn't there before I took my car in for the software update, so it must have been attached at the dealership, but I can't believe they would have anything to do with this."

"I agree and already called them. The service manager is ready to slit his own wrists he is so distraught. And he swears by all his technicians. He promised to look into the logs to see who could have touched your car and will get back to me in a half hour or so."

When Harlan's next call came it was bad news.

"One of the dealer's service techs didn't show up for work. He was just found knocked out and bleeding in his apartment. They got him to the hospital and the man will live. A temp showed up yesterday saying that the regular guy had been called away to a family emergency. Since he was only working the desk he didn't need any service credentials. He didn't work on your car but it's a sure bet he had access when someone wasn't watching."

"And *he* didn't show back up today I'll wager."

"That's about the size of it. Oh, and the reason nobody else spotted it on the final inspection is that a similar box is supposed to remain in that data port for fifteen days to monitor the results of the real software update. They would have called you after a couple weeks to remind you to swing by so they could retrieve it."

Tom didn't like it and neither did the Security chief. He promised to keep the inventor updated on anything else he found.

Within seconds of hanging up, the shared office door swung open and a very happy Bud Barclay stepped inside. He threw his arms open wide and announced, "Taa-daa!"

Then, getting a little serious he asked if Tom was okay. After hearing about the knee and the deadly control box, he was much more concerned than happy, but Tom brought him back by asking about the little display as he entered the office.

"That? Well, you know I was up there with the CanaDair folks, and we were tooling around when I spotted your car going like gangbusters. So, once I knew it was you and did my little tail slipping turn their bigwigs were so impressed that they gave me a round of applause right up there in mid air. Turns out that a couple of the airports they want to fly into, like up in Nunavut and the Northwest Territories, are in tight spots and it takes a little tail wiggle and side slide to land. Nothing else they have seen can give them the jet performance *and* the steerability until they saw that, so they are now sitting over in Purchasing signing a contract for not just thirty, but thirty-six."

"Congratulations, flyboy. It was your quick thinking and skillful maneuver that did the trick. Thanks for being my guardian angel up there. Are we still on for coming to your house for dinner tonight? I'm afraid I'm not going to be able to do the dancing thing, though."

Bud agreed to go see his wife to verify the invitation and tell her of the plan change. "She might have heard about the car problem by being over there in George Dilling's group. But back on a sales matter, I want to make that maneuver a suggested one for all future demo flights. It's super easy, safe as long as you know what you are doing, and is impressive as all get out."

"Check everyone out on it and put it in the book," Tom directed.

When he departed to walk over to Communications where Sandy Swift-Barclay worked, Bud left a contemplative inventor. While it was fresh in his mind Tom called Bashalli at the advertising agency to ask her if she didn't mind no going dancing, although he didn't mention the reason.

"Me. Mind? Oh, Thomas Swift. Of course I do not mind. I love Sandra like my very own sister and always have fun with her and Budworth. The dancing might have been fun but just spending time as family is all I really want. I will not be able to get out of here for another two hours so can you please stop by the market and pick up some of those small potatoes from Canada, and—"

"Potatoes from Canada?" Tom asked, interrupting her.

"Yes, the ones from the Yukon area up there."

Tom laughed. "I think they are just *called* Yukons, Bash, and don't actually come from the frozen ground of the great white north."

There was a pause and then she giggled. "I suppose that makes much more sense. So, I will need eight to ten of them, please. Not too small and not too large. And a small, sweet onion. I have agreed to bring potato salad to the dinner this evening. We have everything else I need."

Tom promised to get what she requested on his way home.

When she arrived at the house she threw herself into his arms and his right knee buckled under their combined weight. Bashalli was horrified and began to cry as she helped him to stand. She believed she had just hurt him.

Tom told her it was okay and described the runaway car and how he had banged his knee earlier... but did not mention the explosives. He took out a small vial of pain pills that Doc Simpson had given him and asked for a glass of water.

By the time they got to Bud and Sandy's his knee no longer hurt.

They had a wonderful dinner with Bud regaling everyone by describing the demo flight. He, too, avoided the more serious parts of the story but did finish by telling his wife that she would need to learn a new maneuver. He gave her a quick description.

"Easy peesy!" she declared. "Give me a Toad, a control stick and a rudder pedal to steer her by!"

The conversation eventually drifted to the current status of the strange sounds coming from below the helium wells.

"To tell you the truth," Tom told Sandy when she brought the subject up, "we don't know where they are coming from. Because they resonate so strongly in the vicinity beneath Helium City we have been assuming that is where they originate. I had Bud take a tour all around the area when we were down there and he found nothing on the ocean floor, but that doesn't mean our mystery noisemaker is definitely down in the caverns."

"I didn't see anything visible," Bud added, "but that might mean there is something that is either well camouflaged or already dug in. Gee, skipper, I hope it isn't another case like the last one where Haz's father syphoned off all that helium."

"It didn't sound like drilling to me, Bud. Not to say it isn't. Heck. Anything's possible."

When the ladies asked if they might hear some of the noise Tom produced his smart phone, found the short audio file he had copied to review himself, and played it for them.

"It sounds like the ground below is having stomach troubles to me," Bashalli declared. "Maybe you need to shove some antacid down into the hole."

Sandy listened a few moments longer before shaking her head. "Has anyone ever been swimming in a fast-moving stream and put their head under the water?" When she received three somewhat blank looks, she continued. "Well, evidently I've lived a more rounded life. I have done just that. If you stay very still and don't let your ears fill up with water you can hear every little pebble and stone as they get moved around by the rushing water."

Tom had a small scowl on his face when he inquired, "And this sounds like *that*?"

Sandy shook her head. "Not exactly. It's kind of like that sound but only if you muffled it a lot. Sounds heard through the water sort of thing. I don't know. It's just sort of like that to me."

Tom spoke a quick note into his phone before putting it back in his pocket. "I'll see if anybody has a sample of that to compare with."

They finished dinner—including the perfectly-cooked artichokes —and the dessert Sandy admitted her mother had made then headed to the living room to play a board game.

The following afternoon the young inventor received a call from George Dilling. "Hey, Tom. I've had one of my people scouring the various audio archives for that sound you said Sandy told you about. Well, we'll have it downloaded in about ten minutes. Want to stop by to hear it?"

Tom told his head of Communications that he would be right over and left his underground office seconds later.

Once they were seated in the audio editing booth, George typed a command and soon their ears heard a combination of a soft whooshing noise—*probably the water*, thought Tom—and hundreds or even thousands of very tiny clicks.

"Are those the little rocks moving around?" George asked.

Tom shrugged. "I suppose so. Can we get Sandy in here?"

Two minutes later she was pulling up a seat. "Let me hear it, please," she requested.

Tom watched his sister as she closed her eyes and turned her head from side to side as if typing to find the best listening position. Finally, when the 30-second piece was finished she opened her eyes and smiled. "That's it!"

Tom was baffled. "Are you certain? It doesn't sound at all like the recordings from Helium City."

"No, silly. Of course it doesn't. But it is the sound I was trying to describe. Now we need to start muffling it."

For nearly an hour George applied various filters to the sound. He used his 24-channel equalizer to bring down certain frequencies and enhance others, especially in the lower wavelengths. Time and again they compared the processed sounds with the recording from under the sea. They got close to it once but anything else they did made it worse.

Finally, George declared, "I've tried my bag of tricks. I'll turn this over to one of our audio engineers who may be able to coax something better out. Sorry, Tom and Sandy. That one is a close as I can get us."

"Not to worry, George. It was worth a try. Now at least I can see, or hear, what Sandy was talking about. And," he turned to his sister, "you are right. There is something there reminiscent of that sound. Rocks clicking but the sound deadened. Well, keep trying, George, and let me know if your engineer gets anywhere."

After leaving Communications Tom headed for Arv Hanson's workshop and an appointment with Linda Ming.

The model maker was standing near a desk with his hands behind his back attempting to look innocent. Tom decided to ignore the look on the man's face and instead turned to Linda.

"So, I've seen the designs and approved them. Everything ought to be underway in the other departments. What did you want to see me about, and why is Arv standing there like the cat who ate the canary?"

She giggled. "Mr. Hanson is standing there because he has a little something to show you. I asked for the appointment because you have been busy with other things the past day or so. I heard about the car. Hope you're okay."

He assured them that his knee felt much better. "Just bruised."

"Great. Okay, Arv, can you please show Tom what you have there?"

"Of course. Here," he said bringing his right hand around and handing Tom something about thirteen inches long, about two-inches wide at the top and with a pair of small propellers sitting about three inches behind the front nose cone. The rest of the body was under an inch wide.

He and Linda looked at Tom expectantly.

For his part the inventor turned the device over and looked at it from several angles.

He spotted what appeared to be a pinhole at the back and five folded objects near it that he believed might be fins of some sort. He was about to ask when he suddenly knew what he had in his hands.

"The sideways probes, right?"

"Exactly. I was going to build them as something that simply gets shot out of the larger probe, but Arv here suggested that the deeper they are the harder it will be for them to keep going out to the end of their tethers on the initial push alone. We needed them to be longer than the width of the probe so they go down stored upright and swing into position before launch. When tests showed that no amount of push would get them farther than a few dozen feet down here, we came up with a pair of ultra-thin electric motor bands that take up just three millimeters inside the body tube, thickness that is, and drive those two counter-rotating propellers. Inside the head is the probe sensor array and the body holds a tiny battery that powers everything."

"So, how long will the battery last?" Tom asked her.

It was Arv who answered. "It's a new type of battery the team in Electrical Engineering has come up with. A HeCe-ion battery."

"Hmmm. He for helium and Ce as in cerium?" Tom asked. "Interesting. Let me see if I get this. The cerium decays and sends out neutrons that collide with the helium turning it into hydrogen and that... what does it react with?"

"Platinum. A tiny plate of it that gives off about two volts of power, and keeps on giving," Arv told him. "Each battery is a fuel cell."

"We just let in a little more helium and the reaction can keep up for days," Linda added. "The hydrogen that has broken down exits from that tiny hole in the back."

Tom smiled. "Well, as they say, color me surprised. I'm guessing the battery is one of dad's inventions."

Arv nodded. "Yes. It's just another of the many little things and refinements your old man is making to enhance the Japanese satellite design. I hear their plans were to try to do an in-space power pack replacement at about the four year mark to give the satellite additional life. Until you get the new space station built and the Tom Swift Satellite Repair and Tune-up Garage completed, it was going to be their only hope. With this battery type, only larger, your dad will get them twice the life."

"And we get the benefit of that research for my probe. Probes, I guess I ought to say," Tom told them.

Linda pointed out that the non-working model Tom held was missing two things. First the connection point that was located inside the small rear hole where the super strong data and retrieval cable would attach to the larger mother probe, and also the final computer equipment.

"We're using both the head as well as an inch or so of the tail end for circuitry."

"Yeah," Arv hastened to add, "Linda's doing an amazing job of miniaturizing things. I have a hunch that we might get some other interesting uses from this sort of probe."

"I shouldn't wonder." Tom said, smiling broadly at them.

CHAPTER 7 /

THE PROBE DROPS

"HELLO, everybody," Mr. Swift greeted the nine men and women seated around the table in the large conference room on the Administration Building's third floor. As they murmured their hellos he continued. "You are, as I'm sure you know, the leaders in your departments, and each of you holds some responsibility in the creation of the forthcoming Swift MotorCar Company. I wanted to get us all together, along with Tom, to ensure that we are going to be ready when the day comes that we open the doors."

"The Construction Company stands ready to begin building all the assembly line equipment," Jake Aturian, the President of that division, told him. "Rumor has it that we're ahead of schedule over there. Any truth to that?"

"Better than rumor, Jake. What with favorable weather, Tom getting the sub-assembly inflatable building up in record time and a host of other things all going our way, we are one month and three days ahead of the original schedule."

Everyone smiled and words of congratulations were spoken all around.

He spent the following half hour detailing where this new timeframe left everyone. Only a single department didn't believe they could accelerate their work. The hold out was Maintenance, and they were responsible for all the surfaces such as roads and runways at Enterprises and the Construction Company.

"Our hold up is in materials, Damon. As you've seen we have managed to do the basic road work around the facility and inside the fence, but there's a shortage of good quality materials to make the large amount of asphalt we require to pave the huge parking and storage lots for finished vehicles along with the general parking for employees. I've got it all on order, but I'm afraid it's going to hold up completion by several weeks. I'm sorry."

Damon thought a moment before smiling. "I really don't believe that will be a problem, unless you can get no supplies in. So long as the employee parking and the front of the grounds is finished we will be spending perhaps the first full month is creating only subassemblies and body shells. No final vehicles will pop out of the end of the line in that time. Let me amend that. Only about a dozen hand-built test vehicles will come down the line during that time."

"You can't imagine how relieved that makes me feel," the man confided. "I'll make that date for sure!"

"Great. Now, there is a small matter of something I think might have escaped most if not all of us." He looked around the room to see if anyone wanted to guess. Nobody did. "Fine. Let me pose this as a question, then. Once we get a batch of cars finished and ready to send out, *how* do we get them down to Albany for general rail shipment or to the bullet train depot to head west?"

"Trucks?" offered the manager of the department who would be producing the interior electronics for the new cars.

Tom spoke up. "I don't think the roads out of the Shopton area can handle that sort of heavy traffic day in and day out. We might be able to convince the county to let us redo things out to the freeway, but even that is in fairly shoddy condition after the last two winters."

Damon nodded in agreement. "I must also tell you all that if we were to go that, ahem, route, we would need to either build a fleet of carrier trucks or buy them. Thirty 10-vehicle trucks at a minimum. I'd prefer to *not* do that. Instead, and this is why I asked Tom to join us, I'd like to propose that we offer the state to rebuild the old rail line that terminates down at Pottersville at the southern end of Lake Carlopa and ties into the main rail lines to Albany at Glen Falls. The old line hasn't been used for thirty years and the state took ownership of the right of way fifteen years ago. In fact, there is an even older track that comes up from Pottersville but passes by a few miles to the West. Other than revitalizing those tracks we would need to build a spur line over to the plant."

Jake raised on hand. "Will you let me tack on a couple of cars to carry some of our other goods that either have to fly out or truck right now?"

"All part of the plan, Jake," Damon assured him.

"So, you want me to build the rail line?" Tom asked.

His father shook his head. "Oh, no, no, no. But, you do have one of your tunnel boring machines sitting in hangar eleven and that has the nifty little attachment to extrude the tracks and cross braces like you did in the transcontinental tunnels. Unless I'm totally wrong I believe that connecting that to your road resurfacing machine might be a winning combination."

Tom's face brightened as he now saw exactly what his father was thinking of.

If a team could go along the rail route removing the old steel rails—simply setting to the sides—the resurfacer could pick up, grind down into a finer material and re-lay the existing stone rail beds and even bind them together for added strength. Then, the extruder would follow which would lay out the new and perfectly spaced rails and ties as the pair of machines traveled along.

"How much track do we need to repair?" he inquired.

"Just a little under thirty-nine miles of old track and then the new spur of six miles."

"I'll get everything ready to go for when we get permission." He looked happily at his father who stood there with an expectant expression. "Oh. Do we have permission already?"

Damon nodded and replied, "Came through yesterday. So, any time you can give to prepping your equipment will be appreciated."

The meeting broke up with the gentleman from Maintenance promising to pull together a crew to dismantle the old rails. "I think we'll borrow a flatbed rail car to haul those down for recycling," he told the young inventor as they left the room.

This was the last week of construction and testing for the probes Tom would take to Helium City to lower into the well there. With not much to do other than overseeing minor details, he was able to spend some time creating the linkage between the paving and extruding units and also to work with Hank Serling to outfit a special truck with tanks sufficient to carry the liquids to feed the extruder.

"I don't have my notes in front of me, skipper," he told Tom over the phone, but I seem to recall that we used about one hundred gallons of the liquids for every mile of the rails."

"That seems to be about right," Tom agreed. The main liquid once activated swelled to many times its volume and set harder than steel.

"Okay, we have a truck bed I can fit the pair of tanks onto; one hundred ninety of the main mixture and another one with the ten gallons of the activator/hardener. So, two miles at a crack, and with the railing setting solid in an hour out in the sun we can either pause and drive back to get more, or I can build you a second pair of tanks that we just helicopter out to the current site."

He would use the large vacuum-form equipment at the Construction Company to build each tank in two halves that would then be sealed together.

"I can have it all in three days if that is okay."

Tom said it would be fine. "The main thing is we need to wait for the crew who will remove the old tracks, Hank. That's going to be at least a couple of weeks, so there's no need to rush this."

When he looked up from his phone call Bud was standing just inside the door, grinning at him. "Yes?"

"Two things, skipper. First I wanted to see if you knew when we are going back down to the well, and then to ask you, what rails?"

"The rails are train tracks, Bud, and we are going to be replacing an old line to transport our cars down for shipping." He filled his friend in on what had come from the meeting.

"Neat!" Bud declared. "Will we be able to run your little track racers along the new stuff?"

Bud spoke about the small and fast 8-man vehicles Tom created to bring new crews into the tunnels, sometimes hundreds of miles from the entrance, to replace the previous men and women working with Tom's bullet train tunnel boring machines. They traveled on the new rails inside the tunnels and were like riding in high-performance sports cars. Capable of more than one hundred seventy miles per hour, inside the darkened tunnels riders felt almost no sensation of speed. However, outside and sitting very low to the ground they provided an incredibly exciting ride.

"I may let you take a trip down and back, Bud, but once we get going with the car shipments there will be practically no time when a car-carrier train won't be on those tracks."

"Just as long as I get my name on the list. So, what about the cavern probes?"

Tom suggested that they walk over to see Linda. He knew she had the complete schedule and was managing almost everything right now.

She greeted them with a smile that told Tom something had come up.

"What's the matter?" he asked, concerned.

"You could tell?"

"Yes. You have the sort of look my sister used to get when she knew something was wrong but hadn't decided if she was at fault or not."

"She still gets that look," Bud confided. "Only now it is usually over whether to tell me she just bought something or to tell me she's had it for a long time."

"This is something that just came up this morning, Tom. I ran some computer modeling as we tested two of the probe packages. We know that the sonar works to some extent in thick liquids like magma and it will really work well in the gassified upper areas of the caverns. But the computer says that as we get into the liquefied helium, maybe as soon as six hundred feet down, it will be too thick to propagate sounds and give us anything close to accurate numbers."

"How bad is it?"

At that depth in the liquid helium we might get good information one hundred feet out from the probe, Go another hundred feet down and that drops to possibly as little as fifteen feet."

Bud whistled. "Even I know that isn't good."

"No," Tom said, "it is not good." He thought for a minute. "Linda, will the little torpedo probes you showed me have the same problems?"

"Well, until the pressure gets to be so great that the helium is nearly a solid mass they will work their way out, just a lot slower the deeper we go. We, and I mean I, didn't take that thickening into consideration enough."

An idea occurred to the inventor. "Can we replace the sonar equipment that isn't going to do a lot of good for us with another version of the shoot-'em-out module but one with larger torpedo probes with more powerful batteries and motors?"

"Same sensor package?" she inquired.

Tom nodded. "Yes. I'm now thinking that we use the small probes up higher, and as we find they begin to have problems moving around, we switch to the larger ones."

She promised to get on it right away.

Tom and Bud left after telling her the planned trip to Helium City for the next Friday was still on.

After calling over to the Electrical Engineering to advise them Linda might be phoning with a new request for their astounding batteries, and suggesting that it was a high priority, Tom placed a call to the Helium City manager.

"I'm sorry, Tom," Dora Mays informed him. "Peter took a really bad tumble this morning and had to be evacuated to the mainland. Got a nasty concussion. Luckily, one of our newer technicians found him. Is there anything I can do?"

Tom told her no, asked her what facility Peter had been transported to, and the call ended.

He headed over to the shared office and brought his father up to date. The news of Peter Crumwald's injury surprised the older inventor. "Did she say what actually happened? I ask because Peter would not have fallen from anything even if there was some place he might have been climbing around. He has quite a history of rock climbing and is about as sure footed as a mountain goat."

Tom promised to find out. When he did, the news was both good and bad.

Peter, although he had been knocked completely out cold and had a concussion and a small fracture of his skull, was in no danger and expected to return to work in four or five days.

That was the good news. The bad news was that on waking up in the hospital in Savannah, Georgia, he made a statement that somebody had attacked him from behind. He didn't see who the attacker was but swore that he was standing upright by the side of one of the buildings when he was hit on the back of the head.

The location of the hit he described was exactly where the fracture happened.

Tom informed Harlan of the attack, and the Security man promised to get Gary Bradley—his number three man in the organization—on it right away.

By the day of the probe drops Peter was back at work with Gary shadowing him everywhere except his quarters. That, secured by a lock that required Peter's TeleVoc signal to be within a few feet before it operated, could not be opened by anyone else in the dome except for Gary with his override code.

The trio of probes sat in a rack just outside of the pressure containment building erected around the gas lock.

First to be taken inside was the unit that would take the assorted images of the areas surrounding the probe as it was lowered into the depths. Since it was tethered and powered from above Tom decided to run all its equipment both going down and coming back up.

The tether connection was double checked and declared to be ready. The overhead hoist was lowered and the probe picked up.

"Sorry, folks," Tom said to the fifteen or so people standing around outside. "Time to close up. We'll let you see some of the video shots on the screen out there." With that the door was closed, sealed and the pressure inside brought up. The five people inside—including Linda Ming whom Tom believed deserved to be there—had to "pop" their ears several times but soon everything was in readiness.

The end of the probe was put inside the now open end of the gas lock and the entire body lowered until it bumped at the bottom. The upper hatch—with the tether cable traveling thorough a special fitting—swung shut and the pressure inside the lock was increased to match that of the cavern below.

"She's ready to lower, skipper," The operator called out.

Tom looked around at the others and nodded. "Let's go!"

The totally dark monitor on the wall suddenly became so bright that the automatic circuits had to dampen the signal. The lights on the probe had come on. Next, the lower hatch swung open and everyone got a glimpse of the cavern below.

There was a sharp intake of breath from Linda at the images from inside the upper cavern she had not seen before.

"That is incredible," she declared. Nobody contradicted her. It was. The giant vertical cavern stretched hundreds of yards in all directions and went down farther than the light could reach.

At about the three-quarters point down Tom pointed out the crumpled remains of the "flying" probe he once used to survey the upper chamber. It was mostly intact except that the dragonfly-like wings were crumpled and torn from the impact it had made just above a small ledge. It was that probe that allowed Tom to come to the conclusion that something was below the bottom of the cavern.

"I'll bet that was beautiful," Linda commented.

Within minutes the probe had reached the point where the down-facing camera could make out what had once been the bottom of the cavern. There was a slightly jagged hole in the floor about seven feet across where Tom had dropped a heavy, pointed weight down and punctured what turned out to be the top cap of a second, even larger storage cavern of liquid helium.

With so many things to do he never had bothered to send anything down this deep to see what was beneath that cap. Now as the time approached when this new probe would pass the former cavern bottom he felt a little apprehensive.

The camera's field of view narrowed as it passed through the hole and only widened slightly for the next fifty feet. But, after that...

"Jetz!" Bud said almost under his breath. Tom had switched them to the rotating side-view camera.

The lower area opened out into a cavern so wide that the sides were lost in the distance.

"It's easily twice as wide as the upper cavern," Tom told them. "Perhaps more. But, look at that!" He pointed to the screen as he switched back to the downward camera.

Everybody immediately saw what he was looking at. The top portion of the cavern was also gaseous helium, but only about a dozen yards below the probe was a veritable ocean of liquid helium. It showed small ripples on the surface and a permanent fog-like layer of the helium as it passed from its liquid state to a gas.

As Tom continued to lower the long probe the lenses of the various cameras seemed to fog up just above the liquid, grow incredible arrays of crystals as the probe dipped down, and then cleared.

With several light sources and imaging elements designed specifically to detect each wavelength of light, and a computer in the pressurized building capable of combining them all and then color correcting to make them appear nearly lifelike, the images were stunning. The liquid seemed to reflect normal "visible" light like headlights in heavy fog and so that source was soon shut off.

Tom's special underwater light source gave them the best long-range images, but as Tom suspected the cavern walls down in this lower chamber were much, much farther away from the path of the probe than above. There was so very little to see and again he switched to the down-facing camera array.

"It's kind of eerie," Bud said, "what with it looking a lot like water but there is absolutely nothing floating around in it."

Linda asked what he meant.

"I mean even where there's no fish or other sea life, well not the big stuff anyway, you always see tiny krill and other things like plankton and a lot of dead material floating around in the ocean. The water isn't like a giant filtered bowl of water. It has... *stuff* in it."

Everybody agreed that it appeared like nothing they ever experienced before.

Down and down the probe dropped. At first it continued at about the same pace as it had in the upper chamber, but by the time it reached three hundred feet below the liquid surface, the speed had been cut in half.

Several hours later a relief team came in to take over. It could be many hours or days before they either reached the bottom, or ran out of the three-mile long tether cable.

The outside temperature was approaching absolute zero and still the probe's weight forced it down.

Tom and Bud took back over late that afternoon. With them were Linda, Peter, Gary and even Dora Mays.

"Well," Tom announced, "we don't appear to be getting close to the bottom but we are nearing the final five hundred feet of our tether. I was hoping to get a glimpse of the floor of this place, but I guess we're out of luck."

Just ten minutes later everyone could see that the sides had reappeared and were sloping quickly in toward the middle where a new, dark hole soon appeared. Near the top of this hole the lights reflected off of what appeared to be a rock formation bridging from one side to the other. It was about one hundred feet across. No light traveled much beyond that.

Tom was pondering how a formation generally associated with horizontal movement of water having washed away the lower dirt had formed so deep under the ocean floor—

"What the heck was that!" Bud exclaimed.

"What was what?" Tom asked in a worried voice.

"Umm, oh, maybe nothing. For a split second there I thought I saw a flash in the haze, like you get sometimes with lightning and thick clouds. Must've been nothing. I guess it was my imagination because it sure isn't there any more."

Everyone nodded except for Tom. His mind may have been occupied with other thoughts but he'd kept his eyes on the monitor.

He had seen something flash, too!

CHAPTER 8 /

NOT HIM AGAIN!

NOBODY ELSE had seen the brief light coming from deep inside this newest cave formation. At least, nobody mentioned it. The two young men looked at each other and a silent signal passed between them. It would not be brought up right now.

"So, how much farther down can you go, skipper," he asked to change the subject.

"Not much. If we had a longer cable and some way to heat up the surrounding liquid we would go farther, but I think we might as well stop now and bring the probe back up. And, sorry, Linda, but we may just as well not spend the time sending down the next probe and its little fleet of probe-ettes or the sampling probe."

"Hey, that's okay with me. After what I've seen, I'd rather *not* use them until I add a few upgrades I want to make. I'll put your idea about heating the outer skin on the list," she promised.

Tom stopped the winch for a moment before reversing its direction.

"Wow! The sludgy helium down there almost froze solid before I could get the thing coming back up. In fact, at the rate the computer tells me we can bring it back up, it will take nearly five hours longer on the return journey. Add that heater system to the top of your list, please." He made a mental note to work closely with her on that. She had an incredible talent with miniaturization, but he had far greater experience with things like surface coatings and heating and cooling systems.

Peter called the relief team back to work.

"I'll let them ride herd on this for you skipper. I need to bend your and Gary's ears a little if you can spare the time." His look was serious and Tom knew that he wasn't someone to ask for a private discussion time without a reason.

"Great. As soon as they get here and I brief them on a couple things we can get out of here."

When they all stepped outside of the airlock in the main dome Tom stretched and looked around. This deep under water there was never any real light to see above them except on very clear days and only when the sun was directly overhead. The rest of the time a series of specially-tuned lamps provided the proper light cycles—a version of bright nighttime moon light, dawn, a full work day, and dusk—to keep everyone's internal rhythms in sync. It was beginning to darken in the dome so it was after nine. They walked toward the dining hall with Bud taking the others on a different route leaving the three men alone.

"The reason I need to talk to you both is that I am getting worried about the safety of everyone down here." When Tom appeared to be ready to say something, Peter hastened to add, "It is nothing I can put my finger on, but there were a couple of odd things going on down here for a week before I got knocked out."

"Like what, and why the heck haven't you mentioned these things before?" Gary chided him.

Peter stopped walking. "The first thing I noticed was a large tank of carbon dioxide. It had been moved from our holding depot during the night and was close to the vent used to recycle existing air with the breathable mixture we take from sea water."

"How large a tank?" Tom asked.

"As large as you seem to suspect, skipper," Peter said seeing the look on Tom's face. "Enough CO_2 if let loose in here to incapacitate everyone."

Gary was confused. "But, I thought that CO_2 was heavy and would just sink to the ground. Wouldn't that keep people safe?"

"Not really," Tom explained. "If the tank were connected into the vent system it would get mixed pretty thoroughly. Just like we have carbon dioxide in our normal air that doesn't sink, it would remain in suspension easily long enough to do the damage."

Gary swore.

"That goes double for me," Peter added.

"Anything else you can tell us?"

"Well, Tom, I had our internal Security man dust it for prints. Lots of them all over the tank and the valve. Far too many to get any idea of whose are most recent. I expected it to be wiped clean but not the way we found it. My guess is that twenty or more people have handled that tank in the last couple of months alone."

He went on to tell them about another occurrence the afternoon just before he was attacked.

"I was doing my daily walk around the perimeter of the dome when I discovered some tools hidden behind one of the buildings. Not the one where I got hit, but about a third of the way farther around the circuit. What I found made me think somebody was out to sabotage the dome until it hit me that even if they made it through the inner layer, the repelatron would still keep out the water."

"You found cutting tools?" Gary asked.

"I found a pocket knife with a four inch blade. Serrated to saw through things. That *had* been wiped of any prints."

"But that one of the forbidden five!" Gary stated.

There were five absolutely "not allowed" items to be brought down to the hydrodome at Helium City. These were:

- **Firearms of any sort**
- **Knives of any sort**
- **Anything explosive**
- **Transmitting devices**
- **Lasers**

Most personnel knew the rules and it was generally only the first two times someone went down that they and their luggage were checked. After that the honor system seemed to work quite well.

"It appears that someone, and probably it is your attacker, didn't want to follow the rules. So, as the new sheriff in town," Gary said giving them a lopsided smile, "it behooves me to declare that I get to start an inspection of everyone's stuff. Now, the usual thing is to call in a support team, so that is what I will do. Not a word, Peter. Nobody is to know until I get my people down here tomorrow or the day after and we do a side-to-side, top-to-bottom sweep."

Tom wasn't certain that it would be necessary, and said so, but Gary reminded him that it was Tom and Damon Swift's idea in the first place to institute searches in case of attacks inside of Swift properties.

And although Helium City was technically owned by the world— the free nations who all shared in the helium it provided and was sold to those with a need—it was just inside of U.S. territorial waters and so a combination of the Swifts and the U.S. Navy were responsible for the mine's safety and security.

The Navy had the outside world while Enterprises was responsible for the dome and all the people who worked in it.

As Tom, Bud and Linda were heading to the surface the next afternoon, with the three probes stored in the cargo section at the rear of the seacopter, they spotted the second seacopter that would be delivering a team of sixteen specialists to aid Gary Bradley in his search. The Security man had promised Peter that the actual search would not be done in a confrontory manner and nobody would have any of their lawful rights violated.

"But once my team gets here everyone steps out and into formation. One minute or they get triple scrutiny. I've got a communications specialist to take that over and people to run the well and other vital equipment. Maintenance will have to stop as will all the administration work, and everyone off duty will need to be awake, but we're fast. I plan the entire search to take less that two hours."

There was little or nothing for Peter to complain about. He knew it was a "must do" thing.

On Fearing the word had gotten around of the forthcoming search. Almost everyone knew Peter Crumwald and liked the man. Some would have gladly taken part in the search and ensured that the guilty party or parties were left with painful reminders of their transgressions.

When the trio arrived, the seacopter technicians who met them all asked if Security had found the culprit.

"No," Tom said, "and the search is only just now due to get underway. We'll keep everybody posted once we find out anything. And, thanks for your concern. We all hate it when one of our own is attacked, and it hurts a lot more if it turns out to be a fellow employee that's gone bad."

With Bud and the controls of the Toad, and Tom and Linda discussing some probe upgrades, they were soon winging back to the mainland and Shopton.

Mr. Swift was waiting near Tom's car. He had requested the control tower notify him of their arrival and came down a minute before the younger Swift walked up.

"Hello, Son," he greeted Tom.

"Hey, Dad. It's close to six. What are you still doing here?"

"Sheer curiosity, Tom. So, what did the probes find?"

They stood leaning against the fender of Tom's car while he related the issues that kept them from launching more than the first one. He also told of the enormous area of the lower cavern.

"We couldn't detect the sides, but they must be a minimum of twice the distance from center as the upper cavern and fifteen times as deep. I'd say there is at least another two hundred years of helium down there and maybe more. We just couldn't get to the bottom to tell." He described how they had seen a lower passage heading farther down, but it was unknown to where or how far it went.

When they parted forty minutes later Tom felt a small pang of guilt. The one thing he had not told his father was about the flash of light deep in the cavern.

He also did not mention it to Bashalli that evening.

However, the next morning he arrived to find Bud waiting for him. "Coffee and conversation, please, skipper," the flyer requested.

At the cafeteria they poured steaming mugs and headed for a remote table.

Bud sipped his drink for a moment before looking Tom in the eyes.

"The flash?" He didn't have to say anything to explain it.

Tom nodded. "Yeah. I saw it, too. And, I have no idea what it was. I'm hoping to see out more when I review the video later. With luck I'll find that the probe moved slightly and the lower lights reflected off something shiny down there."

Bud nodded. "Sure. It beats the alternative." Tom looked puzzled. "That crazy preacher in Florida being right that we're dealing with something evil!"

Tom had to chuckle. "Bud, I may have no idea what could have been the actual cause of that... uh, phenomenon, and that is most probably exactly what it was, but I'll bet you there is nothing supernatural or mystical or with religious connotations about it. Light is light. That was light. Maybe it was ours shining on something and maybe it was some other source." He shrugged and the conversation changed.

"I took Sandy up in the Toad the other day, before we headed down to Helium City, and showed her that tail slip maneuver." He smiled. "I could barely keep her from doing it over and over. I hear that she spent some of the time we were under water trying it out in several different planes and jets."

"What did she have to say about it?"

"Her exact words were, 'It's like a gentle slide into a favorite dance step.' In other words I think it's just become a standard maneuver."

"Some day you're going to have to check me out on it," Tom requested. Although he had performed the same maneuver many times in smaller, single tail planes, the Toad—with its V-tail—handled a little differently than others.

Bud laughed at him. "Right. I'm sure I can teach *you* a flying trick. Ha!"

He returned to the underground office and went back to work on a design for a two-man probe. Every time he thought to add another sensor array he decided that the un-used probes ought to be rebuilt so that they might do that sort of investigation. His cautious side told him that it would be best to get an unmanned probe to the very bottom before anybody might be put in jeopardy.

After several hours he wandered up the stairs and across the tarmac into the building where Arv and Linda worked. Entering the large workroom he sat down on the sofa close to the door.

"Did I forget an appointment?" Arv asked him as he walked over to see what his young boss needed.

"No. I just have been worried about something that Bud and I caught while we were down there with Linda. Nobody else mentioned it so I thought I might talk to her. Is she around?"

"She is not. At this moment I believe she is conducting a test in one of the pressure tanks of the larger torpedo-style probe drive system. Said something about needing to run the thing through compressed custard."

"Well, perhaps a new set of eyes might help me. Can we call up something on your computer?"

Arv motioned for the inventor to lead the way to the nearest computer station. Tom took a seat and typed a series of commands, and he soon had the video he wanted on the monitor.

"Let me fast-forward this to near the halfway point—" he said as he moved the slider control, made a few position adjustments and then said, "—to about here. Watch the screen carefully, Arv."

The model maker had taken as seat and now leaned forward to concentrate on the images. "It's moving very slowly," he commented. "As thick as compressed custard?"

Tom replied, "Uh-huh."

Six or seven seconds went by before Arv sat straight up.

"Go back!" he requested.

Tom reversed the video and they watched the small flash that lasted only two frames. It would have been easy for anyone not concentrating when it first happened to miss.

"You saw it?" Tom asked.

Arv nodded. "I saw it. I don't know what it is I saw, but I definitely saw a flash.

Tom moved the paused video back to the first frame. There, on the screen, was the narrowing tunnel leading down with the rocky "bridge" in the middle and the flash of light that seemed to be coming from deeper down and behind the bridge.

There was no way, Tom thought, that it could have been a reflection.

* * * * *

Tom heard the footsteps coming across the hangar floor. Heavy enough to be male and in hard-soled shoes, not sneakers like he and Bud generally wore. That narrowed it down to only about seven hundred possibilities.

He had to chuckle to himself. There had been more people crossing that floor in the past several months than since the underground hangar had been first built.

"Oh, hello, Harlan," he greeted the man who walked through the open door. "Have a seat."

"I don't mind if I do." The Security chief sat heavily on the visitor's chair across the desk from Tom. "Do you want a little chit-chat first or have me get to the point?"

"*Meaningful* chit chat, or just putting off some bad news?"

Harlan pursed his lips and rolled his eyes. "Guess it shows, huh? So it's get to the point, Harlan. You will recall little more than a week ago Peter Crumwald was struck on the head and ended up in the hospital." When Tom said he did, Ames continued. "Fine. We know who did it. Care to guess?"

Tom was dumfounded. How could he ever guess something like that? He said so to Harlan.

"Lemme give you a hint. I'm feeling like playing a game if you can put up with me. It is safe to assume that you and Peter have something in common. A common enemy, that is."

Tom's mind didn't hesitate to come to a conclusion. "That Reverend Speers guy in Florida?"

"Uh-huh. It was another of his followers. The culprit has been working down at the city for nearly eight months. He is also the person who *found* Peter. Nice kid by all accounts. Good family, educated at Texas Tech. Passed our security screening with flying colors. The only thing we didn't check for, and we can't by law, is any religious affiliations. Just before going back down following his first rotation topside he met a young girl who has been in the thrall of this Speers fellow for more than a year." Harlan reached over with his right hand and massaged his upper forearm, grimacing slightly.

Tom groaned. "Don't tell me. Things started to go sour until he agreed to become part of this church. And then she somehow talked him into trying to disable Peter in order to prove his loyalty?"

"Yes. Pretty much that. But this kid mentioned that he was supposed to kill Peter." Tom was horror stricken at the news. "You're good at this game. He felt really guilty and that's why he was the one who quickly located Peter. So, we have him in custody on Fearing Island where he will receive an all-expensed paid trip to a federal prison courtesy of the FBI. When Gary confronted him about acting really nervous during the snap inspection, the kid tried to run. A couple of the others caught him and he broke down and confessed."

"And, the girl?"

Shaking his head, Ames replied, "Can't touch her until he turns evidence against her, and my guess is he still thinks he can salvage their relationship and live happily ever after! I guess that's all I came to tell you."

He grunted as he got up to leave.

Tom was happily humming to himself a few minutes later as he pulled up the preliminary drawings of his manned probe and went to work bringing in wire-form representations of everything that could be of use inside. He had been at it for nearly an hour when the phone rang again.

"Hello, Tom? It's Harlan, again. Sorry to bother you twice in one afternoon. I just got off the phone with the State Police down in Virginia. They caught a man matching the description of the one who clobbered that auto mechanic and then planted the kill box in your car."

"Do they know for sure it's the guy who tried to make me crash?" Tom inquired.

"Not for certain, but there is one little thing that gives me the feeling they have our man, just not somebody associated with the person whom I assumed might be behind it. He was carrying a small sheet of paper in his jacket. Actually, it had slipped through a tear in the upper pocket and was in the lining where he'd forgotten to get rid of it. I'd say that you can have five guesses whose name was on the paper, but that would be cruel."

"I just had a nasty feeling about all this, Harlan. My first guess would have something to do with Florida again, but go ahead and tell me."

"I'll read the whole thing to you. 'Go to Shopton, New York and find someone working for Shopton Motors as mechanic. Take his place. Wait for TS to take car in for computer update (probably 1 week) and plant new box in ODB. Leave town immediately, disappear forever.' That's about it except for the name on the bottom."

"Okay, tell me, who supposedly sent that note? Not the Reverend Speers?"

"No. It's signed, A. Samson."

"*Atlas Samson!*" Tom gasped.

CHAPTER 9 /

BAD CIRCUMSTANCES

HARLAN WAITED a moment before answering Tom's unasked question. "Yes, Samson is still in prison and has shown no signs of either getting out, or of having any communication with the outside world. Of course, that doesn't mean he hasn't found a weak link in his prison's security. There are always low-level guards who are willing to turn a blind eye in return for large sums of cash."

"But, how? I mean, to what purpose? Is this some sort of revenge plot because of our getting Samson arrested the last time we had strange and bad things happening down at—" he stopped for a second. "Oh-oh. Atlas Samson was involved up to his eyeballs in the last problems we had in the helium well. He goes away but as soon as the word slips out that there are more strange things— strange noises—going on down there, up Sampson pops."

"Yeah. Just like a bad jack-in-the-box. I'll follow up on this with the folks at Interpol and our FBI and CIA people. It may be a hoax or a coincidence. Could be that the note was from somebody named Anthony Samson and not Atlas. The thing is I really wanted to suspect that Speers guy in Florida. This complicates everything."

"Okay, Harlan. While you do that I'm going to call Haz up on Mars to see if he has any ideas what his father might be up to."

Hazard Samson, the commander of the Mars Colony, might have grown up in his father's shadow but he was an entirely different sort of person. A gentle and intelligent giant of a man, he had worked for his father for a number of years until it became evident that the elder Samson was a totally rotten individual and ruthless businessman. It was fortunate that Haz had managed to amass a small fortune of his own and so he could finally break all ties with his father.

Tom headed for the Communications building. When he got Haz on the radio ten minutes later he gave him a brief rundown of the attempt on his life and then the gist of the note in the would-be assassin's jacket.

"What do you think?" he asked.

"Well, Tom, it *sounds* like something the old man would be involved in. The only thing is that my father never signs anything with his last name. Especially something like that note. It would either be A. S. or just *A Telamon*, meaning 'Enduring Atlas.' I suppose that is his little joke."

"Some joke," Tom snorted. "If he is involved, do you have any ideas how he might have managed to get such a note out of his high-security prison?"

"With my father, nothing is impossible. Rather, with his money, not all of which was ever located and impounded, nothing is beyond reason. Was that note actually signed or the name just printed?"

"I'm pretty sure it was printed. Why?"

"Hmmm. If anything it could mean that my father was able to get the word out to someone else who wrote and sent that note, not realizing how Atlas Samson signs things. I'd have Ames check up on an old acquaintance and flunky of his, Damian Goosens."

An icy spike ran down Tom's back at the mention of the name. Goosens had been found at the undersea city of gold near to Helium City half starved and claiming to have been abandoned there to die by Atlas Samson. He had been allowed to leave once his health was restored and nothing had been heard of him since.

It now appeared that his entire condition might have been an elaborate act and that he was back to working for Samson.

"Thanks, Haz. As usual, if you hear anything—"

"I'll get in touch. I do have to say this doesn't honestly sound like something he would do. There are too many uncontrollable factors. It's not his style."

Tom called Harlan and told him about all this.

"Do *you* think Samson is behind the noises down there, Tom?"

"I'm not sure. But one thing that crossed my mind is that Samson might be trying to take advantage of the situation to make another move to take control of the wells. I'm going to call the Navy and have them increase surveillance."

"Have our own folks run a series of seacopters and jetmarines around the area, too."

"Great idea, Harlan. Thanks!" Tom hung up the phone. *Not one but two possible enemies appear to have it in for me,* he thought. *This crazy guy in Florida and now, maybe old Atlas Samson. Sheesh!*

He pushed his chair back and left Communications heading for the Adminstration building. After greeting their secretary Tom entered the big office and sat down in the conference area facing the large monitor on the wall. The remote control he picked up from the table let him place a video call to Graham Kaye, a Swift employee and the man who managed their Key West, Florida, telecasting center.

Years before Tom put the Outpost in Space into its geosynchronous orbit and they were able to take advantage of that broadcasting capability, Damon Swift had decided that the way to assure a consistent and readily available communications network was to have several stations located at strategic points around the country. Kaye and his center were the last of these facilities in operation, and Tom believed his father kept this one going for sentimental reasons.

However, Kaye had proven on several occasions in the past year alone to have a better feel for what was going on in both Florida as well as the entire Caribbean region than just about anyone else.

When his face appeared on the screen, Graham gave Tom a big smile. "Well, hello, Tom. You look like marriage is agreeing with you. To what do I owe the pleasure?"

Tom also smiled. He genuinely like Graham Kaye. "Well, knowing you like I do I have to assume that you have been watching all the news lately. Things like the rumors that have leaked out about the noises under Helium City."

Kaye nodded. "I have. And all of the whinging and moaning and everything else coming from a certain pseudo-religious personage and his followers. Did you by chance call to discuss him?"

Tom grinned and nodded. "Yeah. Him." He filled Kaye in on everything he knew including the attack on Peter Crumald and his own brush with death.

Kaye whistled and shook his head. "I should warn you that this guy is a real nutcase, Tom, but I'm sure you've already guessed that. Before you ask I have looked into him a little. I just knew you would eventually remember me and call."

"What have you found?"

"Harlan Ames either already knows this or will when I send him the file in a few minutes. Here's the basic rundown." He looked down and scanned a piece of paper he seemed to be holding out of camera range. "Walter Speers, born Raymond W. Spears, with an e-a rather that the double e, born sixty-three years ago in Wyoming. Father, unknown. Mother, in and out of that state's women's penitentiary until her death eleven years ago. He was conceived between stints in jail and delivered the day she was being released on another crime. Raised by an aunt, at least when she wasn't in jail."

"Fine family background. What about his church?"

"Oh, I'll get to that. He was just nineteen when they reinstated the military draft after the Government let the numbers grow too low and we were in that policing action in Central Africa. Got his notice to report and disappeared. Resurfaced nine years later as Walter with the new spelling of the last name. Over the next five years he spent a total of nineteen months in jail on various charges including robbery and dealing drugs. During that time he claims to have talked to what he terms, 'the greatest spirit in our universe,' who is supposed to have told him to form his church. *He* calls it a church. It isn't recognized by the state of Florida or by the U.S. Government as a legitimate religion and so he gets taxed on everything he takes in. And that, by the way, is about fifteen million a year. Uncle Sam takes forty-five percent, the church gets about ten percent and the rest our Walter spends on himself."

"And, nobody has caught onto him? His scheme?"

Kaye shrugged. "The guy is charismatic. Over eighty percent of his followers are women, and most of them are under the age of forty. The men are mostly young and get dragged into it by their girlfriends. About once a year he makes a grand proclamation that either the world is about to end—he even gives dates—or that the devil is coming. In either case he makes an appeal to his followers telling them they can be saved... for a price of course! When it doesn't end he takes the credit."

"Anything else?"

"Just that the former Raymond Spears spent some of his teen years behind bars on a murder charge. His aunt!"

Tom sat in stunned silence. Kaye added that before then the boy had been charged with talking a number of young girls into shoplifting for him or ruthlessly attacking other girls he wanted to teach a lesson.

"He has a history going back to about the age of thirteen of getting young women to do things for him."

"Yeah," Tom said, "and now it seems he's getting those girls to get their boyfriends to do bad things to us. Well, thanks for the information. Hopefully Harlan and his team can make something from it all."

He thanked his Key West telecaster and cut the connection.

A day went by with no word from Harlan regarding the information Kaye had sent. But that doesn't mean all had been quiet.

Phil Radnor finally called to report there was not much to report except that Peter Crumwald's attacker had started to name names.

Three more reports of the strange thrumming noises were reported by the people in Helium City. To add to that a U.S. Navy fast attack submarine on a secret course that took them through the area reported their sonar-phones had picked up a combination of very low pitched noises and something sounding like rock rubbing against rock.

The first return of the sounds lasted only about eleven minutes. A period of almost fifteen hours went by before another run of the noises that lasted nearly six hours.

It wasn't until late that same evening before they returned yet again but for less than a minute.

Nobody was certain what it was about the sounds, but everyone agreed that it set their nerves on edge. Five people requested emergency leave due to anxiety and there might have been more but Peter had the medic distribute ear plugs. At the first sign of the sounds the personnel were directed to insert them.

After that, it was tolerable, but Tom knew he had to hurry up and find out the source.

On the plus side there had been no further proclamations by Rev. Walter Speers. In fact, and according to Phil, the man had mysteriously disappeared. One of his followers attempted to get a press conference together but only the local cable access channel sent anybody. Even that person laughed and walked out when the young woman who identified herself only as "Sister Arlene" tried to claim that she had proof Tom Swift had personally come down, kidnapped the reverend and was, "Even now whisking him into space where he will be killed in a devil-worshiping ceremony that will never be seen by anyone!"

When the reporter called the police and provided them with her recording, they paid a call to the church and took the woman with them for questioning. Tom had to laugh when he learned that her one phone call from jail had been to another television station who had promptly hung up on her.

Linda Ming reported that she had been working hard with Arv and Hank Sterling and the people providing the new batteries. She was ready to take the probes-inside-a-probe down.

Bud could not go with them. He'd agreed to replace one of the men up at the *Sutter* involved in the building of the new super space station. Red Jones had been unfortunate enough to be hit rather sharply in the back by a floating supply pallet and had two cracked ribs. He would come back down on the *Challenger* as soon as Bud arrived in her.

In his absence, Tom asked Arv if he would like to come down again.

"You can see the fruits of your and Linda's labors," he said. He also invited Hank Sterling to come along. Both men eagerly agreed.

"I heard about Red," Hank said as Tom set the seacopter on the ocean surface and began the process of reversing its blades for the underwater dive.

"He's going to be fine, but he cracked two of his back ribs and those really hurt when you do things like walk and sit. Doc told me he'll be fine in a week and Bud's very happy to take his place."

"And, Sandy?" Arv asked.

"As I said, *Bud* is happy. But George Dilling is keeping her busy. The time will fly by."

With the advantage of practiced skills assisting them, the team got the new probe upright and inside the gas lock in record time. It soon was gliding down through the gaseous helium with only one of the smaller lights and the downward camera in operation. When it arrived at the breakthrough spot Tom turned on all the sensors and began the drop into the lower cavern.

"I'm going to leave the heat sleeve on the outside turned off until we get about a third of the way down," he told them. "I am, however, going to begin using Linda and Arv's little shoot out probes about every five hundred feet so we get a better ideal of the diameter of the cavern."

That lasted through the first two levels of probing. The first time out the little probes propelled their way out to within yards of the outward-sloping walls of the cavern. They had more than three hundred feet of additional wire that they might have used.

The second time the probes also stopped short of the walls, but this time it was by nearly fifty feet and they had reached the end of their tethers. The cameras showed the walls angling steeply away at that point. They were recalled and stowed.

"We'll send them out when we get to within a thousand feet of the bottom. At least we know where that is," Tom said with a rueful grin.

When the time came he turned on the electrical resistance coating on the probe. It had already slowed down by nearly forty percent. Now, with the area surrounding it warming slightly it picked up about half of that speed. Unfortunately, by the time it got within the quarter mile point of the bottom it was no longer having much effect.

"Can we keep going?" Hank asked.

"Absolutely, but it will be slow from this point. We're still at the liquid temperature of helium, about four degrees Kelvin, but it is so thick it might as well be frozen."

The small lateral probes had a terrible time with the thick, slushy liquid. But they did manage to get out to the point where they came near the wall. It meant that the cavern widened out above and was coming back closer to the cavern center as they got deeper. While they all waited for the larger probe to retrieve the small ones Tom did a little calculation. He smiled and announced that the reserves in the lower cavern were even larger than he might have guessed. "We really don't know. I'm using an assumption that from the point where we could no longer get out to the side walls that they only extend another two hundred feet or so. It could be double, triple or fifty times wider than that. The point is, this lower chamber is incredibly helium rich."

The relief team notified Tom they were ready to come in. The inventor looked at his watch and was surprised to find that almost nine hours had gone by.

"We'll call you when we get to within a couple hundred feet of the bottom, skipper," the incoming hoist operator told them. "By my reconning that will be another six hours at the rate of drop. Have a nice rest, you'all!"

"Skipper?" came the call over the intercom in the seacopter. "Skipper? You awake? It's Hank."

Tom looked at this watch, rubbed his eyes and looked again, this time focusing. He reached for a button on the wall. "Yes, Hank. Just barely, but awake. What's up?"

"Thought you'd like to know that the probe is nearing the bottom, and this time it is going to keep dropping. You've got maybe half an hour before it gets close to that new lower cave."

"Be right there. Is everyone else up?"

Hank's laugh came over the speaker. "Now what sort of Enterprises' employee would I be if I didn't wake you first. Everyone else is next on my list. See you in a few!"

Tom was the first to get to the air lock of the pressurized building and entered. He waited near the back wall only acknowledging the operators as they turned to see who had just come in. "Keep going until the others get here."

In five more minutes Hank, Arv, Linda and a Helium City video technicianl came in. The duty crew filled them in and then asked if they might stay.

"We're all curious, Tom," the hoist operator told him.

"Sure. At least for a bit." He took the man's place and checked the instrument panel. Everything was going smoothly. The drop rate was down to about three feet per minute, but that was faster than the first time without the hull heater.

Seventeen minutes later the bottom end of the probe passed the floor of the large chamber. It was a little eerie to suddenly have their wide-angle view narrowed to a few hundred feet at most. The lights were now able to illuminate everything below.

"If I didn't know that thing was nose down," Arv said, "I'd swear it was a camera going into a horizontal cave, and that bridge thing was a gigantic stalagmite and stalagtite formation."

Tom had to agree at the image.

"The next one down is much larger," Linda mentioned as it came into clearer view. "Can the probe get past that? It appears it will collide with the rocks."

Tom picked up a clear plastic ruler and held it up to the screen as close to center as possible. "It looks like we will just make it," he said as the alignment showed the probe would barely skim past it. "We've got about an hour before we really have to worry about that. I guess we'll see then."

The video was incredible. Even with the computer color correcting based on the various video inputs, the array of colors was fantastic. There were shades of blues, greens and yellows all around the probe, and as the light moved down the walls reflected some new shades.

"Hey," Tom said as he glanced at the control panel. "We're moving a little faster now. A couple extra inches a minute, but it is definitely faster. Look," he tapped one of the digital readouts. "It is warmer. Two-point-one degrees warmer than in the large cavern above. I wonder if there is some sort of magma source farther down that is warming things up?"

Arv chuckled, telling him, "You're the expert in here, skipper. The rest of us are a collection of kids who build things, a girl genius at making things tiny and a group of people standing behind us who keep the world running with the helium they provide."

About a minute later the probe reached the point where it was even with the underside of the first rock bridge. Tom activated the rotating side-view camera and swung it around to take a look. Where the top and sides of the bridge were rough and jagged, the bottom was almost rounded and smooth. He switched the view back.

"We'll have to get a *real* expert in to tell us why that bridge is the way it is," he declared.

Down the probe continued. The rate remained the same and the temperature was now constant.

With everyone now silent, Tom sat watching as the probe dipped below the rock bridge near the entrance to the deep hole. He had to blink several times when he discovered his eyes were drying and there were tiny spots before him. When he managed to get them to go away the probe was now about twenty feet past the bridge and he, and everybody else, could see the twisting and uneven vertical cave below.

In the distance they could now see the other rock bridge, perhaps three hundred feet farther down the hole.

Then, it happened. This time it wasn't just Tom and Bud who saw it. Saw *them*.

"What the—?" Hank cried out as they all saw first one, then another and finally more than half a dozen flashes of light coming from below the lower bridge.

Something was flashing deep inside the nearly frozen helium!

CHAPTER 10 /

THE BIG PILL

THERE WAS no denying it since they all saw it, and no denying it when Tom reviewed the video with his father the following morning.

Linda and Hank remained behind to retrieve the probe and to launch the third one to take samples of the liquid helium while Tom and Arv headed to Enterprises by way of Fearing Island.

"How can anything be generating light down there?" Damon asked dumfounded at what he was seeing.

Tom had no answer, but did admit, "Now I think I should have included a high-speed camera in the probe. We might have been able to see exactly where the flashes originated."

Mr. Swift shook his head. "How could you have anticipated this?" He waved his hand at the monitor.

Tom felt the searing redness of his face as he confessed. "I saw it the first time, but I didn't say anything. I figured that Bud and I only saw—"

"What! Bud saw this? The first time you sent the probe down? Whatever possessed you to not mention that before, Tom?"

Tom, who had been looking down at the floor now brought his gaze up to meet his father's. "What we saw only appeared once, came and disappeared in an instant and appears on just two frames of the video. Even looking at a still frame it is almost impossible to determine anything. I guess I convinced myself that it was a video artifact and not... that." He pointed at the screen.

They rewatched the video. It lasted just nine seconds and there was nothing that could be directly seen. Everything was behind the second bridge or possibly around a bend farther down in the shaft that could just be made out.

"How much farther down did the probe go?" Mr. Swift asked.

"Even though we had another mile of cable we ran into another colder layer. It made the helium more solid to the right and that pushed the probe to the left. No matter how many times I tried bringing it back up a bit and dropping back down, it stopped right on top of that second rock bridge."

"And no further flashing lights?"

Tom shook his head. "We pulled back out after that but saw nothing else." They looked at each other for a couple of minutes, both men lost in their individual thoughts but both contemplating the next move.

"Would there be any possibility of building another probe that can be steered around any formations in the way?" Tom's father asked. "And with a higher output heating system?"

Tom pursed his lips and looked at his father in a meaningful way. "Or, I could go down there and see for myself," he stated. "Other than the cold and whatever possible threat those lights might pose, if any, we detected absolutely zero radioactivity at any level. In fact, if you discount the flashes the only interesting thing we discovered is that fairly narrow band where the temperature comes up a few degrees. Even that, statistically, is practically nothing."

Now Damon pursed his lips a little before he spoke. "I can't say that I will happily give my permission, but I also have to realize that you are not a teenager any more. You are an adult and you have both responsibilities and benefits within this company. There are two things I would ask of you first. One, that you get our rail project going, and two, that you run your plans for a manned probe past me so I can try to justify the safety of it to your mother."

"Yeah," Tom grinned, "and I have to do the same for Bash."

Neither of them mentioned the reaction Sandy would have when Bud told her he would be going. It isn't that she would demand that he not go, it was just that, "her Bud" had received a few injuries while adventuring with Tom, and she really wanted both of them to find a way to stop getting hurt. In her mind that meant Bud should stop going on these things.

He placed a call to the Maintenance manager. "Ralph? It's Tom. Listen, I was wondering how the project to pull the old rails off that line was going. I'm going to be ready day after tomorrow to begin laying down the spur line from the new car facility out to those tracks."

"Well, by a strange coincidence we are starting that today. My crew used one of the heavy-lifting helicopters to take a crane down and attach it to one of the flat bed rail cars they left near the end of the line in Pottersville. We had to spend a few days jacking it up, sledgehammering the wheels off, and then grinding down the rust and reinstalling them. It doesn't have the moves of a ballerina, and it groans something fierce, but move it does and so we can run it down the tracks pulling each old pair off as we pass them. We have enough room to pile about six hundred feet of track on the rail car."

"Hmmm. That's not a whole lot, is it?"

"No, but given that neither the old track bed nor that rail car are in great condition, and that much rail weighs about ninety tons, it's about the top weight we can haul along."

Tom informed Ralph that the spur line was going to require about four days to complete and the weekend would be in the middle of that.

"Plan on my wanting to make the sweeping curve and start on the old bed by next Wednesday," Tom told him.

The combination grinder, repaver and their track extruding equipment had been at work creating the main tracks and the side tracks within the boundaries of the new facility. Another team was preparing to erect a series of ramps and other loading equipment. That work would be finished a week after the spur line and revitalized old tracks had been completed.

"I see you brought one of the track racers out, skipper," Bud said as he walked over to stand next to the inventor that afternoon. Tom had been supervising the alignment of the equipment so that everything would run smoothly from the first rails. The little vehicle was Bud's favorite of the group, the blue racer—each one had been given a color code so that coordinating their whereabouts could be simplified.

"It still isn't for joyriding, Bud," Tom cautioned. "It is, however, for transporting all crews out to the work area, bringing out food and beverages, and letting me—yes, you too—drive out to inspect every so often."

Bud frowned before suggesting in a serious tone, "I think that somebody must volunteer to run the entire length of the track system at some point to ensure that all the rails are properly spaced and that there are no sudden bumps or anything." He looked at Tom hopefully.

The inventor laughed. "Okay, Bud. You win. Once we get the entire line finished you get to go from one end to the other. Twice, in fact. On the way out and down you will go about twenty miles per hour to, ahem, check the rail alignment. Then you can try for a couple speed bursts on the way back."

Bud now had a huge grin on his face. "I knew you'd see it my way, skipper!"

It was getting close to quitting time so Tom bade his friend goodbye and drove off a minute later.

As Tom began drifting to sleep the next night an image entered his subconscious. He fought against sleep to try to determine what it might mean but lost the battle and began to softly snore.

Bashalli, not yet asleep herself, poked him gently in the side causing him to roll over. The snoring stopped only to be replaced by the inventor muttering a few words. She propped herself back up, reached into the night stand and pulled out a pen and pad of paper writing down the few words that made any sense to her.

In the past this had proven to be of some help.

In the morning after showering and shaving, Tom dressed and went down to the kitchen. Bashalli was sitting at the breakfast table reading a paperback book and humming cheerfully to herself.

"Good morning, Bash," he greeted her as she pointed to the cup of coffee waiting for him.

"Good morning to you, Tom. It is a wonderful morning full of the songs of birds, sunshine and the promise of an entire day of relaxation. Your scrambled eggs and toast will be just a few minutes." She got up, kissed him on the forehead and went to the stove. "Did you have pleasant dreams?" she inquired. As the words left her lips she wanted to clamp her hands over her mouth. She knew what was about to happen.

"Dreams? Yeah, I guess so, except—" *Here it comes,* she thought, "—something came to mind right as I nodded off and I can't for the life of me figure out what it was. It seemed mighty important, too."

She came back to the table and pulled a piece of paper from her book, the one she had written his words on the night before. With a deep sigh she told him, "I really had hoped we could spent at least this one Saturday together, Tom."

Tom frowned but opened the paper. A moment later he jumped up. "That's it!" he cried. "Oh, Bash, you're the greatest! This is the solution to what I've been trying to think of all last week. The way to move the new probe inside the big caverns. Oh, wow!"

He was about to rush out from the room when something told him to stop. He turned to look at his wife who was standing, looking quite sad. Tom hadn't yet been a husband for two years but he was catching on quickly. He walked back to her and took her in his arms.

"Listen. If you can put the eggs and toast on hold for five minutes, I'll go make a few quick notes, enough so that I don't lose the idea, and then we'll eat and have a quiet day together.

She let out a pleased squeal and jumped up in his arms wrapping hers around his neck and putting her nose against his. "It is a deal!" She kissed him and let go.

It took seven minutes, but Bashalli was used to "Tom minutes." They were not like real minutes and their span fluctuated based on the task in which he was involved. They were rarely shorter than real time. She felt lucky that today's had been only forty percent longer than those showing on the wall clock.

They did have a wonderful day that included a picnic lunch on the small beach on Lake Carlopa down from the historic Swift home where several of Tom's ancestors had lived.

He even agreed to take her flying on Sunday. Other than Anne Swift—who explained that being married to someone who was a qualified pilot, and had two children who were excellent pilots meant that she did not need to *be* a pilot herself—Bashalli was the only one not licensed. She had been trained by several of the best including Sandy, Tom and Bud and only lacked a little more take off and landing experience before everyone felt she could do her solo flight.

Unlike a number of people who spend all their student time in a single type of small aircraft, she had experience in four aircraft including Tom's Toad jet commuter.

She asked to be allowed to fly the *Racing Pigeon*. Like the successful Swift's *Pigeon Special* the "Racer" was still a single-engine over-wing craft, but featured a more powerful engine and was nearly a thousand pounds heavier making it smoother to fly in light winds.

It was a beautiful day to fly so they headed toward the Atlantic Ocean. On the way Tom told her about what his flash dream and mumbling had been about. As he described what it meant for his new probe even the non-technical Bashalli could readily picture it in her mind.

When she landed back at Enterprises four hours after they left she kissed Tom and told him she would come back to pick him up in a few hours. He looked questioningly at her.

"You go get some of that into the computers so that you may be able to come home at reasonable times the rest of the week."

Tom went to the big office to pick up a new computer tablet he had ordered. It was less of a computer than it was a drawing machine. Outfitted with the latest CAD software it wirelessly interfaced with Tom's larger computer and from there to the company's bank of computers. He walked down the hall to the stairs with it tucked under his right arm.

He ascended one floor coming out at the far end of the hall and walked back in the direction of the office, passing the Legal department on the way. An unmarked door opened to his entry code and he was soon climbing the spiral stairs to the original air control tower for all of Enterprises. The 360-degree wrap-around glass was still there while every other piece of equipment or storage container had long since been removed.

This was Tom's favorite "get away" spot. On a sunny day like it was the temperature was fairly high so he tapped the thermostat to bring air-conditioned coolness to the space.

He sat and turned the tablet on, then rubbed his jaw in thought as he pondered what to do first. Finally he pulled the pen-like stylus from its small recess and began to draw.

In the past few weeks, Tom's designs had gone from an elongated capsule to a squat oval and finally was within a foot of being a ball. It wasn't going to be a radically different shaped craft.

The thing that was going to be truly different is in how the new manned probe would maneuver into and around the upper and lower caverns. While he still would be adding a tether from the top of the probe to the point of entry in the top of the upper cavern, it would not be there to simply lower the thing down and pull it back up. In fact he saw it having only two real functions: to provide power so that only a small backup source needed to be carried; and, as a communication line.

After sketching for nearly an hour he moved the results into the CAD program and began to clean it up. Within another half hour he had a fairly complete wire image that could be rotated, moved up and down, tilted and swung about.

With a smile he pulled his cell phone out and called home.

"Bash? You can come get me. I've got it all in the computer. Oh, and thanks for letting me do this!"

It would take about ten minutes for her to get there so he sent the file off for storage and transferred a copy to his personal system. Before he went back downstairs he turned the thermostat off again and went to the South-facing windows. In the distance sat the new Swift MotorCar facility and his enormous inflatable sub-assembly hall. The late afternoon sun was shining off it giving it a spectacular sheen.

Everything was peaceful out there so he nodded to himself and headed down to the second floor, dropped the tablet off in the office and then went down and outside to wait for Bashalli.

By Wednesday Tom had again adjusted the shape of his probe. With most functions other than visual observation able to be handled by the unmanned probes he felt there was little use in having a taller-than-wide body. Where his very first design had been sketched at nearly eleven feet tall he realized he was bringing the dimensions closer and closer to a sphere. He asked himself, *Why not a ball?* He and Bud would ride in the widest part of the body with their environmental equipment sitting at the bottom and all the electronics wrapped around and above them.

Because there was some slight worry in his mind that the sphere might tip over, he added a weight at the very bottom of the shell. Now, even if it dropped into the liquid helium, it would float with its passengers able to climb out the hatch next to where they would sit.

Of course doing that would mean almost instant death, but Tom had a plan for that as well. He and Bud would wear a variation of his pliable deep sea hydrolung suits; these were the suits that eventually became the genesis for his replacement to the Fat Man egg-shaped diving suits.

Soft enough to be folded and stowed in a box, the suits could form fit to an individual's body in seconds and the material become capable of holding off great underwater pressure. He planned for them to wear the newest version over modern long johns and coveralls and with the helmet hanging off their backs.

When Bud dropped by late that morning Tom suggested they sit for a while and go over everything.

"After all, flyboy, you're going to be in there with me so you need to know how it all works."

Bud had no issues with the computers and equipment inside, nor did he question the shape or composition of the capsule. To him, if Tom said it was necessary, and that it would work, that was good enough.

He did, however, point at the screen and ask one simple question.

"Where does the big cable attach?"

Tom brought the upper area of the capsule into a close-up view. "There. That small plug. Why?"

Bud stood up and walked to the wall monitor pointing at the capsule. "Uhh, I was kind of afraid you were going to say that. What I mean is where does the heavy-duty cable that we get lowered down on, and more to the point, get brought back up with, get attached?"

"That's it, Bud. We won't be using a big cable. What we may use is a large suction hose and fitting that will stick to the capsule long enough to ease us out of the lock but after that we're on our own. But, I see a look of concern on your usually bright and cheerful face," he teased. "Tell me what is on your mind."

"Tom, I try to not question anything your make. If you say we have a suction cup licked and smacked on the capsule to get us into the lock, and that it lets us go, then I believe you. And, I'll assume it works the opposite way when we want to come back out. But *how in the heck* do you intend to have us get around in those chambers without a cable?!"

Tom laughed. He wanted it to be the big surprise finish, and Bud was playing into his plan.

"You understand the Attractatron system, right?" Bud nodded.

A combination of Tom's earlier repelatron technology but now used in concert with a reverse of that effect, the system used a repelatron to both sample the target material it pointed at, but after sending that information to a computer that set up a direct opposite field and sent that back to the object—as a circular sheath surrounding the repelatron beam—the combination grabbed and held tight. The push and pull were balanced so a specific distance could be maintained at all times.

These were first used in Tom's Attractatron mules, small autonomous spacecraft that patrolled space looking for and deflecting any space objects that might otherwise hit the Earth.

"Okay. Sure. Attractatron." He paused. "So what?"

"Well, this capsule has eight of them arranged on both sides of the body. The computers keep them pointed at enough spots to give us a good, solid hold. Then, the beams move around so that we travel using the electronic equivalent of legs. In other words, we walk up and down the caverns getting closer or farther away from what we want to see."

"I see. I think. So, how do we—you and I—actually make the thing move?"

"Two joysticks and a lot of computer power. One handles up and down, the other side to side and thumb wheels do the rotation and pitch." He looked over to see if this was enough information.

Bud was looking at the ceiling, mouthing something. Finally he looked back at Tom. "SpiderBall!" he announced. When the inventor looked blankly at him, he explained. "Eight beamy legs like eight legs on a spider. They climb walls, and we will climb walls. Plus, the capsule is almost an orb. SpiderBall. Get it?"

Tom got it, and like most of Bud's pun nicknames he had to groan at it. The problem was, in this case it was very accurate, and it *had* been a spider Tom pictured that night as he fell asleep.

He rose, shook Bud's hand and declared that the name would be SpiderBall.

"Congratulations on another wonderful name, flyboy. Beats what Dad came up with. The Big Pill!"

The production of the a scale model of the body—coming from the skilled hands of Arv Hanson—was first delivered to Hank Sterling and his team of engineers along with Tom's detailed CAD drawings where they began the pattern-making process for the individual pieces that would become the outer shell.

Although the smaller probes had managed the enormous pressures lower down, Tom was afraid the larger near-sphere might be subjected to far greater pressures, so he had specified that the shell be built as two layers interconnected to each other and the five millimeter gap flooded with a hard-setting insulating foam.

Only the outer "hull" would also receive a layer of electrically resistive material to provide the necessary heat to help the capsule travel through the thicker, colder and much heavier liquid near the bottom of the lower chamber.

And into whatever might be waiting for them below that!

.

CHAPTER 11 /
WALKING THE SPIDER

TOM WORKED off and on for six days getting his design finalized. The body was now definitely a sphere, six feet across with a rather tight compartment taking up the middle two-thirds and everything else either under the two seats and the foot rests or crammed above, around and behind the control panels. It would be a tight fit for them, but Tom anticipated they could manage the planned twenty hour journey with minimal discomfort.

When he wasn't working at his computer or meeting with several departments who would make his designs a reality, he spent time managing and inspecting the rail work.

It was easy to build the spur line from the new facility out to the old tracks. Bud, Hank Sterling and Art Wiltessa took four-hour shifts over three days and got that completed.

When Tom came by to see how it turned out, Art was just aligning a laser measuring device on the inside of the right-hand track. He stood up and smiled. "Just in time to press the switch, skipper," he said. "I was getting ready to take a measurement to see if we stayed in line. Looks so to my naked eye, but this will tell us. Want to do the honors?"

Tom smiled. A few years ago he would have jumped at the chance to be the one to do practically everything, but time, marriage and maturity had softened him a bit. "No, Art. You set it up, you take the sighting." He did not add, *Not that there is anything we can do about it now that the tracks have set solid.*

Art pressed a button on the small hand-held remote and a bright green light lit up on top of the measurement device. It was followed a half-second later by a green light on the remote.

"Nice," Art commented. "Take a look."

Tom nodded his approval. "Within two millimeters of dead straight. Now all I have to do is program that banking curve over to the old rail bed into the machinery. I'm thinking that it would be nice to be able to run the transport train along at about forty-five miles per hour end to end. We can get down to the terminus in about an hour. I just need to angle the track up on the outer side to accommodate that."

"How is the Construction Company coming on the little locomotive engine and the cars?"

"Really well. Since we already had the forms and jigs to build the smaller interim engine cars that are spaced along the transcontinental bulletrains, and two of those, front and back, can do this job just fine, all I needed was for them to turn out two extras in the batch they are producing for the Chicago to Dallas run of the transportation line along with a dozen of the box cars. These ones will not be as tall; just enough to carry two levels of cars."

"Too bad you can't make some sleek little body for the locomotive," Art said with a tone of regret.

"Ah, but Art, I did," Tom said with an emphatic nod. "It isn't nearly as long in the nose as the big locomotives, but it is along the same lines. Sleek with room for two drivers in the front and a single Y8 engine in the back turning a generator that drives the four powered wheels. And those box cars are being configured inside with a floor half way up and pneumatic ramps that can be dropped down at either end to aid in loading. We'll be able to transport a dozen of our first model per car, times ten of the cars."

Art looked confused. "I thought you mentioned a dozen box cars at one point. What about the other two? Extras?"

Tom explained that the Construction Company hoped to use the train to ship some of their goods out. "Those two cars won't always be attached but they'll be able to get hooked up at the end in about three minutes. Eventually I think dad wants to run another spur line over to the Construction Company to make things as easy as possible."

With Art's assistance Tom muscled the blue track racer onto the rails and headed out to the connection point. As he approached he could see the paver and extruder combination where it had stopped. He pulled up behind and got out.

Bud was talking to one of the men from Maintenance about the ongoing work.

"Hey, Tom," he called out. "Bradley just told me that they've got all but the last three miles of the old track pulled up and moved out."

"That's right, Tom," the balding thirty-year-old told him. "We had no problems getting the old rivets out. They practically jumped out, the wooden ties are so old and rotten. Anyway, those old rails were never welded together so they came up nice and easy. The only issue is stacking them. They are warped from heat and age and heavy loads so we can't just stack 'em very well." He shrugged.

"What's happened with the ones you've pulled up?"

"Taken at very slow speeds down to Glen Falls where a metals reclamation yard is paying us two hundred dollars a ton. These are old New York Central Railroad tracks and they used some of the heaviest rails for their time. About a hundred and fifty pounds per yard. These are sixty footers so they come in at just about a ton and a half apiece."

Tom did the arithmetic. "Three hundred dollars per rail? That sounds like too much."

"Six hundred per double rail set. And the reason it is such a good price is that this is prime steel. It's the sort of stuff that armored plating for old battleships was made of, and the girders in skyscrapers that have to hold up a lot of weight."

"Well," Tom told him, "I'm going to have to check to see what the state wants us to do with that money. It will end up being a fairly incredible sum."

When he arrived back at Enterprises Tom talked the recycle money issue over with his father.

"As nearly as I can tell from a conversation I had with the state's office of Budget and Resource Management they don't want it," Mr. Swift told him. "The last word Jackson Rimmer up in Legal got was along the lines of, 'We can't account for that money being shoved back into the state's coffers. Keep it or give it to charity!' So, Son, while I would love to keep that, it obviously isn't ours and to give it away before the state realizes they are passing on just over two million dollars may come back to bite us, I think we ought to put it into a special account and sit on it for at least a year."

Tom agreed with his father's plan.

They talked about the next steps and also agreed to hold off on laying the curve and final miles of the replacement track until the entire old line had been dismantled and cleared away.

So, other than to request that the track equipment at the end of the spur be brought back to the car company's property for safe keeping, Tom set that project aside in favor of taking a more direct hand in the building and testing of the new sphere.

His most pressing need was developing the Attractatron "legs" for moving the sphere around. Creating the design for the swiveling gimbals to mount the Attractatron emitters on was fairly easy. What was difficult was coming up with a material for the gimbals and mounting brackets that could withstand both the weight and the incredible cold. Many materials would have been fine at normal temperatures. Even in a range of zero to minus fifty degrees Fahrenheit most metals or strong plastics—like Durastress—would have no problems. Not so at near absolute zero. Metals got very brittle when subjected to that level of cold. Most plastics as well. His computer modeling tests gave him a pretty good idea that in the upper cavern of gaseous helium there would be zero probability of any issues. Even in the first thirty to fifty feet of the top of the liquid helium where it was more pressure causing the liquefaction than cold, most materials would work. At least, for a while. But not long enough.

Working with his Metallurgy department Tom concocted more than twenty new alloys.

Few, by themselves, turned out any better than those he had tried earlier. However, one "mistake" held some promise.

Tom's instruction for a night shift scientist had been to take the basic components of magnetanium—magnesium and titanium— and combine them with aluminum and an increasing amount of copper. In his haste to write the note, Tom's scribble led to a misunderstanding where the metallurgist added some of the Swift's small supply of ArmAlColite, already an alloy and one found only on the Moon.

The man discovered his mistake and was in a state of despair when he told Tom of the costly error.

Getting Tom Swift angry wasn't difficult but getting him to let you see he was angry was very hard. His great grandfather, the man he was named for, had several favorite sayings, among them, "There is a teacher lurking behind every mistake."

Not so much angry as frustrated, he looked at the sad man, took a deep breath, and said, "Tell me about what you ended up with."

The man, Christopher Adderly, looked up with some hope in his eyes. "Well, it is actually pretty amazing stuff."

He told Tom about both the strength as well as the ability to withstand extremes in heat and cold.

"Once the stuff anneals over an eight hour cooling period it doesn't want to even go soft at the original casting temperature. As for cold, I've only put it into some liquid nitrogen. That's all we have right now in the lab. It held its tensile strength."

Tom's heart was beating faster in excitement over the possible breakthrough, accident or not. While the use of the ArmAlColite was costly at a value of nearly twenty thousand dollars per pound, the man admitted to only using a half ounce for the two pound batch. His entire project would use less than seven pounds of alloy.

"Let me make a little call," he told Christopher. He picked up the phone and asked Trent to connect him with Peter Crumwald in Helium City.

"Hello, Peter? It's Tom. I know that before everyone came back up here that Linda Ming lowered the sampling probe. She told me she left the samples with your folks because you have the equipment to do all the tests... Right. And I agree that is exactly why you have all that nifty equipment and I don't." Tom winked at the scientist across his desk. "So, Peter, how much of the super cold and slushy stuff do you have still... Oh. That much? Wonderful. Can you please get one of those deeper samples sent up to me as soon as possible? I need to use it to test some things for our next probe... Uh-huh. Right. Bud and I will be going down... Probably four weeks. I'll let you know. Thanks!"

Hanging up Tom looked at Christopher. "You will have one cubic foot of highly compressed liquid helium tomorrow. Since I have a pressure setup already in my lab just next door I think it is best to use that for your tests. If you can have your sample and a small strength test rig in there tomorrow I will give you most of the next day as your assistant."

When they got together Tom explained the procedures they would have to follow.

"To begin, I'm afraid that the test devices you've brought are not going to work for us today. It's a bit too large. That part that looks like a tunnel—" he pointed inside the clear tomasite walled test chamber, "—*is* a tunnel and a set of pressure locks. Three to be exact. Our helium sample is at the equivalent of one hundred and sixty atmospheres. Inside the container it is one cubic foot of super-pressurized and super-cold helium almost in a solid state. If that container were to rupture, and always assuming we weren't immediately killed by being splashed and covered with what's inside or crushed in a microsecond against the walls of this room, it would expand to about one hundred-nine cubic *yards* of gas!"

"Whoa! I can't even fathom that kind of explosive force."

Tom had to agree. It was an awesome force. "Although this isn't a really good analogy, think of it having the explosive force of a small nuclear warhead, only so incredibly cold that it would penetrate and freeze your body in under five seconds."

Christopher Adderly gulped. He found that his mouth was completely dry and he tried again. Tom spotted his distress and got a large cup of water from the nearby cooler. "Better?"

"Yeah. Thanks," the man said breathlessly.

As he set things up, Tom explained. "I was fairly certain you wouldn't have the very small equipment I have so I pre-loaded the test rig in the large, round chamber at the end. Because once we insert the gas container we can't add anything else, I need you to place your sample material in that clamp at the open end."

Adderly did as he was told and returned to Tom's side.

"Now, I will place our gas container in its proper spot—" he did it, "—and now I'll close the chamber door."

"Ummm, what if everything explodes in there? Will we be safe?"

Tom laughed. "Yes. And the reason is that the right side wall is a blow-out panel. Before enough pressure might build up in there the wall would slam open. It is on heavy, heavy hinges and would most likely come around so hard that it punctured the wall over here, but the pressure and even that collision would not hurt us. Are you ready?"

With a nod from the metalurgist, Tom tuned and began moving controls. The sample, its clamp and the gas all moved into the tunnel and the hatch closed. He brought up the pressure inside the first chamber as well as the second one to about fifty atmospheres before opening their adjoining hatch and moving things into that second chamber. The process was repeated with the second and third chambers brought to ninety atmospheres.

The final pressurization brought the third chamber and the test chamber to the highest level Tom could achieve—one hundred-fifty atmospheres. It wasn't exactly what he needed but it would have to do.

A closed circuit camera showed them what happened next.

The sample was picked up by a robotic arm that set it into a devise looking like a guillotine with the metal supported on either end but not in the middle. The liquid helium was allowed to flood the entire chamber and left to do its worst to the metal for a full minute.

"So here's the moment of truth, as they say..." Tom said as he pressed the release for the guillotine. It slammed down onto the frozen metal. Both men had been holding their breath but now exhaled as they saw what had happened.

Nothing!

The metal didn't shatter or even bend. The guillotine shaft had cracked. The test was a success.

Tom congratulated Christopher and told him to now work closely with Hank Sterling who was managing the build of the SpiderBall outer hull.

"He'll need to have you work your alloy magic on nine special mounts. Eight for our emitters and one for the data and communications cable to connect us to the outside world. Oh, and thanks for letting me know about the mistake. It turned out just fine, but I might have never known had you tried to cover this up. Good job!"

With what might have been the weak link in the project now

handled Tom relaxed enough to spend a week concentrating on the programming to properly control the Attractatron emitters. No matter what he or Bud might do with the controls, the emitters had to work in perfect unison to compute where they needed to be aimed, measure both the distance as well as the composition of the target materials, make that precision aim and then move on their mounts as a group to ensure the smooth motion of the sphere. All in about a quarter second.

More than one person, on having him explain the intricacies of everything, likened it to attempting to herd cats.

Luck was with him as he only made two false starts on the programming, both times after making a wrong assumption about requiring that all four emitters on each side be constantly working and moving.

Once he realized that at least one emitter on either side had to be off temporarily to move to and set up to use the next location— even if this would be measured in tenths of a second—and then saw that even if two were shut down the sphere could be made to maintain its position, things went quickly.

Arv and Linda came over to his office one afternoon to see if they might assist.

"Hmmm? I'm not sure to tell you the truth. I think I have the programming nearly wrapped up and it all tests great in the computer simulation. What did you have in mind?"

Arv looked at Linda. "You were right. I owe you a steak dinner. He *has* forgotten what you and I do around here. Come on. I guess we've taken up enough of his time."

They both made to leave but Tom stopped them.

"Okay! Fine. You are my chief model maker, Arv, and you are my genius of making things small. Right?"

Linda looked worried. "I was actually thinking I was the Queen of Miniaturization. Is suppose that *genius* has some value." She gave a little sniffle and pouted.

Tom let out a laugh. It was the first one for him in nearly a week and it felt good. They quickly joined him.

"Okay. I know you've done the basic sphere but can you two build me a scale *working* model of this SpiderBall as Bud calls it?"

"As long as two things can be handled. One, your programming gets used by a computer that we already know won't fit inside," Arv told him, "and two, that this won't be tested in anything thicker or colder than water."

Tom held out a hand to Arv. "It's a deal!" He then shook Linda's hand and told her, "I have taken your concern to heart and hereby declare you to be Swift Enterprises' Queen of Miniaturization. Just don't let Bud Barclay hear it or he'll probably start calling you Teeny-Queenie or something like that!"

They left promising Tom they would have the working model for him in two days.

"We've been downloading your CAD materials and already have the body and the mini-emitters and their servos built," Linda told him. "We just need to build an interface and add batteries."

When they came back two days later with a beachball-size globe, Tom was speechless. Around each side—measured by their position of either side of the small hatch—of the sphere were arranged four one-inch emitters. They were a bit larger than the scale of the ball but were the smallest Linda had managed to create.

They demonstrated how each one could swivel and rotate independently from each other. But, as they explained, while they had an interface plug, it would need Tom's programming and also a small computer inside to make things really work.

"I have just the little computer," he told them. "It's only a processor chip and some memory plus a AAA battery, but I can download an instruction set on how to interpret my large-scale program to work with the servos controlling the eight emitters. Come back tomorrow and we can test it."

They did come back along with Bud, Sandy, Mr. Swift and even Chow.

The first thing the inventor did was to have it raise itself up on invisible legs. It was an eerie sight. Then, Tom walked the sphere out of his lab and down the hall. After passing the shared office he adjusted the pair of small joysticks on his controller and the ball paused for a second before moving closer to the left wall and "walking" up it, across the ceiling and back down the other wall.

Tom finished those maneuvers and it nimbly jumped over the ride/walk belt in the middle of the corridor before he moved it back to his side.

Bud leaned over and whispered something in Tom's ear. The inventor grinned and nodded.

"Well, that's about it, folks. Thanks for coming to see the first test. And I declare it to be a success. We'll do a lot more tomorrow." As most of the people moved off Tom maneuvered the silent ball along the corridor and up in the air until it appeared to be resting on top of Chow's ten-gallon hat. He and Bud walked along to keep the twenty-foot cable slack.

Chow turned the corner and entered his kitchen. It was about fifteen seconds later when there was a shout and the sound of pots and pans crashing to the floor.

They raced into Chow's kitchen in time to see the chef flailing his arms at the ball now resting in mid air just out of his reach.

"Consarned ee-lec-tronical varmint!" he told them. "Tryin' ta hitch a ride on my haid! It jest ain't right, I tell ya!"

Tom apologized but had to ask, "Did you feel anything? I aimed two of the emitters down at your hat."

Chow thought about it, now calming down, and replied, "I felt a little tingle but I thought it might be the new shampoo Wanda got me."

Bud and Tom left before they could break out laughing. The very thought of bald-headed Chow Winkler and shampoo nearly had them in stitches.

CHAPTER 12 /

SPIDER INTO THE DEPTHS

FIVE MORE days passed during which Tom used the scale model of the SpiderBall to test his software along with the effectiveness of operating in water under great pressure. Even though Arv hoped Tom would refrain from that type of evaluation, the sphere design needed testing under those conditions. With the few bugs worked out by day three he set up for another test in the main water pressure tank and was just climbing into his deep sea suit when Bud came into the control room.

"I hope you've waited a half hour after eating lunch, young man," he kidded. "Can't have you getting a cramp and drowning, or whatever it was they used to warn kids about."

"That, I believe, was just a ploy by parents who wanted a little after lunch rest time before they had to watch the kids splash around. Besides, I haven't had my lunch yet. Too much to do."

"Mind if I join you in the tank?" Bud inquired.

"Get suited up. I'll hop in and close the hatch in ten minutes."

Once the flyer changed, they eased the SpiderBall model into the open hatch and climbed in after it. Bud looked at the ball as if something might not be quite right. He mentioned it to Tom.

The inventor nodded toward his left forearm. "You probably can see that the ball no longer is tethered to a remote controller. I worked this wireless one up this morning." He held up his left wrist. "Everything I need is strapped to my arm except for the computer which is this—" he turned around so that Bud could see the black box attached to his back, "—that does all the thinking. Are you ready?"

With a nod the flyer reached over and closed the hatch while Tom got on the radio and told the technician to start bringing up the pressure.

The suits they wore—the same ones they would wear in the full-size sphere—would safely allow them to go down to depths of nearly two miles.

"Stop the pressure at three hundred feet, please," Tom requested.

"Roger. Three double zero feet... coming up on that in about one minute."

"Okay, flyboy, here we go." Tom activated the remote on his arm and they could both see a small light pulse as everything went through automatic checks. When a row of solid green LEDs were visible along the top of the arm band he looked over at his friend and smiled.

His fingers moved over the controls, and the ball, which had been floating, began to move down. The tank measured about twenty feet square and was thirty feet deep. As the boys sank down the ball kept pace with them.

Over the next hour the pressure was allowed to build and the testing continued.

When the pressure was relieved and they got out Tom even had the SpiderBall climb out after them and "walk" to the side where it settled to the ground before being turned off.

Bud tossed his helmet back onto his shoulders and smiled. "Success?"

"Absolute success! You noticed that it slowed down quite a bit when we got to the deepest pressure, right?"

"Yep."

"I'm going to have to feed all the data we collected into my computer back at the office, but I think that we only saw about a twenty percent slow down. Of course, the water isn't a thick slush like down in the well but I believe the full-scale ball will still be able to maneuver at about fifteen percent of normal speed, especially with the newer, higher wattage heating system Hank is covering the ball with."

"How hot will it get?"

"At room temperature, about one hundred and fifty degrees."

Bud considered that information before inquiring, "How far out will that reach once we're under the surface?"

"I think, and this is only a partially educated estimate, but I think that the heat will extend about five inches around us. At least to some degree. It will be enough that the first centimeter out from the skin will be warm helium gas and then it will cool then liquefy and then freeze the farther out you go. So, in effect we will travel within a small bubble of helium gas that we drag along with us as the ball moves."

"Too bad we can't make that bubble really big and keep all of the frozen slush a couple yards away," Bud stated.

Technically, Tom realized it could be accomplished using between forty and fifty small repelatron emitters spaced all around the sphere, except they would interfere with the Attractatrons.

"What are we going to do once we get down there?"

"That is a very good question, Bud," Tom told him. "There are a lot of things we might try, but primarily I want to go down as deep as we possibly can, hopefully all the way to the very bottom of that shaft. Beyond if there's anything else below that. We'll take along a few of those ejectable probes Linda Wong came up with, only I don't believe we have the space for the mini-reels to try to recover them."

Bud nodded to indicate he understood the logic in that.

"Okay, so what will they be doing? If that shaft stays that narrow we'll know how wide it is. And a little doo-hickey sticking out of the side of the sphere can give us the temperature. So...?"

Tom smiled. "So, they do have a small camera and light source in them. I'm going to have ours arranged on the bottom of the ball so they shoot down. Anything we can't see around, like corners or more of those rock bridge structures, we shoot a probe past. They can be steered to some extent and will send back some pretty good video."

By the time Bud left he had heard about the three-day air scrubbing system—a modern-day version of what Tom had developed for the original Fat Man suits—the power source, food and water storage, and the fact they would be wearing the deep sea diving suits as a precautionary measure.

When the flyer inquired about bathroom facilities, Tom smiled innocently and reminded Bud about the time they had flown a re-fitted *Pigeon Special* around the world using just the electrical power from one of Tom's prototype nuclear power pods. That flight had been non-stop and required they wear what is politely described as "an adult undergarment" for several days.

"Oh, goodie. Three days of that, again," Bud had muttered as he departed. Just before the door closed Tom could hear him say, "Wonderful. Seventy-two hours of sitting in our own—" and the door clicked shut.

Now that the final dimensions had been set, the task of drilling and outfitting a new gas lock at the former location of Atlas Samson's illegal well began. It was decided to forego mounting a small hydrodome around the pressure building. Tom and his father believed the added pressure from the weight of the water at that depth would be sufficient to keep leakage to a minimum.

And, rather than lose another earth blaster, Tom had a small mechanical hole digging machine built. A rotating disc at the front was outfitted with extra sharp tomasite and Durastress teeth. The disc could be expanded and contracted to bore anything from a four-foot hole to the six-foot six-inch hole they would need for this project.

The main body was nearly three feet wide and featured caterpillar treads set at 120° angles from each other. These would force the machine forward and would eventually be used to back the entire thing out of the hole.

The mini tunnel took five days to complete. As the machine eased forward at about thirty degrees of downward angle it also pulled a rigid sleeve behind. This extended to within about a half inch of the sides of the hole and made the removal of debris using a special vacuum easy.

The final use of the sleeve was to form the inner wall of the hole with a special sealing foam injected around it.

When Tom and Bud arrived with the SpiderBall the inventor swam out to inspect the new gas lock.

"Perfect!" he declared after seeing the results and measuring the inner dimensions. "We can slip right in, close up out here and pop out into the cavern in no time."

"Do we still get that suction cup thing to hold onto old Spidee here?"

"No. We'll just use its Attractatron legs," Tom answered.

Overnight a team of underwater specialists moved the SpiderBall from the cargo hold of a large seacopter, took it inside the pressure building and prepped it for its voyage.

Tom, Bud, Hank, Arv, Linda and the team of engineers and technicians who would monitor everything entered the building at eight in the morning.

By eight-fifteen the boys were in their suits and had awkwardly climbed inside the SpiderBall. Tom gave Hank a few last-minute instructions and the hatch was closed, its seal hissing tight.

Inside, all final checks were made, and Tom reached past But and showed a thumb's up at the window of the hatch. Seconds later the sphere rose on invisible legs and tilted back so it would be able to use at least a few of its emitters to get them into the open end of the lock. A thin yet strong cable had been attached during the night. It would transmit data to and from the sphere as well as act as their communications link. Tom had decided against using the cable as their power source. Enough room had been made for a trio of Solar Batteries, more than enough for their needs.

Once the outer door of the lock closed, Tom asked Bud, "Are you ready for this?" In the fairly dim light of the sphere's control panel he could see his friend smile.

"Ask me once we get to the bottom," came the reply.

"Pressurizing," Hanks voice called out over the small speaker. A moment passed before he added, "At pressure. Good luck, guys!"

Tom requested, "Open the door, please," and they heard a slight rumbling noise as the outer hatch opened. The SpiderBall began to slip downward. His hands flew across the controls and he took the joystick in his right hand, and the ball came to a halt as the popped out into mid air. Around them, as Bud scanned with their side cameras, they could see the nearby wall of the upper cavern.

The inventor set the ball in motion and headed for the center of the cavern. When they reached that point he tapped a button and moved the joystick forward. "That's the descend button," he told his companion. "The one next to it is the ascend button everything else makes us hover."

"What happened to the two joystick approach?"

"Too cumbersome," Tom answered. "We won't be maneuvering very quickly so I made it as easy a possible."

They took turns piloting the sphere as it "climbed" down the upper cavern, and Bud was soon piloting with the expertise of someone born to use a joystick.

"We're passing the breakthrough point at the bottom of the cavern," Tom reported to the people above. "We'll be in the wet stuff in three minutes."

"Great, skipper," came Hank's voice. "Keep us posted."

"Roger. About every fifteen minutes or so," Tom promised.

The sphere was heavy enough to partially sink on its own but had slightly better than neutral buoyancy in the liquid helium. Tom moved the joystick forward again and they headed down. He angled their travel to the left where he hoped to follow the wall down on the eastern side and then come back up on the western side to get a true measure of the cavern—and helium reserves—size.

When they arrived Tom and Bud saw on the screen that the sides were very much like those of the upper chamber. They looked to be natural as if at some time in Earth's distant past trapped gasses had formed them.

It required considerably less time to push their way down than any of the probes had taken. They reached the bottom in under four hours. It was decided that a rest break was in order, and Tom filled the time by running some projections on his computer.

"If the other side wall is about as far from dead center as the one we climbed down," he told Bud, "then the reserves down here are nearly twice what I estimated to dad a month ago. As in, greater than three hundred years worth of helium at a world-wide consumption rate growing five percent per year."

"Jetz! That's great!" Bud said.

Tom took a deep breath before stretching a little and taking hold of the joystick again.

"Down we go, flyboy!"

The sphere started down into the hole. It took just two minutes to maneuver past the first rock bridge. Pausing under it Tom swiveled their cameras up to get a good look. As shown on the probe camera the underside was far too smooth looking. He had no explanation for it and wondered if it had been like that for as long as the bridge had been in existence.

As the ball moved downward again he decided to hug one of the walls. It would give them the best path to skirt the second rock bridge.

That, like the first, looked perfectly normal on the top and along the side they passed, but at they neared the bottom it smoothed out as well.

Below them, about three hundred feet farther down, the shaft took a turn to their right. "That must be a fairly sharp angle," he told Bud. "I can't see more than a few dozen yards past the turn. Time, I think, to send out one of our little probes." He paused their downward motion.

With just six of the probes able to fit in the tight spaces of the sphere he wanted to make good use of them, but blind corners were what they had been brought along to explore. It required a minute to get the first probe ready but they soon heard the *shhhwoooshhhh* of the escaping nitrogen gas that pushed the probe out and down. The bottom camera of the sphere caught the fins sliding into position and the twin propellers start their slow rotations.

He switched to the camera in the probe's nose. Together they watched as the probe moved slowly but steadily down. It was much slower than the SpiderBall but progress was made, and twenty minutes later the probe was even with the beginning of the turn. A slight flick of the control sent it on a new path. But within a minute they could see that the hole now angled back to going straight down starting eighty feet ahead.

As Tom aimed it on the new course a bright light on their monitor strobed twice, a red light flashed on the panel and the camera from the probe went dead.

The boys sat, slightly stunned.

"That flash looked eerily familiar, Tom," Bud stated.

"Yeah. I know." They sat in silence another minute before Tom reported what had occurred to the people above.

"You sure you want to keep going, skipper?"

"Yes, Hank. There are still things to see. We'll go down to the point where the probe, uhh, conked out and then stop and launch another one."

The ball began to move again and Tom found that the close positon of the walls outside was making the steering almost too responsive. He entered a string of commands and was pleased to see that the reaction time was now more in keeping with what they had experienced above.

When they reached the next launch point Bud had the new probe ready to go. It exited and the picture from its little camera showed another section of the shaft that angled straight down, but in the distance—Tom estimated it to be about four hundred feet ahead—the shaft took another sharp turn.

The probe barely got down twenty feet when a light exploded right in front of the lens. Tom waited for the monitor to recover while he checked the probe's data. In was still sending back operational data but the camera had been burned out.

With a sigh, he cut power to the probe and severed the thin cable.

"Now what?"

"Well, Bud, I have a little experiment I have wanted to try. You might recall I mentioned wanting to rebroadcast those sounds we first detected back down into the caverns. Well, I think now is the time to see what that get us."

"I didn't know we brought along a loudspeaker. So, how are we going to sent that out?"

Tom motioned all around them. "This sphere. I had sonar transducers placed between the two hulls touching the outer one and shielded a little from the inner. We'll still hear it, but we will also be able to hear anything that comes back. It'll take me just a minute to get ready."

He busied himself at the keyboard, at one point plugging his tablet computer into a cable that he pulled from a small recess on the control panel.

"I suppose I ought to warn the folks topside," he said with a grin. "Tom to Hank."

"It's Dora, Tom. Hank's taking a breather. It has been eight solid hours after all."

"As they say, time and Bud Barclay fly by. I just want to warn you, and have you pass it along, please, that I am about to broadcast some of those sounds you first captured back at the beginning. I plan to start in three minutes. Tell everyone in the dome to get their plugs in."

"Will do. Hold a minute." She was gone almost two before coming back with, "You're clear to go any time. Have fun!"

After maneuvering the SpiderBall over to the second downward shaft, Tom typed a new command on the keyboard and tapped twice on his tablet's screen. The thrumming noises started. He was about to say something to Bud when several lights outside the small porthole flashed and the sphere vibrated violently.

Another series of flashes lit the interior of the sphere and a small siren went off. Bud glanced out the porthole in time to see another flash nearby.

"Bud! We've lost the data cable. We're—"

It was all Tom got out. With another terrible shake all the power in the sphere went out and they were slammed to the left, to the right and then up into the overhead.

The last thing Tom saw was his friend slumping down and the feeling that they were tumbling slowly out of control.

When Bud came to, he could see that Tom had been busy. The SpiderBall had been turned so it was tilted, but they had lights and he could feel the air purification system was still working.

"Nice nap?" Tom asked almost pleasantly.

"How long was I out? And, did you get conked as well?"

"You were out about an hour. I think I must have been out only ten or so minutes. As soon as I had my eyes focused I got a few of the systems back on line. We were dropping for another thirty minutes until we hit something. Hard. We ended upside down. This past twenty minutes I've been slowly getting us upright. It isn't perfect, and I'm afraid that I can't coax any more out of her. We may be stuck up against something that's not letting us turn any farther."

"Any more signs of our attackers?"

"Just a few flashes I think are coming from below us."

While Bud broke out two water packets Tom kept working at the controls. To Bud's eyes it appeared the inventor was attempting to reroute some functions from the main board to an auxiliary panel on his left side.

"Well," Tom said with a deep breath and sigh, "Here goes!" He reached out and tapped a command sequence on the keyboard and then took the joystick in his right hand giving it a little pull toward them.

"Uhhh. Why aren't we moving, skipper?" Bud asked in a worried voice.

Tom was concentrating on the controls so much that the flyer decided to not bother him by asking again. He sat and watched his friend. Finally, Tom looked over and shook his head slowly.

"We might be in trouble here, Bud," he admitted. "There is an outer hull tear along the right side we took while we were scraping down the tunnel. It severed some of the heating circuit connections so most of your side of the body is getting frozen. It also took out two of the Attractatrons. No heat means we're stuck. I can't get the remaining two attractatrons to swivel on that side."

"Oh. Well," he said hopefully, "can't you use the ones we still have to push us away from this wall?"

"If I do use them in their current positions it'll push us farther down the hole and closer to those energy flashes. I really don't know what to do. I'm sorry!"

CHAPTER 13 /
"THOSE CAN'T BE…"

NOW, BUD shook his head. "I won't believe that you don't have some idea what we can do," he said. "You always have a back-up plan. Heck. I'll come up with a back up plan!"

Tom didn't want to discourage his best friend, so he waited while Bud pondered what to suggest. Twice he appeared to have something but quickly decided to not mention it.

Finally he did have something. "Call me crazy, but if the Attractatrons can't be aimed from inside, why don't we go outside and aim them ourselves?"

It the situation weren't so dire Tom might have laughed. But, he stopped and thought about what Bud had just asked. "Are you suggesting that we open the hatch, climb outside and reach around and swivel the emitters by hand?"

Shrugging, Bud replied, "Either that or find some way for us to push the entire ball around so the good side of emitters is one hundred eighty degrees around and then use the good ones to push us up and out of here. Or, is that a really stupid idea?"

Tom checked their power situation before answering. "On the surface of it, your idea sounds like a foolish thing to try, but there might be some way for us to do exactly that. I need to run some numbers to see how long we can survive in these suits surrounded by the nearly frozen helium. Give me a couple." He picked up his tablet computer and called up a scientific calculator program. For the next eleven minutes he did calculation after calculation before finally setting the tablet down and turning back to Bud.

"How cold have you ever been, Bud?"

"Uhh, pretty cold. Almost hypothermic once. I fell through some ice at Lake Tahoe in Eastern California on a Christmas vacation when I was about eleven. My core temperature got down under ninety-four. But, I didn't pass out, and—" he wiggled his fingers at Tom, "—I didn't lose anything to frostbite. Do I want to ask why?"

"You do, and it is because I figure that I can override the safeties on the hatch and get that open. It'll be slow and the slush outside will start to seep in almost immediately when our inside heat warms things up a little. Then, it is going to take both our strengths to push the hatch far enough away so we can get out. Then, and assuming that we can move into the slush we will have to turn around, grab onto the open hatch and start to pull and push it counter clockwise. One hundred and thirty degrees ought to be enough. Then we have to drag ourselves back inside, nearly shut the hatch and get things heating back up so the helium goes gassy and escapes. Then we close up, repressurize, aim the Attractatrons and get out of this hole."

"I see. Just those things. How much time will we have?" Bud asked, biting his lower lip.

Tom reached up and scratched the top of his head. "Under four minutes," he finally stated.

Giving an exaggerated gulp, the flyer's next question was, "What if it takes five?"

The inventor placed a hand on his companion's knee. "These suits are only here in case of a hull leak. I never planned extravehicular activity. If they had a larger power pack and if I had made the material thicker we might get six or even eight minutes, but I'm afraid that we get four. I really wish that our tumble hadn't severed the communication link. I'd love to have dad in on the planning."

"It's just you and me, Tom. You tell me what I need to do and the let's practice everything a few times before we get too far into this."

They spent nearly an hour walking through each step. At first it was verbal descriptions coming from Tom, then it was Tom saying what he was doing and Bud describing his own movements.

They only managed to get things down to about four minutes and sixteen seconds.

Tom called for a break. He needed to rethink a few of their moves.

"You know, Bud. I believe that if we get the working side as hot as possible, and then only open the hatch a little, the air bubble that will begin to leak out plus a tiny push from the lowest emitter on your side might help carry us around part of the way. Even if we only get perhaps fifteen degrees of rotation, that will cut the rest of what you and I have to do enough to get back in before the four minute mark."

"Let's do it!"

They sealed their helmets and started their suit heaters. For a few moments they were going to be very warm. Tom typed several commands into his control keyboard and they heard the hissing of the hatch seal as it deflated. Almost immediately a thin stream of slushy helium began to enter the cabin. With Bud pushing against the hatch and Tom measuring the progress, the small stream was soon a slushy helium waterfall. But something *was* happening. The

SpiderBall was turning in place. It went past ten degrees before the slush inside had reached their knees.

Both young men pulled their feet up and out, crouching on their seats. It would give them several precious extra seconds.

The ball rotated past fifteen degrees and only slowed down after twenty. When it stopped at about twenty-five degrees their feet were back in the liquid helium and both were getting chattering teeth.

"Time to shove!" Tom announced. Bud braced his shoulder against the hatch and Tom pushed at his backside. It moved outward as if pushing against a raging torrent, but it did open. "We're eighteen seconds ahead. Now we get out and push."

With great effort Bud first and then Tom got outside. In the light from the sphere they saw the sphere was very close to one of the walls. Bud's heat trail made it easier for Tom so he took the first grip on the ball, braced his feet on the rocks and pulled while Bud took a ten-second breather. He quickly gripped the opposite side of the open hatch and pushed. The ball was moving. And, it was moving faster than they could have hoped for.

The readout on Tom's heads-up display in his helmet was just reaching the two-minute mark.

"That's it," Tom said panting. "Back in."

Bud grabbed Tom's arm and tugged him toward the hatch. "You... then me..." he stated also heavily panting.

There was no time to waste arguing so Tom—his arms and legs aching from the cold that was now overpowering the suit's heater—gave a superhuman pull and got his head inside the hatch. Bud pushed at his rear end and legs. As soon as the inventor's knees were inside Bud pulled himself right behind.

It was now three minutes and fifty-three seconds.

It had taken longer to get back in than they planned for.

Moving the hatch back almost into place took nearly all their reserved strength, but Tom managed to get a hand out to press the button turning back on the environmental systems of the vehicle.

Neither of them could move. Tom's vision was graying out and Bud was shuddering so violently that he was setting up ripples in the helium.

Both of them were fading quickly, faces and all other visible flesh now turning blue.

Tom took a deep breath and screamed out, forcing himself to remain conscious. He fought to turn his head to see how Bud was. He panicked when his vision went white and hazy and was about to give up when his nearly frozen brain sent him an image of the area just above the liquid helium in the lower cavern. The same white fog covered that area.

He willed his eyes to open as wide as possible and was rewarded by seeing that the level of liquid in the ball had dropped by more than half and the fog cleared. It was accelerating as it turned into a near gas and leaked out of the ball.

Three minutes later he was able to reach over and move the hatch closing mechanism. The seal hissed and Tom realized that there was some sort of atmosphere now inside the entire ball. His suit, no longer fighting the losing battle against the icy helium started to warm him.

Bud's suit was doing the same thing for him and he was slowly moving his arms and legs and his head as he began to thaw.

A minute later the cabin had been flushed of the last of the helium and they could open their helmets.

The air was icy cold but they were alive!

Through chattering teeth, Bud remarked, "Not so bad. A bit too refreshing, but we did it. Can we go home?"

Tom flexed his fingers until they seemed to be working the way he needed them to before checking the control board.

"If that had been water we'd be in a bad fix. But, the helium didn't cause anything to arc or burn out. Give me a second here and I'll see if we did the trick."

Bud gave out a cheer when the sphere rumbled and started to move. It was in the right direction. Up.

It was still incredibly slow going but the SpiderBall began to climb back out of the tunnel. Within three hours it passed the lower rocky bridge and an hour after that the upper one.

They both saw the severed communication cable end pass by but neither wanted to suggest going out to retrieve it.

Hour after hour passed and their progress continued at the same pace. With two fewer Attractatrons on the one side Tom had to do a near perfect balancing act. He was bathed in sweat long before they emerged from the lower tunnel.

Bud took over for an hour every two hours so that Tom could rest. He carefully mimicked everything the inventor had been doing. It worked.

After being in the caverns for nearly twenty-four hours they were only just approaching the upper third of the lower chamber.

Tom called a halt.

"We've got to take a break, flyboy. Food, sleep, bathroom stuff, everything. I'm setting the controls to keep us in one spot and neither you nor I will be moving us a foot further for at least eight hours."

They barely finished eating when they fell asleep.

Tom was the first one to open his eyes. The clock told him he was just a few minutes shy of the intended rest period so he had a drink and checked the instruments. They were still in the position where he had stopped.

"Are we there yet, daddy?" Bud asked as he stretched. He looked at Tom's face, that registered a relaxed look, so he figured they were just fine.

"We have about five more hours of climbing in liquid and then I think about two in the upper chamber. Hopefully somebody is watching to see if and when we reappear. I'm not entirely certain how we might knock to see if anybody is at home!"

Bud was silent so Tom looked over at him. The flyer was deep in thought about something.

"Penny for them?" Tom offered.

"Huh? Penny who?"

"No, Bud. A penny for those deep thoughts of yours. We are going to make it, you know."

Nodding and with a shrug, Bud replied, "Yeah, I know and I even can get over the whole bit about how Sandy and Bash and everybody is probably beyond panic about us and maybe even giving up. We'll show up, they'll be ecstatic and life moves on." He sounded completely unconvinced of his own words.

"So, what is it?"

"The lights. The flashes. I know they weren't zipping through that cold ooze, but is there anything, ummm, they remind you of?"

Tom had been wondering about the lights. And he, too, had come to a startling conclusion about what they seemed to represent.

"I mean," Bud continued, "those can't be alive, right?"

"I'm not sure, Bud," Tom answered truthfully.

"Okay. But we've both seen that sort of electrical thing zipping down from space. Or am I crazy?"

Tom was quiet for a minute. "No. You're not crazy. Not any more than I am, but other than telling dad about them I would like to keep this very quiet. I don't think the world is ready to hear what we think we've seen down there. Not until I get this sphere fixed, upgraded with even more heat capabilities, and we go back down for a close look. Are you with me?"

Now Bud, Tom's best friend, brother-in-law and companion on many, many adventures clapped his hand on the inventor's shoulder, gave it a squeeze and grinned, telling him, "You bet!"

Nursing the remaining Attractatrons by rotating so the damaged pair were on the side nearest the cavern wall, Tom set them back in a climb. It was slow going and twice he had to use the opposite side emitters to push them against the wall to hold position while he reset a tripped circuit breaker.

After the second occurrence Bud asked, "What's causing that to blow?"

Tom grinned sheepishly. "I keep hoping to coax a little bit more out of what we still have operating and put just a tad too much power into the working emitters on that side. It's just that I'm really worried what Bash and Sandy and my folks—heck, *everybody* up there—might be going through. I have to be a bit more gentle. What's that old saying? Softy softly catchy monkey?"

Bud laughed. "Right. Also known as slow and steady wins the race!"

"Uh-huh. Well, unless I cause something bad to happen we'll be at the entrance to the gas lock in two hours plus about ten minutes."

They continued the slow climb with Tom avoiding another instance of the circuit breaker issue.

"Okay, Bud. We're within about two hundred feet. Time to put on your thinking cap. How do we go about announcing ourselves?"

The flyer had been doing practically nothing *but* thinking along those lines for over an hour.

"It's easy," he said. "You maneuver us right to the side of the hatch, we seal up these suits—even with the really nasty smells inside—and I open our hatch, climb out and bang the hatch with something solid. Like my head."

"It's going to take a lot more solid thing that your noggin to make enough noise to get up to the other end. See what you can find under us."

Maneuvering space was very tight. It took everything Bud had to get turned around and crouched in the space where his legs had been. He pulled his seat up exposing some of the machinery below. He felt a tap on his shoulder and turned to see a small flashlight being held out to him.

"Thanks."

The light illuminated several potential candidates that he quickly disregarded as they appeared to be vital to the working of the Attractatrons. After ten minutes, his legs falling asleep, he cried out, "Yes!" Putting the end of the light in his mouth he reached down with both hands and undid a small cover. It came away freely and he put one hand inside, grabbed a handle and yanked.

"I'm getting a warming light up here," Tom told him. "Did you just grab what I think you did?"

Bud got his upper body back out of the hole and began to work his numb legs to get back into a seated position.

"Yep! One of the air scrubber canisters. It's an exhausted one so I figure the machinery won't mind it not being there."

"I don't know how to tell you this, Bud, but I designed the system to require that all five of the canisters are in place. We now have about fifteen minutes of breathable air in the sphere plus what we have in the suits. Maybe an hour. Let's hope they're listening for us."

"Oh. Uhh, how soon will we be in position?"

Tom checked his instruments and the monitor on which he now had the upper camera view.

"Five minutes. There is one flaw in all this. I hate to mention it but our pumps are out, so once we get ready to open the hatch I have to purge the atmosphere in here. If the signal isn't heard then you are going to have a really bad time trying to get that canister back in. With your helmet sealed you won't be able to get as far in the hole."

Bud held up one finger. "Ahhh, but I can come back inside fully upside down and reach back down there."

"Well, it's nearly time to give this a try. Are you ready to seal up?"

The flyer nodded.

They both reached back and brought their clear helmets over their heads hearing the seals click and their suits' breathing systems come on.

"I'm busy with keeping us from tumbling, Bud. Can you do the cabin pressure and atmosphere stuff?"

"Roger." Bud moved one hand over to the auxiliary panel and pushed several buttons. Slowly the gauge indicated that the breathable atmosphere was bleeding out of the cabin and being replaced by helium. The pressure inside rose, but the two inside noticed nothing other than the fog forming inside. "I'm unlocking the hatch. Tell me when we are close enough so I can open and give the door a little rap."

Tom called out their position as he carefully moved the sphere closer and closer.

"Fifteen feet... twelve... nine... five... three... two... one. Okay, Bud. Do your magic!"

Bud swung the handle around and pushed on the hatch. He had expected it to be as difficult as it had been far below and so he pushed with all his might.

Tom barely had time to reach out to grab the back of Bud's suit before he would have tumbled out. With only gaseous helium between them and the floor below, it would have been a fatal fall.

"Thanks, skipper!" Bud gulped in a breath. "I'm okay. Let me lean a little out here and—"

Inside the sphere Tom could hear the five solid blows Bud gave the outer hatch before the flyer let out a curse.

Bud climbed back in and sat there staring at the thing in his hand. It was the handle of the air scrubber canister. The rest was now missing. It had broken off from his using it to try to signal.

"Oh-oh. I hope they hear us, Tom, because I just ruined our chances of getting that canister back in place!"

The inventor looked over at his friend. All he could do was nod.

A minute passed, and then another and then two more. They sat in the sphere sealed in their suits in silence. This wasn't the first time they had faced death. All the other times there had been some level of hope. But, now...?

"Hey!" Tom cried. "Look!" He was pointing at the gas lock hatch outside their own doorway. A red light was blinking. It was the signal that the hatch was cycling and about to open.

Ten seconds later the right edge popped out and the entire six-foot-wide hatch swung to the side.

Tom lost no time. "Get our hatch shut," he commanded as he began to move the SpiderBall around. There was no time to twist the sphere around or to turn it so they would be entering on their backs. There was precious little Tom could do other than to shove them inside.

The outer hatch clanged shut and they both heard the hiss of air as it was pumped in replacing the helium. Soon, the inner hatch opened and Tom used the remaining Attractatrons to reach up and grab onto the inside of the pressure building.

The SpiderBall pulled itself up and out of the tube and settled to the ground.

When Bud popped their hatch it was to the rousing cheers of about twenty people who had all crowded into the building.

They were carefully helped out of the sphere. It was only as he tried to stand that Tom realized his legs had fallen asleep. He had to be helped. Bud's legs collapsed as well but more from relief than stiffness.

Five minutes later they were assisted over to a waiting seacopter that took them to Helium City where they endured a brief check-up by the medic.

"You two had us in a right old panic," Hank told them as he stood to one side, letting the medical corpsman finish his assessment. "As soon as the data cable snapped and we lost contact we did everything we could to see if we could get you back."

"Did you give up on us?" Bud asked. "Oh, and how did Sandy and Bash and Tom's folks take the news?"

Hank smiled. "We never got the chance to worry them with such a small detail!"

CHAPTER 14 /
THE BETTER PART OF VALOR

BY THE TIME Tom and Bud got back to Shopton the word had been circulated that they had "run into something unanticipated," but "were just fine." Of course, Damon Swift had been privately advised of the loss of contact, and it had been his decision to not mention it to anyone else.

Doc Simpson insisted on giving them both a complete physical examination before sending them home.

Tom was declared to be okay but Bud had a slight concussion and also a broken little finger. It was on the hand he had used to beat the air scrubber canister against the hatch.

"It's a wonder you shattered that canister case and not your entire hand," Tom told him. "They are supposed to withstand being dropped from thirty feet. I'll assume that it isn't a manufacturing fault and that you were under the influence of adrenaline at the time."

"Something like that. I guess it was that near fall out the hatch that got my blood flowing. I kinda don't remember much that happened after that until we were back inside the tube."

"And, that is why you are going to have two days of bed rest, *mister* Barclay!" Doc cautioned him in as stern voice. "It wouldn't hurt you to take one or two days off as well, Tom," he suggested in a less threatening tone.

"Bash will like it," Tom responded. "Sandy will read Bud the good old riot act about getting himself injured and I'll get the brunt of her anger tomorrow about 'breaking Bud,' or something like that."

The three men shared a smile for a moment before Doc told them to take off. "Remember, Bud. Three days of bed rest. Period!"

"I thought you said two?"

Doc shook his head and winked at Tom. "Nope. Must be that concussion. I said three, and you believe you heard two. Hmmm? So, four days it is." He left the examination room before Bud could protest.

"Don't worry, Bud. I've been there many times. You'll grow to hate it!" Tom told him.

By the time he got home Bashalli was just pulling up into the driveway. She jumped from her car and ran to him, putting her arms around his neck and giving him a big kiss. "I had a terrible dream last night, Tom," she admitted before she let him go. "Something about you being held down and not allowed to come home to me. I am very happy to see that it was just a dream."

Tom smiled at her and felt guilty as he assured her it *had* just been a dream.

When she went upstairs to change Tom place a call to his father.

"Hey, Dad. The big answer is yes, I am fine. Bud got bumped around and we had a heck of a time getting the sphere back up, but we made it."

"You are speaking to a very relieved man, Son. Of course Hank let me know as soon as he heard the banging on the hatch of the lock. I haven't mentioned a thing about this to any of our assorted ladies or to anybody at work. But, after you've had a day or so I want a full rundown of what happened, good and bad. And, I want to warn you that I might be putting a foot down over you trying that again."

Tom sighed. "I guess you're right, but after we talk you may change your mind. The SpiderBall took a real licking but I have some ideas to make her stronger and safer so no more near disasters!" They spoke another minute with Tom agreeing to come see his father the following afternoon.

He hung up before Bashalli came back down. What he didn't realize is that she had been standing at the top of the stairs for the last half of their conversation, her right index finger knuckle between her teeth nervously trying not to sob. She wiped a few tears from her cheek, checked her makeup in the mirror in the hallway and put a smile on her face that she really didn't feel.

Over dinner Tom sensed that something was wrong and he asked her what it was.

"Nothing," she said without conviction.

He decided that he must tell her what had happened, or at least an abbreviated version. He left out the part about nearly being stranded near the bottom of the lower cave and about Bud's last-ditch effort with the canister that could have spelled their doom had it not worked. Instead he concentrated on how, with a few glitches, the SpiderBall had performed and about their encounters with the energy flashes.

"And," she began before a small sob came out, "you and Bud did not almost die down there? Please tell me the absolute truth, Tom. Please?" she practically pleaded.

He took her hands in his and pulled his chair close to her.

"We had a couple of malfunctions that we were able to overcome. It meant we were down there about a day longer than I anticipated, and Bud and I had to use some ingenuity to get things working correctly, but I've told you many, many times. I *will* come home to you, Bash."

She gave him a brave smile and kissed him gently.

The next morning she called into her work to tell them she wasn't coming in until after the lunch hour. She and Tom spent the morning sitting in the living room reading and making plans for a possible vacation. It was something they had tried to do after the launch of Tom's High Space L-Evator, but had not come off as planned.

"I would like to go some place other than into space or under the sea," she requested. "Perhaps Tahiti where we could try all the different rum drinks. Or, Scotland where we could visit old castles and perhaps a distillery where I could bring my father a special bottle of whisky or something."

Tom agreed and told her to go ahead and plan for something in a month or so.

When he sat down opposite his father that afternoon the two men only chatted about some of the unimportant aspects of the trip inside the helium well for the first few minutes. Finally, Tom nodded.

"Okay. Time to tell you all about what went right and what went wrong."

Over the next two hours he detailed as much of the trip as possible leaving nothing out. He made certain to let his father know that even with the damage caused by what he now knew to be a collision with the cave wall, the SpiderBall had still operated.

"If I go back in there I want to rebuild the shell with a hundred or so fingers that can be extended and used to move the ball into a better position."

"That's a big if, Son. Now, I am not suggesting retreating from trying to figure out what's going on down there, but as they say, that often is a better part of valor. It may not be retreat but it may mean going back to probes that do not require you and Bud risk your lives. In fact, let me ask you bluntly, can your SpiderBall be made to operate either autonomously or by remote control?"

Tom nodded, reluctantly. "Yes. Although I would hate to gut it just yet and convert it."

"All right, then can you build a second, possibly smaller version that could be remotely operated?"

The younger man thought a moment before he answered in the affirmative. "Without the requirements for a two-man crew it could be made at least half the current size. I would want to program it to do whatever is necessary to return at least to the surface of the liquid helium on its own if we lose contact."

"Why do you suppose," Mr. Swift asked, "your data and communications cable separated from the sphere?"

"It was burned through, Dad," Tom replied. "I took a good look after Bud and I got out. Scorched almost as if a welder's torch had been used. The thing is, it must just have been electrical power from those flashes. And when one or more of them hit the cable it didn't just cut it, it sent so much power surging into the sphere that every circuit breaker tripped. Three of them were fried and it was a good thing I took extras."

"Then I suggest that you rig up a master breaker for the cable. One that not only stops surges like that from going into everything, but one that can be either remotely or automatically reset." He looked at Tom before adding, "Probably several times. I don't want to jump to conclusions for which we have no actual data, but you cannot deny that those flashes, the ones I've seen from the video Hank uploaded yesterday, look quite a bit like the energy being you call Exman."

It was something Tom had been considering but having it verified by his father came as a shock.

"They aren't moving, or if they are it is very slow," he stated, "and I can't tell you the same thought hasn't occurred to me, Dad. But," he paused a moment "what do we do about them if they are like Exman?"

"I can't tell you that, Son. What I can say is that I strongly believe that if they are like the Exman energy being, don't you think that he... it would have mentioned the possibility of them to you? And, with so many of them down there it would seem to me that Exman would have not just mentioned them, he would have actively requested that you assist in bringing them back to the surface. That supposes they are down there on accident," he added, ominously!

Tom felt a shiver run up his spine.

Carefully, he asked, "And, if they *aren't* down there by accident?"

Mr. Swift shook his head but said nothing.

* * * * *

Over the following three days, including the weekend that fell on days two and three, Tom and his father spent more time discussing the various possibilities and scenarios regarding the energy flashes deep under the ocean floor.

"I believe that we owe the courtesy of letting the President and even the Joint Chiefs of Staff know about this," Damon said on Monday.

Tom agreed and so a call was made to Senator Peter Quintana of New Mexico. Both a personal friend as well as their guardian angel in Washington, Senator Quintana was a man who could be relied on to open connections and make things happen. When Damon explained that he could not give details over the phone, the Senator suggested that he travel to Shopton to meet with them.

"That is, assuming this can wait another day," he said.

His U.S. Air Force jet landed at nine-fifteen the following morning, and he was driven straight to the Administration building.

Tom, Damon, Hank Sterling, and Harlan Ames met with him in the shared office. Damon opened the meeting with a briefing on what had been going on inside and below Helium City followed by Tom giving a detailed explanation of what had been found by the probes and the manned sphere.

"So, you see, Pete," Damon concluded, "this isn't something we feel good about keeping to ourselves. This could escalate at some point, or it could simply go away. The point is that nobody knows and that is why we feel the President needs to be briefed."

Peter Quintana took a handkerchief out of his pocket and wiped his glistening forehead. It wasn't hot in the office but he had broken out in small beads of sweat at least three times during the two-hour meeting.

"I agree, Damon. I also have to tell you, Tom, you have incredible intestinal fortitude, sheer guts, to have gone down there like you did. I know that you are aware how vital that helium supply is to us. To the world! I do not agree with you regarding the Joint Chiefs, though. They are military men first and foremost. Bombs and bullets are what they understand and prefer. This is not a bombs and bullets situation. One bomb down there might take care of any possible threat and then end up blowing the entire top of the mine apart letting all that helium out. No, this needs to be carefully discussed with the big man."

He stopped and thought about something. As he took out an odd-looking device form his briefcase he said, "I happen to have a very private line in. Let me call and see if he is available."

He typed in a series of numbers, placed his eye against what Tom recognized as a retina scanner and then typed in more information. The device, some sort of phone that neither of the Swifts had ever seen before, beeped softly making the Senator smile.

"Got it right on the first try!"

He waited three minutes before speaking into the mouthpiece.

"Good morning, Sir. It's Pete Quintana. Do you have five minutes for a class pink?... Good."

He spent four minutes summarizing what Tom and Damon had spent two hours on and didn't leave anything out.

"So," he said concluding his report, "I hope you will agree this is not something to bring our uniformed men and women in on at the present time, but I also feel strongly that you need to hear and see everything the Swifts have. Is there a time when we can have two hours in your schedule, Sir?... Fine. Let me ask." He put one hand over the mouthpiece. "The President is flying to San Francisco tomorrow morning starting at eight. Can you both be on Air Force One with a portable video and audio presentation?" Tom and Damon nodded. "Mr. President? They will be at the base by seven-thirty. Thank you, Sir." He hung up and put the phone away.

"You will have hours two and three during the trip. He has pressing business to attend to from before takeoff until then. If you don't object I think I'll avail myself of your hospitality tonight and tag along tomorrow. We'll all be back in D.C. by ten P.M., by the way."

He helped pare down and practice what could be accomplished in about one hour fifty minutes leaving the President ten minutes for questions.

The flight went off exactly as planned, except that the President had nearly twenty minutes of questions. At the end he thanked them all for the information and let the Swifts know that he wanted updates every three days until things were completely understood, or immediately if things got worse.

"Do *not* hesitate to call in the Navy," he told them. "Call Admiral Hopkins first, though."

With so much to do at work Damon asked if they might be allowed to take their own transportation home. It was agreed, so as the jet flew over the Western border of Kansas a message was sent to Enterprises requesting the *Sky Queen* meet them at SFO.

With its superior speed Tom's giant jet arrived at San Francisco just fifteen minutes after Air Force One touched down and was waiting for them by the time they were allowed to depart the presidential jet ten minutes after that.

They got back to Shopton two hours later having traveled at supersonic speeds at one hundred thousand feet in altitude. No sonic boom was created by the giant jet and so they could travel at that speed over land.

Peter Quintana said goodbye to them on the tarmac and climbed into the waiting smaller jet, taking off before Tom and Damon got back to the Administration building.

After he checked his emails, Tom walked over and spent another two hours with Arv and Linda discussing building of another model of the SpiderBall. He had come to the conclusion on the trip back that the answer was not in downsizing the current sphere but in making a model larger and one that was more feature packed.

"I'd also like to give this one extra legs," he told them. "Maybe double what we have. It's going to make my programming trickier but I believe the amount of movement control and failsafe I want built in demands it."

They agreed with him on the resizing of the scale model but Linda cautioned against too many legs. "As it is, Tom, things work well because there is no chance that the Attractatron beams will ever cross and touch. Like that old movie, crossing the beams is not good. Unless we add motion stops to keep that from occurring I fear that you might suddenly and accidentally lose control when two or more cancel each other. Could we perhaps try one additional set and put them at one hundred-twenty degree positions?"

Tom moved to a large white board and began drawing. He wanted to assure himself that having the triad of emitters would do what he needed.

"Well," he told them ten minutes later, "it looks like it will work just fine. So, and thank you. Linda, we will go for the three sets, but I want to make it sets of five. Two on the upper curve, two on the lower curve and one straight out from the equator." He looked at them both to see if there might be any question or feedback. When he got only smiles, he concluded, "Then let's go with that!"

The following week was a flurry of activity. Hank cranked out the special hull components. Arv and Linda made good on their promise of the now four-foot diameter sphere just in time for Bud to come see it with Tom. He immediately dubbed it, "Spidee Junior," and was rewarded by having Arv throw a binder at him.

Tom, between checking on their progress and adding a few refinements, spent most of the time adapting his current SpiderBall control software to incorporate not only the extra set of emitters but the fifth one in each set.

On receiving the new sphere he found that it was nearly perfect with only two small changes needed. The following two days people all around Enterprises left their desks and wandered out into the area between the main group of buildings to watch Tom as he "walked his spider." He had asked Arv to give it a coating of a chrome-like polymer so that it shone reflections of everything around it, including shining the sun off the surface.

The sight was eerie. The young inventor with what appeared to be a small electronic piano keyboard hung from a wide strap around his neck just walking along with the shiny ball moving up and down walls and it between buildings, sometimes resting in mid air and sometimes racing along overhead.

By the end of day two he was fully satisfied in the maneuverability and control of the new sphere.

While it contained an array of sophisticated cameras and light sources like the larger ball, one thing it did not have was the sonar transducers, Tom decided early on that he did not want to recreate the sounds from down below. It had been his attempt, he felt, that caused the electrical charges to react so violently and to sever the data cable.

Tom's final test of the autonomous programming was to take the ball up in one of his small, one-man Wasp helicopters and drop the sphere from five hundred feet between a couple of buildings.

It accurately sensed that it was falling, found appropriate locations to grab with its emitters and stopped itself a full nine feet above the ground.

The test was an unqualified success.

After the weekend Tom, Bud and Mr. Swift headed to Fearing Island with the new sphere and from there down to Helium City. As with the manned sphere it was attached to a heavy-duty data cable, placed inside of the large gas lock and launched into the depths of the helium well.

The trip down into the low shaft area went as all probes had before, and it accurately determined the appropriate path to take around the bridges and the first, second and third corners.

It was just after it made that final turn that everyone watching the monitor saw the flashes begin.

First there were two, then five others and finally at least thirty lights coming from different locations below and near to the sphere. A few seemed to repeat their flash but with at least two minutes between. The walls lit up with the reflected light from the sphere's shiny surface.

Everything was being recorded and processed in real time.

Tom looked at one of the readouts.

"Those may be like our Exman energy being, but they aren't moving very much. I detect only about two inches of travel in the most active of them. Most are just hovering there."

"Let's stay right here for ten minutes to see if that's true," suggested his father.

As that time was passing Tom noted that the flashes were coming at faster intervals, but they still showed very little by way of motion. The quickest among them was also the one closest to the heat of the sphere.

"I'm satisfied they aren't able to attack unless they happen to be close enough to the sphere. That's probably the only way they were able to get to Bud and me."

With that said, he sent the command for the sphere to continue down. The next stop he wanted to make was the very bottom!

CHAPTER 15 /

A SHOT IN THE DARK

DOWN AND DOWN the sphere traveled. Even with the additional strength imparted by the extra Attractatrons the going was fairly slow. About fifty feet a minute.

By the time the probe had dropped another two hundred feet the electrical beings—if they actually were that—had disappeared above them. After looking at what had been recorded Tom told everyone, "They seem to be located in a band of about two hundred feet."

Something bothered him about their location, but he couldn't put a finger on it. He jotted down a note on his tablet computer and went back to watching the scenes unfold on the large monitor.

Twice more the shaft veered to one side or back to going straight down, but after the last turn the lights revealed the bottom. It was just fifty feet or so below the probe.

Tom sent a command to stop and two seconds later the picture stabilized.

"That looks to be about that," he stated. He was about to add that he now wished they had outfitted the sphere with at least one collection container when his father spoke.

"Look at the temperature, Tom. It's below what the helium has been at any other point. So close to where it ought to be frozen solid. It has to be the enormous pressure that is changing the state enough to keep it from being a solid block of helium ice!"

"I think you're right, Dad. And see the outer skin temperature readout? For some reason that is lower than it has been. If we had the ability to measure the area right around the hull I bet we'd find that there is no longer a helium gas bubble but a liquid layer. Wow. Well, unless anyone has a curiosity to see how long it might take to freeze the probe into place I'm all for bringing our small spider back. Objections?" He glanced around the room and saw none.

Unnoticed on the last leg of the journey down, Tom now saw that the sphere was traveling upward faster than before through this new, ultra-cold layer. But fifty feet above the turn the temperature rose a few degrees again—back to what they expected —and the ball slowed down slightly. He had no explanation for this phenomena.

As he neared the final turn before the area where the flashes were anticipated Tom decided to see if the sphere's natural buoyancy could let it continue upward.

"I'll be anxious to see if having the Attractatrons off will keep the energy beings from getting very active."

It didn't seem to work. As soon as the sphere neared the zone flash after flash could be seen above it. Tom reenergized the Attractatrons and pushed up and through the area. Rather than disappearing behind the probe as expected, everyone could see occasional flashes somewhere above the sphere in a location the cameras could not show.

The intermittent flashes slowed but continued as the ball neared the first of the rock bridges. As the probe got to within twenty feet of the rounded bottom, the microphone inside picked up the thrumming sounds.

Five seconds later it became very noisy to everyone in the building as well as those in the hydrodome nearby.

It made everyone reach for their ear plugs. It also had the effect of making the flashes go away. In fact, something scraped along the hull and could be seen dropping quickly back down the shaft. It was dark and difficult to detect a shape, but it must have been clinging to the hull.

"Did we almost bring up one of those energy things?" Bud asked in a slightly shaky voice.

"I think we nearly did," Tom told everyone. "I also think we have solved one of the mysteries down there. Why are the rocky bridges there and why is the lower portion smooth and rounded. It looks like some sort of security device designed to keep those energy beings trapped down in the shaft."

Tom turned to his father and shared a very concerned look.

Neither had expected this and neither was happy about the turn of events.

The sphere was recovered and stowed in the seacopter. An inspection of the outer case showed that a series of scorch marks had been made at the top, close to the data cable and out of range of the upper camera.

An investigation was called for. Tom had the sphere transported back to Enterprises to be safely encased in a tomasite box. He gave instructions that nobody was to touch the actual sphere and showed a technician how to make the ball climb into the box on its own.

Back in his large lab Tom used the pantographic arms in his test chamber to open the box. It was impossible to get a scraping of the hull materials so he made due with getting a sample of the darkened area using both fine Durastress sand paper and a sterile wipe. The results were fed into his spectrographic analyzer.

He received exactly what he expected. It was simply slightly burned hull material.

It gave him no clue other than to set him on a course to test to see how much electricity would be required to recreate the marks.

By the following day he had increased the power upwards of sixty thousand volts and at twenty watts. Finally a new mark was made on the small plate of the same material as the hull of the sphere.

It was enough power to kill a herd of elephants. The thing that amazed him was the lack of spread. Each mark measured between three and four millimeters across, had made nearly zero incursion into the material, and showed no telltale streaks of a growing or dissipating energy burn.

He was mildly pleased that only about two microns of the material had burned from what he felt must be classified as attacks. There could be little else to call it. An energy being had attached itself to the top of the sphere, hitched a ride upward all the while attempting to do some damage. That it had been a failure was probably only luck.

At least until the sphere had reached the lower of the rock bridges.

Clearly they represented some sort of protection device. That was made clear when the lower one emitted the incredible thrumming and rumbling noise that had disable or even neutralized the energy. It must have been the energy being that had dropped away and sank.

Now that he considered it, the energy being sank a lot faster than might be expected.

Did that indicate a great mass within such a small space?

Another two days were spent analyzing the video from the probe. This included charting each of the energy flashes on the way down and the way back up to see what, if any, movement there had been. All but one of the flashes during the return trip corresponded within centimeters of their positions earlier. The odd one out? One that had moved at least two feet putting it right over the top of the rising sphere.

When he showed his father the results both were curious about that particular energy being's movement. It seemed completely out of place, but there was no ready answer for it.

"Frankly, I'm stumped over this, Son," Damon admitted. "One thing I would like to see is an overlay of another of the non-moving energies. Can you pull up the same one so I can look at one thing, please?"

Tom didn't bother to inquire what his father might want to see; he selected one from the downward journey and found it again as the sphere had passed the same point coming back up. In seconds he had them on the screen sitting side by side.

"Fine. Now, if you will zoom in on them equally, then place the downward shot over the top of the upward one."

Tom complied. They both let out a small gasp.

The energy was noticeably smaller—by perhaps ten or fifteen percent—on the upward frames.

Tom repeated the process for a half dozen more of the energy spots with identical results.

"Now, do that for the one that burned the area on the hull. I have a nasty hunch that I hope this will disprove."

Tom captured the two frames and overlaid them. The result was shocking.

"Why, that energy has grown by nearly fifty percent!" Tom said as they looked at the screen.

"I think that if we were to check each of the other energy points and had some way to measure their, well, loss, and then equate that with the growth of the one that attacked the sphere the conclusion we might draw would say that energy, somehow, was transferred from the group to the nearest one to the sphere. That shows some level of planning and cooperation between them."

Tom turned to face his father. "But, that would indicate they have some intelligence."

Damon nodded somberly. "Yes. And that means we have to take into account they might not have been attacking so much as trying to get your attention."

Tom disagreed and said so. "What Bud and I went through was no friendly, 'Hi. We're here,' signal. It was a malevolent attack. I'm sorry to not support your idea, Dad, but those are not the sort of energy beings we both might like to imagine. They are not at all like our friend, Exman."

"Fine. I'll accept that for now," Mr. Swift told him, "but I think that another excursion with the unmanned probe is called for. One with greater measurement capabilities."

Tom said that he would get started on re-outfitting the probe as quickly as possible.

While he would have liked to have Hank Sterling involved, the engineer and pattern maker for Enterprises' products was due to leave the following morning for the *Sutter* and his turn managing the forthcoming giant space station for two weeks.

So, Tom had Arv and Linda come to his lab where the probe sat connected to his computer.

Their meeting began with Tom showing them several of the overlays and then the one featuring the "attacking" energy. They both gasped when the meaning hit them.

"They transfer energy between themselves?" Arv asked in disbelief.

"It looks like that," Tom told them. He launched into a discussion of some of the changes he felt needed to be made.

"Of course, we will need a way to accurately measure the charge they put off. I believe I have a way to do that at a distance, but the only way to be certain I have the algorithm correct is to let the sphere get attacked again and measure what hits it."

Linda was scowling slightly as she asked, "Why don't we see if we can capture one of them?"

Tom laughed. "Let me tell you something that we didn't broadcast around a few years ago. When the first energy being came to Earth, and into the robot we named Exman, it took some time to get it to calm down and to stop trying to break free. Of course, when Chow put a piece of chewing gum inside the head of the robot, thinking he was being nice to an alien being, we nearly had a catastrophe." He laughed again at the memory.

"Anyway, what we learned from that is the energy is extremely powerful. Not just in volts or amps or that type of measurement, but in raw physical strength. We were fortunate that after a few hours our Exman energy calmed down and became very cooperative. But, if left alone it might have flung the thousand pound robot body around like a rag doll!"

"And we can't assume the same calming behavior for the energy things down there. Right?" Arv suggested.

"Correct. So, Linda, while it could be a good suggestion in nearly any other case, I believe we have to err of the side or extreme caution for the time being."

They came up with a list of five changes to make, and Arv and Linda departed to start on the parts they would be responsible for providing. Tom remained in the lab and began to disassemble the insides of the probe carefully setting aside everything that would be going back in and placing in storage containers that which would not.

It took a full week before the revised spherical probe was ready to take back to the helium wells.

Arv and Linda begged off from the latest trip.

"It isn't that I don't love going down there," Linda told Tom, "it is just that I have had as much fun waiting around as I can take for a few months. Plus, I promised your father to come up with a miniature, ejectable black box for one of the latest orders of the SE-11 Commuter jet. A customer in Asia has requested that feature. If you will send the video feed back here I promise to watch as things unfold and offer any remote help, but I can be as productive sitting here as down in that underwater shack."

"Sure. In fact I am not even asking Bud to join me. This is going to be a solo trip down and back. With the addition of the extra solar battery you managed to cram inside, I can run the probe down and up even faster. So, perhaps five hours down to the first bridge, then three hours down for measurements, and then I let the relief team bring it back while I look over the results."

When Tom finally retrieved the probe he had two hours of incredibly accurate measurements, some of which he had reviewed while still at the underwater facility.

The rest he waited on until he could look at them with his father.

Mr. Swift spent an entire day with his son looking at everything. There was an accurate census of the energy beings. Thirty-eight of them had been photographed, measured and catalogued. One particularly weak one was spotted hugging the wall.

"Do you think that might be the one that expend all that energy attacking the probe before?" Tom asked.

"I think that is a reasonable assumption but one we will never prove," came the answer.

By the time they completed the review Tom had also called up data and video from their visitations by the Exman energy being. Those images and other data were compared. Neither was particularly shocked to find a great number of similarities and several differences.

"Whatever they are down there," Damon stated, "it is certain that they have been down in that shaft a long time. I would say that means that even if they are like our Exman energy being, they must be very old. Kind of like comparing an old Model T to a brand new Swift 100 coupe—at least once we start building them. Both automobiles have four tires and internal combustion engines and seats and steering wheels, but so very, very different!"

Before heading home they discussed sending the probe down for one final test.

"To begin with, I'd like to set things up so the ball is sitting in a bubble of helium at least two feet thick," Tom said. "I want to see if these energy beings can travel through a gas, or if they are mostly stuck inside the icy liquid."

"Can you do that?"

"Sure, as long as I can pack in a few more batteries, change the outer skin a little and remove most of the other stuff inside."

"Okay. But, how do you plan to get them to attack the sphere. It seems that they remained clear of the probe the second time it went down."

"I plan to put back in the ability to broadcast the original thrumming noises. That really agitated them when Bud and I were there."

After rubbing his jaw in thought a moment, Damon asked, "Are you prepared to lose the probe if they attack in force?"

"I'm hoping that they can't do that, but yes. If it comes to that I can live with sacrificing the probe. I hadn't planned to send it back again after this."

"Tom?" Bashalli started to ask as she sat down on the sofa after they had dinner. "I want to go for a walk. With you. The weather is nice and I feel the need to stretch my legs. Will you come with me?"

He looked up from the engineering journal he had been reading. "Sure. Give me about three minutes to finish this article and I'll put on my walking shoes."

As they left the house he asked, "Are we just doing our neighborhood or did you have somewhere else in mind? We could always walk down that old access road. It's going to get dark in about an hour so it will be extra spooky!"

She shuddered. A couple years earlier she and Sandy had been chased down that dirt lane and taken hostage by a crazy man dressed up like a shabby wolf. Since that time neither of them had ever ventured down the road again.

"No. Not that road. And maybe not the neighborhood. I am getting tired of the same six blocks by four blocks." She looked expectantly at him.

"Enterprises?"

"No. You might be tempted to 'just look into the office for a moment, Bash,' and then I would be stuck there. Someplace new... with a good view, please."

It hit him. He knew a perfect spot. "Why don't we walk the new neighborhood up the hill above Enterprises? It's beautiful, we own the land, and it is protected from lunatics in wolf's clothing." He grinned at her.

"I like the sound of it," she declared.

They climbed into her small 2-seat sports car and drove toward Enterprises. Just across from the main gate was an up hill road marked with signs informing would-be sight seers that the property above was private and no unannounced visitors would be admitted.

Tom turned onto the uphill road just as a small puff of dust rose in the dirt next to the car. Neither of them saw it.

As they neared the top of the curvy road the guard station came into view. But the thing that was even more noticeable was the tall tower sitting toward the front of the hill. It was the combination Enterprises and FAA aircraft control tower.

They were immediately cleared through the gate by a pair of U.S. Marines who gave Tom a snappy salute. He pulled into a parking space near the gate and they got out.

Hand-in-hand Tom and Bashalli walked along the nearest street. It was lined with beautiful, new homes set on very large lots. Only about half the number of homes originally planned were ever completed and no more would be placed inside the walled area.

When Enterprises took the property over—the former owner had hoped to use it as a front for industrial spying on Enterprises— the decision had been made to turn it into housing for visitors and important temporary workers. The old two-story apartment building below had been torn down and now held the Propulsion Engineering building, doubling their square footage.

Forty minutes later they passed the tower. From below it was even more imposing as it loomed over their heads. The sun had begun to go down, and the lights shining upward from hidden locations on the ground gave it a majestic look. The street lights came on within a minute, and the air took on a coolness. Tom hugged Bashalli as he suggested they head back to the car.

While they walked along Tom told her about a plan he thought needed to be put in place down in Helium City.

Bashalli was about to agree with him when a distant *crack* sound was heard echoing off the various houses. Half a second later Tom slapped at his right upper arm.

He pulled his right hand away and Bashalli let out a shriek.

Tom's arm was bloody.

He had been shot!

CHAPTER 16 /
THE RETURN OF "EXMAN"

THREE THINGS immediately happened. First, all the street lights became about three times as bright, shedding near daylight on the ground. This was accompanied by a search light shining down from the tower and across to the direction the shot had originated. It was the newest version of Damon Swift's giant searchlight.

Second, an alarm went off followed by a public address system announcing that an ambulance had been called for. Every area of the neighborhood was watched on closed circuit television. The guards knew exactly where Tom and Bashalli were and what had apparently happened.

The third thing to occur was that the robotic guard devices that rode around a rail mounted to the top of the perimeter wall all converged on the location where the shot seemed to have come from.

Tom and Bashalli sat on the ground where she tried to shield him from any further attack. There was none, and he had pulled his handkerchief out and was pressing it onto the wound within seconds. He tried moving the shoulder around and found that it caused no additional pain. That meant nothing was broken.

"I'm pretty certain it didn't hit any bone, Bash. Just muscle. Doc will get me patched up in no time." He placed his good arm around her and carefully turned her body away from where the shot had come.

In the distance they heard the siren of one of Enterprises' ambulances, but they also saw the headlights of the military jeep that screeched to a halt a few yards away twenty seconds later.

A Marine jumped from the passenger seat even before the vehicle completely stopped. He had a large canvas bag with a red cross on it. Reaching them he knelt down and asked what happened. At the same time he was pulling a large gauze compress out of the bag along with one of Tom's automatic-shaping splints. The bloody handkerchief was taken away, the compress applied and the splint slipped up Tom's arm and pressed into position. It inflated holding the compress with just the correct pressure.

He placed Tom's handkerchief into a plastic bag as the ambulance entered the compound. The siren cut off and it now raced down the two streets to reach them.

The emergency medical technician and his assistant, a young

girl still in her teens, climbed out and hastened to the inventor's side.

"Hi, Debbie," Tom greeted her. Debbie Bates had once proved to be a natural when it came to wound care. She was still in high school when she helped seal up a nasty head wound Tom had received. Her work has been so good that the hospital people in Shopton had refused to believe that anyone other than a skilled doctor or physician's assistant had done the work.

Doc Simpson had been so impressed that he immediately offered her a job on weekends and during her summers off from school.

"Hi, Mr.— sorry. I keep forgetting to call you Tom. And hi, Mrs. Tom," she said to Bashalli. Debbie was a very bright girl, and she assessed the situation immediately. "Why don't you come over here with me?" she suggested to the frightened woman. "Between what this nice Marine did and now with Keith taking over, I think Tom is in great hands."

The inventor gave her a grateful nod and smile. "I'll be fine, Bash. Debbie can tell you all about how there is nothing to worry over."

Three minutes later, and after thanking the Marine, Tom and Bashalli sat in the ambulance heading for the gate. Debbie promised to drive their car back down to Enterprises.

The duty physician's assistant in the Dispensary injected a pain deadener before checking the wound. "Through and through," he declared as he set about cleaning and stitching things together "Muscle only. That's pretty lucky." He gave Tom a second anesthetic shot for the pain and then asked them to remain in the treatment room while he did a check of the blood from the wound.

"Why would he need to do that?" Bashalli asked after he left them.

"My guess is that he just wants to make certain there were no nasty germs on the slug," he told her, but he too wondered about it.

Five minutes later the young medic was back. He gave Tom another shot, this time an antibiotic.

"We're waiting on one final test. I called Doc and he wants us to do a toxicology test. There is most likely nothing, but we can't be too careful with your husband, Mrs. Swift." He reached up and tapped his collar, activating his TeleVoc communication system. He appeared to be listening to something for a few seconds before nodded and smiling. The pin was tapped again and he turned to them.

"All clear, Tom. Oh, and Doc told me on the phone to tell you

154

that you need to keep the arm very still for three days, so you're getting a sling. Debbie will come in and put that on. If you have any other troubles—"

"I know what to do," Tom said with a rueful grin. This wasn't the first time he had been injured or shot in the past five or six years.

Bashalli drove them home attempting to apologize all the way. Tom asked her to stop the car about half way there. He turned to her and kissed her.

"I'm going to be fine. Really. Other that my arm being stiff for a while I'll get over this. Besides, it ought to be me apologizing to you. You could have been hit by that bullet. I don't know what I'd do if—" his voice choked and they sat hugging in silence for nearly five minutes before going home.

Harlan called him an hour later.

"I heard about the incident, Tom. A search team located the gun and two shell casings. It was a thirty-ott-six rifle. No prints so far, but I've got the boys and girls at work trying to earn their keep by dusting the other shells in the magazine and any place else they can find.

"Any idea who did this?" Tom asked. It was supposed to be impossible for anyone to sneak up to the perimeter walls of the neighborhood. Sensors surrounded it.

Harlan sighed. "I'm afraid that we do and we don't. We do have video of someone running back down the hill. We're fairly certain it is a male from the body shape. What we also have is one area of the sensors that appear to have been turned off. That's what let him get up the hill and even on top of the wall."

"I need to do something about that," Tom told him. "Put in a feedback loop to notify you if any individual sensor or group of them gets damaged or deactivated."

They talked for a few more minutes, each trying to take responsibility for the situation. Finally, Tom told him it was a draw. "We both need to amplify the security up there," Tom stated.

His arm ached for five days but the inventor worked through most of it. He now had two projects on his agenda. The rework of the unmanned probe to provide a way to keep the nearly solid helium in a gaseous state for the intended twenty-four inches turned out to be the most difficult thing. It meant that the outer case had to be remade, but not redesigned. The change was the addition of a higher-capacity layer of the metallic fabric that would heat the shell, now to more than two hundred and ninety degrees.

It would be, Linda agreed with him, enough for their purpose.

She had a few internal changes to make including the downsizing of the multiple light array. Now that they knew what penetrated and what did not, she removed two of the lamps and their circuitry, and increased the power of the wavelengths that did penetrate the icy, sludge-like liquid.

Tom also scoured the schematics of the security system up the hill.

Harlan had discovered that a single wire—supposedly buried but now sitting on the surface severed in two—had deactivated the fifteen-degree arc of cameras and sensors. Mr. Swift suggested replacing all wired connections with wireless ones.

"Is there some way to build on your TeleVoc technology, Son?" he asked. "By that I mean not in the way it reads brainwaves, but in how it transmits on an unblockable frequency. Perhaps set up an array of antennas on the tower so that even the wall won't impede signals."

It was to this end Tom spent two of his healing days. Since each sensor was self-powered—taking sunlight in a special solar panel by day and using it at night—and there was easily much more than required by the sensors, some of that could be directed into transmissions. No sensor would be farther from the tower than about one-point-six miles, well within the TeleVoc range, so it was turning out to be a very easy task.

By the end of the second day he was telling his father about it.

"Not only does it make for an uninterruptible signal out, I also will have the new sensors built so they recognize our current TeleVoc pins. For our twice-monthly manual checks we have had to turn off sections so the alarms don't go off. Now, Harlan's people can swarm the hill with no problems."

"And the antenna array?"

"I've got a small crew getting ready to wrap that around the lower part of the tower disc. It's one continuous band with three-inch mini antennas every five feet. They'll use the window-cleaning platform on top to lower down and apply it. The band only needs a single power and data cable and that can be drilled though easily!"

"Good." Mr. Swift now changed the subject.

"Now that you believe you know what those lights are down in the well, what do you intend to do next?"

Tom smiled. "I think it is time to invite an old friend to come visit. I was going to bring the Exman robot body out of storage, give it a shine and beam out an invitation, but I think I need to start from scratch. If anything can tell me I'm right, it is Exman."

The energy being everyone called Exman came from somewhere far outside Earth's solar system. He—nobody could be convinced that the being had a gender but the voice Tom created was male—had been able to tell the inventor approximately where his point of origination was, but not being human, or any other type of living being, his points of reference were very different.

Tom first built a relatively simple robotic structure for Exman. It consisted of a bullet-shaped lower body and a star-shaped chamber to contain the energy being. A learning interface eventually allowed Exman to speak and move the body.

A second body had been constructed later for his return. It was more elegant but had limitations. Tom realized this as he looked the robot over. It would not be sufficient.

He decided to provide his "friend" with a streamlined body capable of walking on two legs and outfitted with a disc-shaped head—more of a flattened ball—with sensors that the energy could move around for 360° vision.

Mr. Swift smiled, but with a hint of concern. "And, you believe that Exman can help, or are your just looking for verification about those... well, whatever they are down there?"

"Perhaps a bit of both," Tom replied. He told his father about his intended changes to the robotic body.

"That would be incredible," Mr. Swift told him. "You did a nice job back when you built Ator and Sermek for the Citadel and a couple other robots, but I have always thought you have it in you to come up with something that truly recreates human movement. I'm assuming that is your intention."

"I'll say it is," Tom said, smiling.

For more than a week Tom labored over an array of servo motors, pulleys, tiny but incredibly strong cables and artificial joints. His work revolved around a magnetanium skeleton built to mimic a human bone frame. Each leg alone held thirty-eighty servos allowing identical movement to a human leg.

The body would be filled with the incredibly powerful computer needed to operate everything and would need to run so fast that Tom had to ensure it was kept extremely cold inside. That meant a liquid helium cooling jacket and that required that he add the same warming layer of metallic fabric under the "skin" to keep anyone touching the new Exman body from getting frostbite.

Linda Ming did an exceptional job with the miniaturization of dozens of interim computer boards that each coordinated several types of movement. She also adapted the gyroscope and repelatron technology from the pogo stick.

The Exman would not just walk upright and with great balance, it would be able to jump—repelatron assisted due to its weight—twice as high as a human might.

With only a few days before he believe they would be ready, Tom broadcast a message out asking that Exman be sent to Earth. He knew that the energy being was not an autonomous creature but a type of powerful energy probe. It would be up to "his" masters whether they would send him.

Two days passed with no answer. In the past it had taken much less than that for a returned message.

Tom decided to up the ante.

His next message wasn't just an invitation, it was a description of the reasons.

> Exman. Tom Swift on Earth calling. My
> previous message unanswered. We need
> communication. Have discovered a large
> group of possible energy beings here
> on Earth. They pose great danger.
> We require your help. Please answer.

This time it took only about one day before a message came through. As before it was not directly from Exman but from its masters.

They asked for verification of Tom's message. He sent it. Another day went by during which he and Linda—along with a team of specialist—complete work on the new Exman robotic body. While waiting he also put the body through a series of agility tests.

Finally a return message came through.

> Tom Swift of Earth. The energy you call Exman
> no longer exists. A new energy will be sent to you.
> New energy given all old data. No new instruction
> to be required. We request full data transmission
> of findings of possible energy beings on Earth.
> Do not interfere with energy beings. Danger.

It gave him the GPS coordinates of where to place the robotic body and named the arrival time. Tom jumped to his feet when he saw that the location was five miles away and the arrival was scheduled for twenty-three minutes later.

He grabbed the remote control, pressed an override button and spoke directly to the robot.

"Follow me."

He ran for the door and was pleased to glance back to see the robot follow at the same speed maintaining the same distance they had before starting out.

Together they left the building and ran to Tom's car. Not entirely certain the robot would understand the command to "Get in" he stopped on the passenger side and opened the door.

"Repeat my motions," he instructed As he slid into the passenger seat.

There was a clang as the robot did exactly what Tom had done, only without the benefit of having moved over so it might use the car and the seat.

"Stand. Repeat my motions into this vehicle once I move out of the way."

This time, and with a groaning of the car's suspension system, the robot body got into the car. Tom closed the door and ran to the other side.

They left Enterprises as quickly as possible with Tom turning to the left out of the gate and heading for a nearby country road. An excellent driver, Tom managed to avoid several potholes in the ill-maintained road and soon they were driving up a nearby hill.

His GPS beeped indicating they were within one hundred yards of their destination. Tom looked at his watch. Still one minute to go as he slammed on the brakes.

He ordered the robot to get out and nearly had another accident when he realized he had forgotten to open the door.

"Override!" He ran to the other side of the car, yanked the door open and repeated, "Exit car and stand up."

The robot did and Tom quickly maneuvered it the rest of the way to a small spot that looked suspiciously like it had been recently cleared.

"Open energy hatch," Tom told the robot.

The top of the head disc revolved a quarter turn and it lifted on a hidden hinge at the rear. Tom stepped back.

Fifteen seconds to spare.

His eyes searched the sky. It was fairly bright so it wasn't until the streak of light was about a half mile away that he spotted it. It was coming in too fast. Anyone but Tom might be forgiven for believing that it was about to slam into the robot or the ground, but the inventor knew better. In a half-second it slowed to almost a crawl and stopped just a foot above the open hatch.

To Tom's surprise it pulled back a few feet and began to circle the area. Slowly it dropped, about one foot per rotation around the robot body, until it was inches from the ground. Then it shot into the air by ten feet, hovered a second and plunged into the open hatch.

"Close energy hatch," Tom directed and the top came down and rotated to lock.

The inventor had been careful to faithfully duplicate the old Exman voice programming. People working with Exman had become accustomed to that voice. He hoped it would continue that comfort.

"Nrrwwww," came a sluggish sound from the speaker. It repeated this three more times. There was no other sound except for the small motor that swiveled the sensors inside the "head" around. Tom had used smoked polycarbonate and could see the array as it moved in a complete circle.

"Hello, Exman. Welcome back to Earth. In case the new energy doesn't remember me, I am Tom Swift."

"Nrrwww," said the speaker. "Nrrw. Nerr. Newww."

Tom was pleased. The new Exman was learning. "Yes. The body is new."

"Neww baaaaad eeee. New baadee. New bowdee. New body. Tommmm Swfffft. New body."

"Yes. I am Tom Swift and *you* have a new body. My body is the same as it was."

Tom spoke the override command to the robot body and they returned to the car. This time the robot was able to complete the task without further instruction. Not only would Exman need to learn to control it, the robot body was designed to learn so that it could repeat motions.

They drove back to Enterprises.

Tom took Exman to the same secure office he had taken the first version. Not precisely a cell, it was reinforced and been able to contain the first body when it went on a little free will spree intending to explore its surroundings.

The new Exman body had a safety built in. If the energy being attempted to run amok, the robot would simply freeze and send out a distress call.

Exman had said nothing until the door closed.

"Tom Swift. I mmmm Eggsmannnn?" It sounded like a question.

"Yes. You are what we call Exman. I am glad to have you back on Earth."

"I mmm Egxmannn. Your arrrrr Tom Swift. I mmm baggk on Errth. I ammm Egxman. I amm Exman. I am Exman. You are Tom Swift and I am on the Earth."

Over the following hour the energy being tried out its vocabulary. With each attempt and a little correction from Tom it was soon speaking in a nearly normal tone, although without any hit of emotion or real inflection. The inflection would come with practice even if the emotion was impossible.

"I am different. You have slight changes."

Tom was very please at the observation. "Yes. That is correct. I am older. How are you?"

The head sensor array swiveled another 360° before the answer came.

"I am Exman and I am worried, Tom Swift. I sense other energy on Earth. I am Exman and you are Tom Swift and there is other energy on the Earth."

Puzzled, Tom asked, "What do you know about them? I only suggested the possibility they might be from your planet when I sent the message to have you come."

Exman didn't answer him directly. "Other energy resides on Earth, Tom Swift, and is not of this planet." The voice now sounded determined. "I detect this energy, but it is very slow. I must investigate this energy!"

CHAPTER 17 /

THE DISCOVERY

TOM WAS surprised that Exman was able to detect the other energy beings at this distance, but he reminded himself that the previous versions of Exman had also surprised him.

What shocked him even more was what the robot now told him.

"I must spend five complete days in familiarizing myself with this new body. Please take me to an area of seclusion were I may remain without freedom for this period."

He may have argued the point except he knew that the energy being would be the best gauge of its own abilities and requirements. Twenty minutes later he led the robot into a secure storage room in the basement of the Administration building. It had once been his father's private lab before the older Swift came to the realization that an explosion in the basement would be much more destructive than one in a room at the top of the building.

During the five days Tom helped finish the rail line work for the new automotive factory. With the spur line and the sweeping, banked curve stretch of track complete, and the last of the old rails removed, the repaving machine had been hard at work taking up the old rail bed stones, crushing them into a smaller and more uniform size, mixing them with a binding agent and then relaying it all down in a compacted and laser-smooth new bed.

Because the new compacted material wasn't as porous, Tom had specified that drainage tubes be laid cross-wise to the bed every twenty feet. Because of this extra work, the decision had been made to not drag the rail extruding machine along as the road bed was revitalized.

On his first day Tom laughed as he spotted the answer to a problem he though they might encounter: how do you move along a rail bed with no rails to keep you on track?'

The solution had been to borrow a harvesting machine from a local rye grass rancher. The wide-set tires perfectly straddled the rail bed, and a laser-measuring device and a version of an auto-pilot kept the machine perfectly straight. Only a special hitch had been added to the tractor, and the extruder had been coupled with its feed tanks held in the hopper of the harvester.

For the three days while Tom worked the track they were able to lay about six miles per day. He headed back to Enterprises with nearly half of the total rail run complete.

Near the end of the fourth day Exman signaled that it was ready to leave the storage room.

"I have reconfigured several of the programs in this robotic body so that I can operate more efficiently," it announced as Tom opened the door. "If you disagree with my work I will return the robot to the original state and will attempt to work within the constraints."

If Exman had been human, Tom could swear that it would have now smiled and winked at him.

"No, no. I want you to operate at peak levels," he replied. "If that means your upgrading my work, most of which was based on your predecessor, then by all means. May I ask the nature of the revisions?"

"Yes." The robot stood there saying nothing further until Tom realized that it took questions literally.

"Please detail for me the changes you have made."

"There are three primary changes and several thousand minor changes made necessary to support the primary changes. Do you want all of these detailed?"

"Just the primary three, please," Tom requested.

"The first change is in my interface to the mobility features of this body. The original programming was not designed to take advantage of the full range of motion or speed capabilities. The body can now operate at three-point-two-five-five times the original speed in forward and backward motion. The second change is in the processing of visual, audio and tactile inputs. These have been enhanced by a factor of two. The third change is in the isolation of the holding chamber for my energy being. I have set in place a non-destructive field to protect my energy. Please refrain from inserting anything into the holding chamber as it will be violently rejected."

Tom felt he had to ask. "How violently would something be rejected, Exman?"

"Reaction time of one-ten thousandth of one second with a result of a twenty gram object being ejected to a distance of eighty-five feet."

Tom gulped.

"We will not open your holding container without notifying you and requesting that you disable the rejection field. Will that be acceptable to you?"

"Affirmative, Tom Swift."

"Exman. The addition of my last name, Swift, is not required when we converse. Tom is sufficient."

"Affirmative, Tom."

With quitting time close at hand Tom tried to decide what to do with Exman that evening. The extraterrestrial visitor helped him make that decision.

"Tom. The data from those who came before me indicate that you and other humans require relaxation and partial shut-down every night of your existence. This is known to me. During this night period I will input and review all data regarding the energies I have detected. Do you have this data?"

"Oh, boy, do I have data for you," Tom answered. He spent a few minutes providing a broad description of the noises, the probes and the attacks. Exman remained silent throughout. Only on the subject of the computer files did the robot say anything.

"What will you wish me to accomplish the remaining hours of the night, Tom?"

The inventor laughed. "How long do you believe you will require?"

"Approximately three hours to download. Processing and analysis will occur concurrent to the download process. Final analysis will be available one half hour after final data input. I inquire again, what should I do following that?"

Tom decided to also provide all the specifications of the various probes and spheres that had been used. After informing Exman about that data he requested that an analysis be made regarding suggestions for any further use of existing probes or additional construction of new probes.

"Please provide a report electronically with what you believe is required."

He took Exman out of the Administration building, across the tarmac and down to his underground office and lab where he connected an interface cable between his computer and the robot.

"Once you finish please allow the robot to go into stand by mode. I will return at nine in the morning tomorrow."

"A question, Tom?"

"Sure. What can I tell you?"

"Is the data correct that my response now should be to tell you to experience a pleasant night?"

Tom laughed. "Well, the saying is 'Have a good night,' but that is primarily correct. You have a good night as well."

Exman decided that a response was not required and began to

download the data.

When Tom got to the office the next day Exman had unplugged the data cable and was standing in one corner.

"Good morning, Tom," it greeted him.

"Good morning, Exman. You don't have to stand around, you know. It is permitted for you to sit. This body is much lighter than the previous ones and I am pretty sure the furniture will take the weight."

"I will store that information. I have analyzed everything in your computer and in the broader based network at this facility. There were several security provisions that I discovered. I endeavored to leave them intact, and therefore I do not know if there is additional data I might utilize."

"Well, our security chief will be happy to know that you didn't breach those. Can you give me a synopsis of what you now understand?"

"Yes."

"Sorry. I'm wording things incorrectly. I should request that you now provide me with a synopsis of what you know after reviewing the available data."

"Should I adjust my responses to assume a request for additional information instead of a simple affirmative?"

"In most cases, but for now go ahead and keep things as they are. I will adjust to you."

"I have a question for you, Tom. Why did you fail to mention the barriers near the upper portion of the downward shaft?"

If Tom didn't know better he could almost hear a tone of reproach in Exman's voice.

"I wanted you to learn about that after you had assimilated most of the other data. Now that you do know about it, what can you tell me?"

Exman spent nearly one hour relating the details of his analysis. About ninety percent of its conclusions were identical or near those of the inventor, but the other percentage surprised him. There were things such as recognition of distinct shape differences and light outputs among each of the energies. Plus, each one moved at a different speed. He had reviewed the very first video from the SpiderBall voyage with Tom and Bud and compared that to all other, newer videos and had sent a 3D chart to the computer showing where each energy had been and its probable path of travel over the weeks between video recordings.

"I will require an additional probe visit to the energies to make special observations. Details of the instrumentation I require can be found in your computer under the titles of 1X33456 and 1X33457. Please advise me if these are not possible using Earth technology."

The inventor sat down and called up the files. The first was for a high-speed camera operating in a light wavelength not visible to humans. It was, however, possible to build.

The second file showed an interim data processing computer that was, Tom had to admit, pure elegance. Sadly, he had to inform Exman that the technology available to build such a system was many years from being available to him.

"That one bulbous component, the one you describe as a data fluidity inverter and pre-processor is something even I can't imagine."

Exman was silent for nearly two seconds, a near eternity to his robotic and energy being minds. "I can find no analogy to that component in any of the data I have recorded. It will mean that I will require an additional fifty hours of processing time once I have received the uplink from the probe. Will you allow me to use the storage room once again for this purpose?"

Tom told his visitor—he found it difficult to not think of Exman as a male and so decided to refer to it as a *him*—it was possible for him to use whatever location best suited him.

"I can leave you there in the dark, or even take you up to my favorite thinking spot at the top of this building. Whatever you wish."

"The top of this building features the disused aircraft controlling facility for this company." It was a statement and not a question. "All data connections were removed. Can one be installed?"

"Sure. If you want to have access it will be easier to drag a cable up there than to try to drill a hole through the safety door in the basement. I'll have that installed as soon as possible. So, about the changes to the sphere..."

They discussed the details and Exman sent page after page of diagrams, parts lists and instructions for the sensors he needed. Tom called a temporary halt at lunch time to speak with Arv, Linda and Hank and to ask them to join him. He called to Chow to request lunches for the four of them.

"Right way, Tom! Cain't wait 'til ya try my newest recipe fer alligator fritters. See ya in an hour!"

"Hey, Chow? Why don't you bring an extra serving? I'll just bet that Bud would love to try something new. Thanks." He hung up deciding to let the lunch be a surprise for everyone.

As soon as they all arrived Exman continued with his assessment of the situation. He was about to conclude when the elevator door opened across the hangar floor and everyone heard the sounds of Chow's rolling food cart.

Exman, who was standing around the corner from the door stated, "The sound combination approaching is not stored in my memory. What is it, Tom?"

"That, Exman, is Chow Winkler, our chef, and he is bringing our food. You have met him before."

"Chow Winkler? That name is in my memory. Chow Winkler is the one who cause my first energy being to almost go insane. Will he attempt this with me?"

Tom assured him that the previous issue was just a mistake in judgement. As Chow rolled through the door the robot voice was agreeing to make judgments based on current and not past interactions.

The cook did a double take on seeing the robot, and even if the form was new, he smiled and said, "Well, hey to ya, ole Ex-feller! Howdy and welcome back ta Enterprises."

"Greeting to you. Please refrain from inserting substances into this robotic being."

The cook reddened. He had hoped the energy being might have forgotten the past incident with some chewing gum.

The food was served at Tom's workbench and everyone, even the inventor who knew what was in the fritters, complimented Chow as he stood watching them.

"Great stuff!" Bud told him. "Chicken?"

"Better'n that, Buddy Boy. But, I got ta admit it does taste a lot *like* chicken. Well, gotta go, hombres. Ya keep yerself warm an' dry, amigo," he said to the robot, giving it a little pat on the shoulder.

After lunch they concluded the report by the energy being and everyone forgot to ask what actually had been the mystery ingredient in the lunch.

Exman requested that he be taken down to Helium City as soon as it might be arranged.

"While I can detect other energies I am unable to determine the extent of them," he told Tom.

Frowning, Tom asked, "What do you mean? We know how many there are already."

"Term of reference incorrect. My meaning is I am not able to determine level of activity, level of individual power, and level of awareness of their surroundings."

Bud, standing to one side, snorted. "They sure seemed aware of us when we were down there. Made a beeline to attack us. Well... it was a beeline as if moving through molasses, but you get the point."

Exman's sensor array has turned to point at the flyer. "Awareness in this instance refers to their self-awareness. If these are energies from my planet, they were placed into minimal awareness activity. Human reference would be induced coma."

"Ahhhh," Bud replied. "I see. So, you need to know how much they may have woken up."

"That is the meaning of my previous statements, Bud. Tom? Should I recalibrate to provide additional, simple terms when addressing Bud Barclay?"

"Hey!" Bud said as everyone else laughed. Tom came to his friend's rescue.

"No, but I want you to be prepared for a variety of interpretations of any statement you make. It depends on the individual and points of reference they might already have."

"Thanks, Tom, I guess," Bud said warily eyeing the robot. "And, thanks for not coming out and saying you think I'm slow, Exman."

Exman must have sensed that no response would be appropriate so he remained quiet.

The following morning Tom, Bud and Exman climbed into his Toad and jetted down and out to Fearing Island. Word had spread that a new version of Exman was coming and several dozen people crowded around the jet after it taxied and stopped at the control building.

The robot was able to recognize and identify by name a dozen of the people. He had interacted with them in the past.

He also paid silent and close attention to the operation of the seacopter they took down to the hydrodome. Once they docked Tom reached into a duffel bag he had carried aboard and pulled out a pair of what looked like strange, wide slippers. Exman was requested to raise each foot in turn and they were slipped over his metal and plastic appendages.

"Why the foot gear," Bud asked.

"I made his feet approximately a human male size ten, but with the extra weight he carries the per square inch weight is near the limit the hydrodome floor material can handle. These spread out the weight a little and also make any hard angles softer."

It was, according to the robot, not necessary to travel out to the larger gas lock building. He asked to be taken to the original lock building and to be left alone for a period of twenty-four hours.

There had been odder requests and so Tom led him to the building, opened the door and watched as the robot knelt down, lowered its posterior to the ground and finally laid out on its back, the head not quite touching the ground.

After he closed and locked the door—not to keep the robot in but to keep overeager people out—Tom paid Peter Crumwald a visit. He filled the city manager in on what had been discovered by Exman and about the one-day data gathering visit taking place.

"He... it...? Oh, phooey, *he* can sense what's down there all that way and into the twisty shaft? Amazing! I guess all we can do is wait, huh?" Tom agreed. "Say, I want to show you something I received yesterday. Came in the good old physical mail delivery. I can't recall the last time I got a paper letter. Anyway," he said, shuffling through a short stack of printouts, "ah, here it is. Take a look." He handed a single sheet to Tom.

" 'Mr. Crumwald,' " Tom read aloud, " 'I owe you a greater apology than I can ever make for my attack on you. It was an act of a coward and I can't imagine how I would feel if I had killed you. You must have heard that my ex-girlfriend put me up to it. Her and that son of a— well, that miserable guy who takes her money for what he calls his church.

'I now understand that she duped me all along. It was part of a plot to ruin Tom Swift. If you see him please apologize for me. I was supposed to wait for him to come investigate your attack and then kill him. I think it is a good thing that I am almost scared of my own shadow. I could not hit you too hard and I do not think I would have actually killed Tom, but she promised me so many great things if I did all that for the Spear guy.

'I am in jail now and will be until the trial (and for maybe ten years after that.) My father used to sing an old TV song, something about if you do a crime you'll do some time. Something like that anyway. I did it so I am here. But, I promise you and Tom that I do not think you are responsible for this. I did it. I won't bother you again.' "

Peter took the letter from Tom's hands and set it back on the desk. "I could almost feel sorry for the poor chump, but then I feel the lump that's still on the back on my head—"

"I'll see if Harlan Ames can get him to go to court and implicate both the girl and Mr. Speers. Maybe he can do a plea deal and get his own sentence reduced. I can't imaging rehiring him, but he probably deserves a second chance."

Right on time the following day Exman indicated he was ready to emerge. The door was unlocked and the robot walked out, stopping in front of Tom.

"My detection was insufficient to determine the level of danger. The situation has escalated beyond a benign state."

"What can we do?" Tom asked.

"I must go down into the mine and see these energies at close range. I must confront them. If necessary, I must neutralize them!"

CHAPTER 18 /
THERE MAY BE TROUBLE AHEAD

EXMAN REQUESTED to be left inside the pressure building inside the dome until Tom returned with the completed probe. The explanation was that he believed continuous monitoring might be advisable.

Tom could not argue and so left him behind with instructions to get in contact if anything was discovered.

"I must spend one day running the final tests of the new rail transport system, but can be reached at a moment's notice. I will return in three days."

"I will not leave the building," Exman promised, "unless ordered to by you or by the commander of this facility. Is that sufficient?"

Tom said it was just fine.

By the following day when he arrived out at the farthest point of track extrusion he was pleased to see that there was just another two mile section to go. With one extra hour of work it would be finished that day.

An Enterprises truck was parked nearby and he asked to borrow it. Moments later he was driving beside the rail bed heading for the end point where he knew the final tie-in work would be accomplished the next day.

What he found surprised and bothered him.

Someone, probably on seeing the other tracks being pulled up, had come in and stolen at least two sixty-foot pairs of the old rails, tearing up the track bed in the process. Standing by the truck he made a phone call back to Harlan Ames, asking to have a security detail placed there overnight.

He had just hung up when an older black man wandered over to him.

"You want to know what happened 'bout those rails, mister?"

"I would be very much interested, sir," Tom replied, nodding. "My company is in the process of getting this line back into operation and we really can't have tracks disappearing."

"Didn't disappear," the man said giving him a grin. "Murphy took 'em!"

"Oh. Who is this Murphy?"

"Mean old son of a gun and 'bout the biggest crook around here.

Thinks he's some all-powerful crime boss the way he struts around and flaunts the local laws." He told the inventor he had been sitting in his house, an old disused box car parked on a side railing sixty feet away, when Murphy and a couple of his thugs pulled up the night before with an old flat-bed car hauler, sledge-hammered the old rivets out of the ties and used the carrier's winch to drag the rails onto the bed.

"He's not too smart, old Murphy, so I bet you can find those rails at the reclaim yard. Uh," the man now looked a little uncomfortable. "Can you do me a favor and not mention where you heard that? Unless Murphy goes to jail he'll just come around and beat me for telling on him."

"I'll not only do that but I will pay you to keep a watch here for me. I'll have my people come give you a special phone to use if you see anything else going on, and we'll pay you for your time."

"I don't want too much. I'd only go back to drinking if I have more money than I need for food," the man told him honestly.

They agreed on two hundred dollars per month plus a bonus any time he had good information that saved Enterprises time or money.

His next stop was to the metals recycling yard. As he suspected the four rails were sitting on the ground near the front gate. The owner came out to greet him.

"I had them dump the rails here so you could come get them," he told the inventor. "I've already called the police on Ricardo Murphy and his gang of thieves."

Tom thanked him, told him to go ahead and recycle the steel and to keep the money for his thoughtfulness in handling the situation.

If those crooks could get the rails up that easy then I probably need to replace that much track anyway, he told himself as he drove back to the terminus.

His new, unofficial night watchman came over when he pulled up. "Get 'em?"

Tom explained the situation before pulling out a couple of twenty-dollar bills and handing them over. "That's your first bonus," he explained.

"Just so you know, they had a dickens of a time with the second set of rivets. At least those timber ties seem to be in good shape."

When Tom looked at the other rails he knew the man had spoken the truth. Perhaps the crooks had actually done them a favor.

He made a few notes and a sketch on his tablet computer regarding how he hoped to tie the old and new rails together. His plan was to have some of his men grind down the end of the rails for a few feet and then extrude the end of his new rails over that like a tight-fitting sleeve. There was little he might do short of either relaying or thermite-welding all the steel tracks into one piece that would keep the new train from experiencing the old-fashioned *clickity-clack* of the wheels running over the small gaps between lengths between this point and Albany.

On his return to the office he sent notes to the team leader detailing his ideas for completing the line.

He spent another full day helping to complete the rebuild of the four-foot sphere. It now featured a new outer look. Gone was the mirror-like surface to be replaced by what appeared to be metallic gauze under a thin clear coating.

"That's the new heat system in case you couldn't guess," Arv said. "Other than that we have everything inside you specified plus a little thing Exman asked for early this morning." He gave Tom a look that said, "Imagine that!"

"Uhh, how? Did he get Peter's folks to make a call?"

"Email. Came through about three-fifteen today. He's asked for a magnetic field analyzer with the probe tip coming out of the bottom. I did it, so I hope you aren't too bothered."

"No, if he wants that then he gets it, I guess."

By the next morning it was time to pack up and head back to the hydrodome. Bud and Arv came along. Linda was still completing her project for Damon Swift.

Exman met Tom at the door of the pressure building. Peter Crumwald had opened it at the robot's request an hour earlier.

The robot had nothing more to report regarding the energies registering from below.

"I have reanalyzed all the data you have provided with no additional results. I continue to detect energies and have found the level of energy fluctuates only slightly even though one energy might dim and another brighten periodically."

"Then I hope we get some more information for you by sending the probe back down. Uhh, and that brings up a question. Do you wish to control its movements or will you accept my control or Bud's control?"

Exman's visual sensor swiveled from Tom to Bud and back. "Is Bud trained to your level of expertise?"

Tom confirmed that he was.

The sensor made its back and forth movement again. "How long will it require to acquaint me with the operation?"

"Hey! Don't you trust me, Ex-ie?" Bud asked.

"I do not trust that which I do not know. Skill level is an unknown quantity in you and in Tom. I only wish to be allowed to take control once the probe reaches the lower depth. My reaction time is superior to either of you and I may be able to keep the probe from harm."

Tom looked at his friend and shrugged. "He has a point. Okay, Exman. Let's sit down and I'll show you what to do."

Ten minutes later the robot had absorbed everything and was exhibiting complete understanding of the controls.

"Let's get our spider probe out to the drop point," Tom told them. It took about an hour to get the probe to the larger gas lock building, dry it thoroughly and run a complete systems check. It all looked good so the ball was moved into the top of the tube. Tom set the controls to use minimum Attractatron power to hold it in the tube.

Sixty-seconds later the inner hatch was closed, the tube pressurized with helium and the outer hatch was starting to open.

As before the probe headed downward, but even faster than before. Tom now knew that he could arrest it's dropping speed rapidly and so let gravity take it nearly three-quarters of the way to the bottom of the first cavern. It also moved more quickly down through the liquid helium.

As the probe neared the bottom of the lower cavern Exman pointed to the screen. "Tom. That cross extension has been damaged. Can you see how narrow it is on the one end?"

Tom had seen it before, but until he had concluded the rocky bridges were some sort of security device for keeping the energies contained, he had assumed them to be natural. As such, they would most probably be uneven. Now, that took on an ominous note. He wondered if the breakthrough between the two caverns might have had something to do with the damage.

"I see. How bad is that?"

Exman was silent longer than Tom felt was necessary. He repeated the question.

"I am attempting to determine, Tom." He paused again for five seconds. "The upper retaining emitter is damaged. It operates at below thirty percent. My observations from your earlier videos shows that the lower emitter is in good condition. The upper one was placed as a precaution only."

The smaller SpiderBall continued climbing down, passing the lower bridge where Exman asked Tom to pause it. Three seconds later he declared it to be functioning within acceptable limits but at only seventy-three percent of original power.

"It will be sufficient," he stated. "May I take control now?"

Tom relinquished the panel and the robot moved into the now empty seat. As the probe headed down Exman experimented briefly with the controls. Finally, he declared, "The functions of the controls is slow but within my ability to compensate for."

Tom looked at Bud who grinned and shrugged, mouthing, "What are you gonna do?"

The first and second corners were navigated and the downward movement continued. The probe arrived where the energy beings were. Flash after flash started, some weaker and some stronger, but as they watched most of the flashes began to be similar if not identical.

"They are cross-sharing energy, Tom," Exman stated.

"Are they energy beings like you?" Tom asked but wasn't certain he wanted to know the answer.

"They are not like me, however they come from my planet."

There was silence for half a minute, then Bud asked the question on everybody's mind, "Why are they here?"

Exman paused the probe about three yards above the uppermost energy flashes.

"At a time which equates to approximately fifteen thousand years in your past my planet had been using energy probes to explore our own solar system as well as five others within your term of reference as thirty-one light years. Yours was not among those as I now can compute your solar system and mine lie sixty-eight-point-three light years apart."

"Jetz!"

"While I do not understand the meaning of your word I recall you use it as an expression of surprise. To continue, the living beings of my planet could not bring themselves to destroy an energy being after it had been put to use, but after one or two voyages to another star system there was degradation in the integrity of the energy being.

"Because they would not be deactivated—effectively destroyed—they had to be accommodated. However, occasionally one energy being would become a danger. At that point it was decided to deactivate the dangerous energies but the attempts failed. They achieved individual awareness and became self-powering."

"That sounds like a recipe for disaster," Arv said.

"It was and became worse when these dangerous energies took on a combined mentality. The analogy I find in your language is a 'hive intelligence.' Many of the living beings on my planet perished because of attacks by the malfunctioning energies. A scientist devised a capture system. You might refer to it as a vacuum bottle. If opened in the near vicinity of one of these energies, it would be drawn in and the top closed, containing the energy within a powerful magnetic field."

Tom cleared his throat, signaling the others he needed to ask the next question. "How did they get here?"

"It was," Exman explained, "decided to find a planet with suitable subterranean features. Deep areas under either liquid water, helium or even chlorine. Your system had only just been discovered so a swarm of new energy probes came here. Of the possible satellites around your larger planets nothing deep enough was discovered. It is regrettable, but on the Earth, even with intelligent life coming into power, several deep and viable caverns were discovered. Many under dry land plus this system of caverns under water."

"So," Tom tried to conclude, "the bad energies were brought here and sunk under all the liquid helium."

"No. The caverns were volcanic in nature and contained only trapped gasses rich in sulfuric compounds, something the beings on my planet needed. They had a surplus of helium and so placed the container with the bad energies in the deepest part of the caverns and filled what is now the lower one with liquid helium. It was sealed—what you broke through—and the upper chamber left alone."

"Ah," Bud now said, "so the bad guys were down under there, the bridges were set up in case they ever tried to move higher, and the upper chamber just had the helium in it."

"No. The upper chamber was filled with normal breathing air. It has only been through the millennia that helium has seeped up from the lower chamber to replace that air."

Tom inquired, "Does that mean your people knew the liquid helium would slow the bad energy beings down?"

"Yes. It was hoped that they would remain undiscovered for many more millennia, if not forever."

Exman went back to moving the probe up, down and through the energy beings. As he did this several attacks were made when the probe touched one or more beings, but these soon diminished. It was evident to Tom that the beings had a limited amount of energy to use in such attacks and must be now conserving that.

For more than an hour Exman moved the probe, stopped it periodically to make observations, and then moved on. He took the SpiderBall to the very bottom of the shaft. There, using the repelatron of one emitter only—something Tom did not remember programming in as a capability—he caused the debris at the bottom to shift.

"There," the robot stated flatly, pointing at the monitor. "That crumpled object mostly buried is the containment vessel for the errant energies. If it were possible to remove and examine it we would locate the point where the energies burned through it. The power for the magnetic flux field should have lasted approximately ten Earth centuries." He paused and rotated his visual sensors around to look at Tom. "It had been hoped that the energies might have perished by that time." His eyes rotated back to the control panel.

Exman suggested that the humans leave him. "I will require another fifteen hours to complete my remote exploration. Unless there is a lack of trust in my abilities then it may be successfully accomplished with no supervision."

While the inventor wasn't certain he fully liked the idea he had to admit that having the group of people just standing around was accomplishing nothing. He agreed and they all left via the air lock ten minutes later.

From the seacopter Tom radioed his father with a report. He included everything Exman had revealed about the origin of the energy beings.

"I was afraid something like that might be the case. They used the Earth like the British used Australia. Ship out the bad ones and wash your hands of the affair. Do we know if they are doing that now?"

"I'm pretty certain they are not. He mentioned that they now routinely deactivate energy beings after they have reached their best by date. That's why our Exman energies have been three different energy beings. The trip out here and back just about exhausts their usability."

Damon, sitting at his desk rubbed his jaw in thought while Tom waited at the other end of the call. Finally he asked, "Did Exman give any indication of resentment among the energy beings when they are due to be shut off?"

After considering the question a moment, Tom replied, "It is very hard to say. Exman has said nothing but probably because I never asked that question. I'll put it to him when we go back inside to bring the probe up. Anything else?"

"Yes. Ask our friend what the people of his planet intend to do now these rogue energy beings have been discovered."

Tom promised he would do that.

When they entered the building late that night Exman was just sitting there. On the monitor Tom only saw the walls of the shaft, but had no hint of where in the shaft the probe might be at that time.

When he asked, Exman rotated his "eyes" and replied, "I completed my work three hours ago and have raised the probe to just below the final turn to the up shaft and lower cavern. I have been in contact with my home planet. I am waiting for their reply."

This surprised Tom. Being as deep as they were he hadn't considered that communication across galactic distances would be possible.

"Can you tell me... wait, I mean please tell me what you reported."

Exman related his communication giving Tom details about his findings of the abandoned energy beings, about how they were more active than they should be and that a solution was requested.

"As of this moment they have only acknowledged receipt of my communication. What do you want me to do?"

"Well, why don't you slip out of that seat and I'll go ahead and bring the probe up. That is, if you are ready."

"Yes." The robot rose and moved to stand to the side.

As the inventor sat down he inquired, "Were the energy beings finished with their attacks when you pulled back out?"

"The energies had become almost indistinct. I believe they have used up too much energy in their attacks and require much time to re-energize. The last video I took was of them drifting above and to the sides of the probe. I waited five hours and could see nothing more of them."

"Good," Tom told him. "Let's get that probe back home."

He began maneuvering the probe up. As it came within a few yards of the lower bridge the thrumming noises began. They were not nearly as loud as before and he was puzzled. With a shrug Tom continued the climb.

At the upper bridge the thrumming started again but so weak that it barely registered on the internal microphone.

Tom paused again, asking, "Why do you think those alarms are going off?" When Exman had no answer he ran through the series of cameras and all their angles. There was nothing to be seen around them.

He set the monitor to show the upper camera and started moving the probe upward. But three seconds later there was a brilliant flash all around the probe. He immediately switched back to the bottom view.

As the probe rose its lower camera caught the sight of nearly three dozen energy beings—small but quite visible—dropping away and hovering above the upper rock bridge. They had hitchhiked on the hull of the probe, just out of camera range, to get past the gate and were now in the upper chamber.

With another sudden bright flash they all headed in different directions.

Tom's heart sank. He had just unleashed them, and he now had no idea how to get them under control!

CHAPTER 19 /
THICKENING THE PLOT

TOM FELT sick. He had known the energy beings imprisoned in the lowest depths of the wells were intelligent. So much so they had learned to hide on the bottom of the probe in order to pass the "gates" keeping them contained.

Now, the upper chamber of the well was filled with the escaped energies and they were zipping around down there banging into the walls, breaking off small pieces of the rock. A constant din of their collisions could be heard and felt by everyone in the hydrodome and the other building.

"The fortunate thing is they haven't discovered anything above the one-third point up the cavern. I dread to think what we are in for if they try to break through the top of the well," Tom said to his father over the radio.

"Then, while you have some time I suggest that you work closely with Exman and see if some sort of solution can be found. Have you heard if he has received a return message from his planet?"

"No. I gave instructions that he is to notify both of us the moment he does."

"Then get back to Enterprise, work up a possible evacuation plan for the city, and we'll see what either of us can come up with."

The next two days were spent working out multiple scenarios for dealing with the energy beings, and for the potential need to remove all personnel from Helium City. Toward that end the largest four jetmarines were sent down and attached to the four docking points at the city. Between them all personnel could be loaded within two minutes and removed from the area.

Tom's days were spent watching a video feed coming in while working on a solution. He was finding nothing that would not be potentially destructive to the helium well and was about to give up when a report came in that the energies were remaining down near the bottom of the upper cavern. It gave his a little relief so he decided to leave early on Friday.

It became Saturday and Tom was enjoying a day off. The Shopton High School football team was playing rival Thessaly High and for the first time in more than three years he was sitting in the bleachers along with Bashalli, Bud and Sandy.

"You know," Bud was telling his wife in a loud voice as he attempted to drag her back down to her seat, "the more you yell and scream for penalties, the less likely the refs are going to throw flags."

"But, they're not calling fouls on those Thessaly bums and all sort of flags are shooting all over the place for our team!" she wailed.

"That is because our team keeps holding or jumping off sides or roughing their passer!"

Sandy sat down as the field commentator announced the end of the first half. A cheer went up and about four-fifths of the crowd rose and headed for the refreshment stands or bathrooms.

Tom felt the vibration of his cell phone and held up a hand. "Bash. You go with Sandy and Bud. I've got a call." She gave him a dark look but he shrugged and pulled the phone out.

"Tom, it's Harlan. There seems to be quite a bit of noise on the line. Should I call back?"

Tom explained where he was.

"Oh. Well, I've got some big news. Actually, it is very good, big news. Is there some place you can get to where it's a bit quieter?"

"Yeah. Hang on." Tom stood and headed up the stairs toward the announcer's booth. He knew the man behind the microphone and quickly explained that he needed a few minutes of privacy in the enclosed room.

"Hey. Not a problem, Tom. Glad to be of service."

As he stepped out and closed the door, Tom raised his phone again. "Okay, Harlan. Shoot."

"Interesting that you should use that term, Tom. I called to tell you that the FBI has a very bad man in custody. Our former Reverend Speers." Tom gasped. "He was picked up in Key West based on a sighting by our own Graham Kaye. It seems he was headed for a charter boat and a trip to Cuba where he hoped to disappear."

"That's great news," Tom exclaimed.

"Right. It is, but it also is the key to a lot of things. As we suspected the out of control car and the attack on Peter Crumwald, even the leak to the press of the subterranean noises were all courtesy of him and a group of young women who apparently will do anything for him. It also turns out that the bullet you took in the arm came courtesy of Speers. As in he drove up here with a stolen rifle, managed to disable one sector of the defense perimeter up the hill and then lay in wait. We'll probably never know where the second shot went. I believe that if Bashalli hadn't suggested that walk, and you hadn't gone to the new neighborhood that he would have sat up there trying for a long-distance shot into Enterprises."

"That was quite a shot for him, wasn't it?"

"Yes. But he seems to have spent a lot of time at a firing range this past year. Almost like he was planning something."

"So, Speers is going to be behind bars for some time I imagine," Tom stated.

"Oh, and not just for the attacks on you. No, it turns out that he has been a naughty boy all along. He spent some time in a psychiatric hospital after convincing a jury he was insane. That was after he killed his first wife. Plus, when he left the country to avoid military service, he murdered another man in Mexico. They would love to have him if our charges don't stick."

"Do you have any idea what is going to happen to the young ladies he seemed to control?"

"Well, the word I get is that most are guilty of various crimes ranging from petty theft to attempted murder, so my guess is they will each receive prison sentences. Hard to say for how long, but as this all appears to be some part of a conspiracy, that will tack a little extra on—at least eighteen years—to anything else they might receive."

Tom thanked his security man and left the booth patting the announcer on the shoulder as he passed him on the stairs.

"Thanks, Rocky. I appreciate the space!"

"Any time, Tom. Any time."

Tom got back to his seat as the other three came up from the ground level, drinks and snacks in hand.

Tom gave them a fast recap of what Harlan told him and they forgave him for not coming along with them. As he was telling them about the man murdering his wife, Tom's phone vibrated in his pocket. It was Harlan again.

"Tom, I almost forgot to tell you that the FBI found out about that note we all thought was from Atlas Samson. Can I come see you?"

"Sure. I can leave the game and be in the big office in a half hour. See you then." He explained to his unhappy companions that it was necessary to leave them.

"You stay and enjoy. If I can get back before the end I'll do that."

When the Security chief walked in Tom was waiting for him at his desk. "I take it from what you said that the note turned out to not be from Atlas Samson. Who, then?"

"Someone right in front of the FBIs nose at one point." Harlan shook his head while rubbing his left shoulder. "In one of those coincidences that really make you wonder, it turns out the A in A Samson is Arlene, and she is the girl who put that technician up to clobbering Peter Crumwald. She is also the one who tried to hold that press conference where just one junior reporter turned up. And, when taken in for questioning she freely gave her full name to the agents. The kicker is that she is Speers' daughter. By the murdered mother. She took her mother's maiden name about ten years ago when she turned eighteen. Quite some family, huh?"

Tom was shocked, but had to ask, "Does she know her father killed her mother?"

"That's the sad part. Yes, she does, but she is so devoted to the man she has chosen to ignore that all these years."

Tom thought a moment, "Do they have her in custody?"

Ames looked at his boss and made a "harrumph" sound before saying, "In another *coup* for the FBI, they managed to make a statement to the press down in Florida that they were about to make an arrest. She saw that and disappeared. Or, she is trying to. Proving they can do *something* right, they have photos of her passing through three toll booths and also have charge slips for two meals. All heading south. We think she might be trying to catch up with her father in Key West. His arrest has not been publicized."

Tom nodded as Harlan added, "Oh. And one other little tie up. You remember Damien Goosens? The one we thought might be part of this Samson thing? It turns out he died in a traffic accident five months ago in Monaco. Absolute positive ID of the body." Ames was now rubbing his left forearm.

"Well, that's something. May I change the subject?" Tom asked. There was something new that bothered him.

"Of course. What's the topic?"

"Your heart," Tom stated bluntly. Several months earlier Doc Simpson had, as part of his contract with Enterprises, approached Tom and Damon to tell them their chief of Security had been suffering chest pains. Both had promised to keep it quiet, but Tom had been watching Harlan across his desk and had seen him rubbing his left arm.

"Doc tattled?" he asked, almost looking relieved.

"He had to, Harlan. Both from a physician's standpoint and as an employee. Just like you are required to tell us about any infraction here, he is sworn to not keep health matters from us. We haven't told anybody, but it looks to me like you're having some issues right now." He inclined his head toward Harlan's arm.

"It might be indigestion," suggested Ames, hopefully.

"No, Harlan. It probably isn't. Why don't you start by putting in for a couple weeks of leave? You're owed it, for goodness sake. And if Phil Radnor and Gary Bradley can't take over for that short period of time, then you've been hiring the wrong people. According to Doc you need to have an angiogram and get a stent inserted in one of your arteries. That's all. We have more than thirty people on the Enterprises employee roster alone with stents. Even Jake Aturian at the Construction Company and Bashalli's father have one or two. It's supposedly nothing. A quick procedure followed by a day of hospital rest to make sure there is no post operative bleeding where they go into your upper thigh and then only light lifting for a couple weeks." His look of concern was so serious that Harlan had to relent.

"Okay. I have to admit that I am having problems especially if I try to run up several flights of stairs. Truth is, my index finger and elevator call buttons have become good friends this past couple of months. I'll call Doc. Promise!"

After he left, Tom sat at his desk a little worried that Harlan might change his mind. Fifteen minutes later his phone rang, startling him from his thoughts.

"Tom? It's Greg Simpson. I don't know what you did or said but Harlan Ames just dropped by my office to schedule his heart work. He said you convinced him. Well, done, skipper! He's on for day after tomorrow at Shopton General."

After hanging up Tom called his father and related the news.

"I'm very glad. For him as well as for the company. I have plans to keep Harlan's skills at work here for many years to come," Mr. Swift said. "I'll have Trent get flowers and a card sent to his room."

"Great. Keep me in the loop, please. I'll try to go see him that evening."

He stopped by the hospital on his way home two days later for a quick visit. Harlan was sitting up reading a "hard boiled detective" crime novel when Tom knocked on the door jamb. "Feel up to a visitor?"

"Hey, Tom. Sure I do. Come right on in and pull up a... well, *the* chair."

The inventor did and sat down. "Should I ask how you feel?"

Harlan laughed. "Oh, if you only knew how good I feel. I hadn't realized it but that blockage in one of my arteries was really holding me down. I feel like doing cartwheels the change is so significant!"

Tom remained for twenty minutes before a nurse came in to chase him away so Harlan could eat. The security man promised to follow doctors' orders—his surgeon as well as Doc Simpson—but winked and told Tom, "I'll be in the office day after tomorrow."

When he got to work the next day Tom reviewed data from the various light and receptor combinations. One, good old incandescent light, seemed to go unnoticed by the energy beings. Or, at least they avoided it. That would be put to use in what he began building. By late in the day he finished a new remote camera that could be lowered from the original gas lock in the hydrodome. With it he hoped to be able to watch the energy beings and to map their movements.

With twin receptors set as far apart as possible he would get a stereo image that would assist in distance measurements.

It was sent to Fearing that evening and a small team delivered it and instructions to Helium City before morning.

By mid-day he was receiving good video and data.

"They seem content to remain down in the lower thirty percent of the cavern," he told Bud as they lunched. "Right now they are just banging into the walls as if trying to find an exit."

"Can you do something to keep them down low?"

With a shake of his head, Tom had to admit he wasn't sure.

"Okay," Bud said, rubbing his hands together, "what will the Swift/Barclay team be doing next?"

"In truth I think that Exman holds the key. He hinted this morning that he may have an idea what to do. The thing is he is keeping pretty mum about it."

When they parted Tom went to the large office only to find his father and Exman standing just inside the door. He stepped in and moved out of the way as they seemed to be in a serious discussion.

Damon faced the robot. "Exman. I know that you recognize me as Damon Swift, but do you also recognize of understand that I hold a higher level of power than Tom?"

"Yes, Mr. Swift."

"Fine. I need to ask you several questions, but I want you to understand that I do not mean for them to be accusations. They are just so I may be certain of particular pieces of information. Will you answer me truthfully?"

"Yes, Mr. Swift."

"Okay. First, did you arrive on Earth with any data or instructions regarding the energy beings in the helium wells?" He looked at Tom as he asked this.

"Yes, Mr. Swift. And also no, Mr. Swift. Tom sent a message to my home planet using the words 'possible energy beings.' My instructions were to discover if this was true."

"Then, were you instructed to go see them for yourself?"

"No. My instructions were to scan and confirm energies not of this planet."

"I see. Well, in that case did you realize that you would be bringing them up with the probe into the upper cavern?" It was asked somewhat harshly and even Tom had to gasp slightly.

"No. Unlike recent energies like myself these have developed a way to hide their energy signatures. This turn of events has taken me by surprise."

"Oh." Damon had thought he might be onto something. "Have you received any other transmissions from your planet regarding these energy beings?"

"Yes. To amplify my answer the message I received stated I am to determine if they pose immediate threat to Earth. If so I am to stop them."

Tom couldn't help asking, "How?"

Exman turned his body to face the younger Swift. "In truth, I do not know, Tom. But it has become imperative that I stop them, whatever it takes."

"But you must have some notion," Tom stated.

"Only that I am certain to ninety-seven percent that I must go into the upper cavern if I am to succeed in returning them to their exile, or to destroy them."

After a nod from his father Tom went to his desk and ordered that the original full-size SpiderBall be checked over and prepared for shipment back to Helium City.

Exman spent the weekend in the old control tower reprocessing all of the data and attempting to come up with a plan of action. When Tom came to get him Monday morning the robot wasn't there. A brief search showed that the robot was already in the large office waiting for the inventor.

"What have you decided?" Tom inquired. "Or, you and your handlers."

"I must go into the upper cavern."

"Fine, but beyond that. What will you do?"

"There are many things I might do but I have computed that the energies' cycle of power and weakness will meant that at precisely three-sixteen plus eleven seconds tomorrow afternoon they will be at their weakest point. At that time I must be among them. I will attempt to overload them using one of your e-guns." He pointed to a gun on Tom's desk. "I have upgraded that to allow an external power pack. The additional power will allow the gun to fire energy approximately five-point-two times greater than the normal high setting."

"That would be nearly the kind of power they used to scorch the probe," Tom said.

"Yes."

"Then, let's get going. I have several things to do but we can depart for Fearing at eight this evening."

The flight out was made in one of the small cargo jets so they could haul the SpiderBall with them. Once it was loaded into a seacopter Tom and Exman departed for the Hydrodome.

When he awoke the following morning it was to a knocking on the door of his quarters. The door popped open and Bud's smiling face came in.

"Forget to ask me along?" he accused his friend with a laugh. "I came down in another seacopter."

"I've been told by your darling wife that I have to stop dragging you away from hearth and home all the time. Sorry. But, I'm glad you're here."

The SpiderBall had been moved to the large gas lock building and was waiting when the three arrived and swam to the airlock. Exman's body was wiped dry before he climbed inside the ball. For the single passenger, even one slightly taller than Tom or Bud, one seat had been removed and there was more than ample space.

Moments later the sphere rose and moved into the lock. It was sealed, pressurized with helium and the other end opened.

Tom switched to the overhead camera dangling under the hydrodome. They could see the SpiderBall as it moved down the east wall almost mimicking an actual spider. In ten minutes it was nearly at the level where the action was occurring.

"They must have noticed him," Bud said as the noise of their collisions with the walls increased. "Can we zoom in?"

Tom complied and the ball could be seen standing still. But, not for long. In a moment one of the energy beings zipped close over the top, ricocheted off the nearby wall and caromed away at an odd angle.

"That was close," Tom said. "I hope they don't sever the data cable. I really don't want Exman down there all alone." He opened a channel to the sphere. "Are you okay, Exman?"

There was a pause. "Yes, Tom. I am fine. The sphere is fine. I am preparing to drop lower and then to try to overload them. I will not be able to communicate again for the time being."

They watched as the sphere began to go farther down. Soon it was nearly surrounded by the energy beings. None of them stopped but they did slow down.

Movement of the hatch was seen as Exman manually opened it. One arm extended holding the enhanced e-gun. It moved almost imperceptibly before the first bolt of energy erupted from it's barrel.

"A direct hit!" Bud cried out joyously. His joy turned to dismay as they both watched the single energy that had been hit. First it flared brightly, then dimmed but three seconds later it regained most of its original brightness and zipped off to the other side of the cavern.

Exman's plan had gone bust!

CHAPTER 20 /
GENIE BACK INTO THE BOTTLE

"IS THERE any way to seal them back down in the lower chamber without cutting off the helium?" Bud yelled over the noises.

"I've got to rebuild the bridges down there. That's what kept them trapped all these millennia, Bud! I was afraid something bad was going to happen once if they found a way to rise into the upper chamber. Without the pressure nearly holding them still, they're zipping around down there, banging into the walls and releasing energy that's shaking things. And, they've now damaged that upper bridge to the point I think it has stopped."

"Is that new banging around the increasing noise?"

Tom nodded. It was easier than shouting. He grabbed Bud's arm and pulled him toward the nearby airlock. Once inside the noise was reduced to a low din.

"If I can't safely raise the pressure in the chamber to slow them down, and I'm afraid that doing so might cause the top crust to blow out, then we must force them back down to where they will remain harmless until Exman can come through on his promise."

"But, if they won't willingly be put back into the pit, how do you corral them? Trick them somehow?"

Tom looked at Bud and a sly grin crossed his face.

"You know, flyboy, there are times that you are pure genius. That is precisely what we are going to do." He told Bud his plans and the flyer soon had his own grin broadly spanning his face.

The video feed from below showed no change in the activity of the energy beings. They continued to slam from one side of the cavern to the other, bouncing at odd angles, sometimes hitting the sides of the SpiderBall, and only doing slight damage. Fortunately their energy had relatively little mass. Unfortunately that mass still was sufficient to cause the constant vibration noises. And those ebbed and increased depending on where in the cavern any concentration of the beings happened to be.

Tom was amazed that there were no detectable collisions between them. It was like watching a crazy, frenetic flight of a million bats from a small cave where each of them seemingly maintains their own space and every one gets out without damage in spite of how chaotic it all appears.

He ordered Exman to return.

It took the best part of the next two days to get everything ready to try Tom's plan. Several new pieces of equipment had to be brought down and dozens of specialists visited and left on almost an hourly basis. But, by midnight on the second day everything was ready.

Tom walked to the waiting Exman.

"I need to have your assistance, please."

The large robot turned to face Tom. "What is it that you would ask me to perform, Tom?"

"A point of interest. If you get surrounded by the other energy beings, will you be able to remain safe and not allow them entry into your body?"

"With a certainty of ninety-three point two-two-five, that is the case. As additional information, much of this depends on you sealing me inside this body when the time arrives. While I still have the capacity to open the shell of this body and depart, it might be possible for a concerted effort of the energies to force the shell open, allowing them ingress."

Tom patted Exman. "How 'sealed in' will you need to be?" He was nervous what the answer might be.

"Permanently."

"But, you can't agree to be sealed inside that body forever," Tom insisted. "You have said that you value your freedom to come and go, and that your handlers expect us to abide by the agreement to not trap you."

Exman did a human gesture... he nodded. It was the first time the inventor had ever seen him do that, and he was amazed.

"I have communicated with my handlers. While they do not find this to be a positive measure, the alternative is for them to come to the Earth and take charge of the prisoners. If they do that your large storage of element number two will need to be released. They compute a deleterious effect on your atmosphere with that much of the gas released at one time. Even though it would rise and eventually dissipate into space it would still be captured by gravity and would cause a shift in the light spectrum for the planet. My way is the only way if you wish me to go into the chamber."

"But, how did you know that was my plan?"

"It seems to be the only viable plan of action. It has been the only viable plan of action for two days. That is why I have already discussed it with my handlers."

With a deep sigh, Tom told the robot to follow him. "We'll rig the seal and then have you go down."

The work required only a few minutes. A tomasite sealant, self-hardening in seconds after application, was run around the entrance hatch in Exman's robot head. The hatch clicked shut, rotated into position and the seal became permanent.

As Tom had been performing this task, the technicians had attached the data and power cable to the top of the sphere. This time it was a more heavy-duty cable and the first five feet had been given a coating of tomasite to ensure nothing could cut through it.

He followed Tom back to the pressure building above the gas lock. Exman picked up a heavy duffel bag. Tom didn't ask what the energy being had inside it. Without any words, he again nodded to the inventor, reached out his left arm—another previously unseen human gesture—and gently shook Tom's hand before climbing into the sphere.

Bud came in through the airlock just in time to watch Tom shut the sphere's hatch.

"Will he come back?" Bud asked meekly.

"I don't know, Bud. I have no idea. Get ready to bring the building's pressure to twenty-two P.S.I.," he called out to the operator on the control panel. "Okay. Now." The man turned a small wheel and a hissing sound could be heard just above the racket of the ricochetting energy beings. Tom and Bud's ears popped three times and it became a little laborious to breathe, but they had to keep going.

Tom raised his right arm and made a twirling motion with his index finger telling the man on the control panel to open the inner hatch of the gas lock. The SpiderSphere rose and slid inside with the hatch closing behind it.

"Flood with helium and equalize pressure," he commanded.

Once this had occurred, he requested, "Open the outer lock door." The proper inside pressure in the tube kept the pressure inside the gas lock from flinging open the outer door and maintained the purity of the helium inside the well. Tom made another motion and the capsule containing Exman swung over the open end and began its downward journey.

A moment later the cable went slightly slack. Bud gasped until he realized Exman had simply begun using the Attractatrons. The outer hatch was closed and sealed.

"I guess it's now or never," Tom said to everyone, but only Bud commented.

"Fare thee well, Exman."

"Drop our pressure to normal, please," the inventor requested, and everyone's ears again needed to be popped. "Let's see how he is doing."

Three camera views were available from the sphere on the large flat screen by the control panel. Camera one showed the interior of the capsule where they could see Exman sitting very still. Only Tom spotted yet another human affectation.

The robot's right fingers were slowly drumming on his right leg.

Keying the microphone, Tom asked, "Exman. First, how are you doing and second, do I detect some finger movement?"

"Hello, Tom and Bud as well. My energy self is fine and my mechanical self is also fine. The noise level is high and so I am communicating via the electronics in the capsule rather than verbally. In response to question number two, I am... I do not know what this feeling is. Strange."

Tom looked at Bud and mouthed "Feeling?" Bud shrugged.

"It is a variation on what I understand to be anticipation of the passage of time. It appears to me to be running far too slowly. I wish the events that are about to occur would arrive sooner."

Barely able to stifle a chuckle, even given the dire circumstances, Tom replied, "Why, Exman. If I didn't know better I would say that you are anxious. Perhaps that plus bored."

He now switched the view to the camera mounted at the top of the sphere. It showed that the area close to the cavern roof was clear of energy beings. For whatever reason they had never risen to more than the halfway point. Even then, only two of the energy beings had ventured that high.

"Tom. I do not fully understand *anxious* or *bored*. I wish that I had additional time to study these energies, but I sense that the time to begin this operation is nearly at hand. Before I start, I must tell you that I have a sense of deep satisfaction in having known you and having worked with you. It is strange because as you know, my energy self is not capable of feelings." He paused three seconds during which Tom changed to the camera mounted on the down tube of the original gas lock. It aimed down and everyone looking saw that the sphere was now nearly two-thirds of the way down, and the energy being were whizzing around but were coming closer and closer to the capsule.

"Tom. What happens to energy when it no longer contains viable electrons?"

The inventor got a lump in his throat. He tried clearing it but his voice was husky with emotion. "In humans we call that dying, Exman. With you it would mean that all that is you, the energy self, will cease to exist, I guess. But let's not jump over that chasm before we get the chance to see there is a safe bridge nearby. Okay?"

"I understand the reference. It is time. Please lock the sphere cable in place for stability."

Tom did so and switched to the interior camera in time to see Exman unbolt the hatch and swing it open. The robot leaned forward and Bud cried out.

"Jetz! He isn't going to jump out, is he?"

Tom was also startled by this maneuver but shook his head. "It isn't quite part of the plan. Let's watch."

As they did the robot leaned farther and farther out of the sphere, but by switching back to the first camera Tom could see that both of the robotic arms were firmly grasping handles on the inside.

There was a sudden commotion as the camera was nearly overwhelmed by bright lights swarming up to and then inside of the sphere.

Tom's worried face changed into smile as he saw what was happening. "Come on, Exman. That's the way to do it. And, come on all you energy bad guys. Get in." His voice was low but as you could already hear a pin drop—all the banging and thrumming noise stopped the moment the swarm began flowing to the sphere —the inventor might as well have been shouting.

Nothing other that flashes of bright light could be seen and very soon the interior camera's receiving chip burnt out.

Tom switched to the top of the cavern view, and now they could see that the sphere was practically covered with a solid layer of energy. It pulsed and wiggled. For all the world it looked like a large crowd trying to squeeze through a narrow gate at a sporting event.

As the seconds passed the outside energy diminished. There were no visible individual energy beings in the cavern, just the ones around and inside the sphere.

As suddenly as it began, the lights went out except for what seemed to be a bright beam coming from the hatch, which quickly closed, and then it was gone.

Tom looked at the screen for a minute. He turned to Bud. "I guess that is it." The sphere hovered in place for more than a quarter hour before Exman's voice came back over the speaker.

"Please allow the sphere to move freely, Tom."

He reached over and released the winch operating lever. The readout above it marked the drop rate and distance as Exman piloted the sphere downward.

In nine minutes he announced, "It's passing through the hole between the upper chamber and the lower one."

They continued to watch for another four hours. With only the two outside cameras working they really had no idea what was happening inside, and Exman was only giving occasional and somewhat terse reports.

"They ought to be nearing the bottom," Tom told them with a catch in his voice.

The plan now called for Exman, if he were still functional, to travel down past the security bridges and around at least the first corner, open the hatch flooding the sphere with the super-pressurized nearly solid helium and then closing the hatch again. That would trap the energy beings back down where they belonged. Or rather, where they had been dumped on the Earth and left.

The bad guys would have been put back in prison, and hopefully this time for good. But, Exman would perish. Tom felt a wave of sadness.

Because bringing up the sphere would just set things back on the road to destruction, Tom had built in a guillotine to sever the cable at the top of the sphere. It would automatically cut everything at the 24-hour mark. There was nothing more to do until it was time to bring the cable back.

Tom and Bud returned to the hydrodome to the cheers and shouts of the assembled Helium City residents. They acknowledged the accolades, but both young men felt miserable about the demise of Exman.

The lack of noise inside the hydrodome was as powerful as the pressure waves of the thrumming. It was so powerful that over the next several hours about half of the residents visited the small dispensary to get aspirins for headaches they developed.

The cooks put on a wonderful celebratory dinner that evening where everyone, including those who had to remain on duty, had a wonderful time.

"You really got the bad Djinn back into the lamp, or bottle," Peter Crumwald told Tom when they had a moment to talk. "Will it last?"

"Well, from what we learned from—" Tom's voice caught. He took a deep breath before continuing, "From what we learned from Exman, those energy beings were originally despicable criminals on their planet and transported in a magnetic field before being placed at the bottom of that cavern and the liquefied helium pumped on top. That was more that fifteen centuries ago. I think it's safe to say we have at least that much time again. And maybe between now and then, the beings from his planet can be convinced to come take them back."

He walked away and headed for the airlock. He and Bud would spend the night in one of the two seacopters before witnessing the cable cut and withdrawal the next early afternoon.

They both tossed and turned and finally got out of their cots about 5:00 a.m. There was little to do for another nine hours but Tom spent about half of that sitting in the pressure building watching the view from the camera high at the top of the cavern. It showed the unmoving cable heading down to the lower cavern and nothing else.

Only the top camera of the probe still functioned and only poorly. He pivoted and zoomed the camera around, seeing absolutely no energy beings. Exman had been able to get their attention and as a group they had swarmed him. And, as a group he had trapped them and taken them back where they would no longer be a nuisance or danger.

Tom shut off the camera. He didn't want to see anything more during the final two hours.

With just five minutes to go Tom made the decision that it needed to be him to cut the cable, forever dooming Exman to join those he took with him. He already had dictated wording for a plaque that would be mounted just outside the pressure building praising Exman as a hero.

Nobody spoke the countdown as it neared time.

5... 4... 3... 2... 1... Tom's finger hovered over the button. He knew it was hopeless but his brain told him to wait. Even if it was for a second or two.

Press.

The button went down and the signal came back ten seconds later that there was no longer any response from the sphere. Until then a small red light had blinked every minute showing that the capsule was still there.

Tom reached over and activated the winch. It began spooling the long cable back up.

"Why's it moving so slowly, skipper?" one of the technicians asked.

"The helium is almost frozen solid and the cable is just in the grip of the ice. It ought to go faster once a half mile or so gets reeled in."

With nothing to really see he got up and he and Bud left. An hour later they were saying their goodbyes to Peter Crumwald and several of the resident when a communications young tech came running toward them.

"Don't leave!" he shouted.

He arrived short of breath but only took a few seconds to compose himself.

"You've got to come. Something is still attached to the cable. They think we're dragging those energy things back up. Please!"

He turned and ran back toward the communications building.

Tom, Bud and Peter also broke into a run but headed for the seacopter. They struggled into their diving suits on the way and swam out of the airlock and into the building's lock as quickly as possible. The inventor raced inside and took the seat vacated by another technician. His eyes swept over the readouts. Sure enough, there was a weight on the end of the cable.

There was a gasp from the five people now standing behind him.

"Should you drop it back?" Peter asked.

"If it is the sphere then it ought to still be sealed so it won't hurt to get it to the bottom of the upper cavern. Then we can see what's there and make the decision at that time. How much longer before it gets to that point?"

"At the current rate, thirty-two minutes."

"Then, we wait."

About a minute before time, Tom zoomed the camera attached to the upper gas lock to its highest setting and aimed it at the gap between the chambers.

A few seconds later Tom let out a gasp.

Coming up out of the hole was something metallic. Something vaguely human-shaped.

Something that looked exactly like Exman!

A cheer went up and Tom joined in.

Exman was gripping the end of the severed cable with both of his mechanical hands. As they all watched his head tilted upward.

Tom slowed the cable rate so that there would be little chance of accidentally shaking the robot body loose.

In just eighteen minutes it was over. The winch had brought Exman up into the gas lock chamber and the lower door swung closed.

Tom raised the pressure in the building and soon the upper hatch was opened. The ceiling winch lowered its connector and the robot carefully let go with one hand to grab the new cable. In seconds he was pulled from the lock and set on the floor.

"Wha— I mean how— I mean... I don't know what I mean, but it's great to see you, Exman."

As everyone crowded around the robot's voice, its speaker element damaged by the enormous cold, rattled out, "Touched down. Opened hatch. Energy stopped but not mine. Climbed out... clamped on... waited..." He stopped.

"Don't worry old friend," Tom directed. "We'll get you back to Enterprises and fixed as good as new and then you can tell us everything."

The word had gotten out of the unexpected retrieval of the hero, and everybody not on duty or asleep lined the inner edge of the hydrodome. They waved as Tom piloted the seacopter past them then headed up to the surface with Exman carefully loaded in the rear cargo compartment.

For the first time Tom flew a seacopter directly to Enterprises and set it down on the tarmac near to the Mechanical Engineering building.

The robot body was moved inside and a two-day overhaul was undertaken. It was found that the seal around the hatch holding Exman's energy self had cracked under the enormous pressure and cold so it was an easy task to open the door. Exman, in spite of the opportunity, chose to remain inside.

As soon as possible, his robot body was interfaced with the computer system and Tom and his father sat in their office now in communication with Exman.

"What happened down there?" Damon asked.

"As I opened the hatch inside the cavern I felt a great electrical scream as the other energies sensed me. As I anticipated, they rushed into the sphere. Once inside I closed the hatch and used the e-gun I had in the canvas bag. I waited until I had a good shot that would not hit the controls, shot at each energy and as it darkened and went idle I put it into a container of sea water I also took with me."

"What did that do?" Bud asked.

Tom answered first. "I believe I understand. They can't operate in salty water. Is that it?"

"It is the case. It is also the final safety measure to keep them from escaping. Once I had captured them all I sealed the container and maneuvered to the bottom of the low shaft. The other energies had recovered slightly and tried to overwhelm me. They could not escape the container but their malevolence stunned me. I did not become aware again for nearly the entire time before the cable was severed. I opened the hatch flooding the sphere. My robot self was generating enough heat that I was not frozen in place. I struggled to get up and out and was able to force my way through the ice and to grip the cable. I thank you for making my robot self so strong, Tom Swift. Without that strength I would remain trapped with those pitiful beings."

"Did you manage to get the hatch of the sphere closed again?" Tom asked hopefully.

"I was unable to do that, Tom. However, I detected no movement and no output from within. The almost absolute zero temperature will have frozen the water solid and they will remain there for as long as I can compute."

"How can we properly thank you, Exman?" Damon inquired.

"Mr. Swift. There is no requirement for thanks. What Tom has given my energy self is a gift that reaches far beyond anything I may have accomplished."

Just after the robot body was declared to be back to full operation early that evening, Exman announced that he would be leaving Earth.

"I must return to my planet and report to my handlers. They need to be provided with a full report of what has occurred, and I am certain that I can impress on them the necessity to devise a way to quietly and secretly remove those criminal energy beings from your planet."

They walked outside to stand in the dusky evening air.

Exman turned to Tom. "I do not comprehend the true meaning of thanks however I do have a positive impression regarding what you have done for me. Some day I hope that another energy being might arrive on Earth and remain permanently. Good-bye, Tom Swift."

Five minutes later and with no fanfare, Exman opened his own head hatch and the energy Exman shot into the sky.

Bud clapped a hand on Tom's shoulders.

"He'll be back, skipper. I feel it."

"I hope so, Bud. I believe Exman has been picking up some human attributes. I'd like to see where those take him."

"Yeah, me too, but for now I'd like to see my wife. Let's get out of here!"

As they walked to their cars Bud called out, "Now that you've saved the world, again, what's your next trick?"

Tom really didn't know, but he was soon to be embroiled in a fight against a terrorist plot and an effort that could lead to him ruining his own newest invention.

"Not sure, flyboy. But I'm not feeling very subterranean right now. Maybe not for a long, long time. Besides, I'm about to disappear. Bash and I will be taking our vacation to Tahiti starting the week after next!"